A DEATH IN HARLEM

A Death in Harlem

A Novel

KARLA FC HOLLOWAY

TRIQUARTERLY BOOKS/NORTHWESTERN UNIVERSITY PRESS

EVANSTON, ILLINOIS

TriQuarterly Books
Northwestern University Press
www.nupress.northwestern.edu

This is a work of fiction. Characters, places, and events are the product of the author's
imagination or are used fictitiously and do not represent actual people, places, or events.

Printed in the United States of America

10   9   8   7   6   5   4   3   2   1

Library of Congress Cataloging-in-Publication Data

Names: Holloway, Karla F. C., 1949– author.
Title: A death in Harlem : a novel / Karla FC Holloway.
Description: Evanston, Illinois : TriQuarterly Books/Northwestern University Press,
    2019.
Identifiers: LCCN 2019013938 | ISBN 9780810140813 (trade paper : alk. paper) |
    ISBN 9780810140820 (e-book)
Subjects: LCSH: A Harlem (New York, N.Y.)—Fiction. | African Americans—
    New York (State)—New York—Social conditions—Fiction. | African American
    police—New York (State)—New York—Fiction. | Homicide investigation—
    New York (State)—New York—Fiction. | LCGFT: Detective and mystery fiction.
Classification: LCC PS3608.O49417 D43 2019 | DDC 813.6—dc23
LC record available at https://lccn.loc.gov/2019013938

For the Friday Night Women.
A sisterhood bound in books . . . and love.

Contents

Author's Note

IN THE TRADITION OF AFRICAN AMERICAN LITERATURE, THIS IS A "talking book." It means that spoken words—whether whispered, intimated, shouted, shared in conversation, muttered to oneself, or simply intuited—are ways and means of revelation. Voices matter as much as they vary.

This is also a book of historical literary fiction. Its era is popularly known as the Harlem Renaissance, or the Jazz Age, or simply the Roaring Twenties. Certainly there are novels and social histories aplenty that engage this extraordinary era. Their echoes haunt *A Death in Harlem*. The reader who knows these histories well will discover nuggets that whisper some distantly remembered reading; or might recall the brash Harlem glitterati like Zora Neale Hurston, who of course could not stay away from the drama in a story like this one—even if only for a momentary appearance. Harlem folk, the siditty and the regular, find a way to make themselves heard as well. Some readers might even discern the voice of Harlem herself. Why not? She was there.

But even more present in *A Death in Harlem*, and absolutely its origin story, is Nella Larsen's 1929 novel *Passing*. Larsen's novel ended on a provocative note—did Clare Kendry jump, was she pushed, or was there some other explanation of her death? The policeman at the scene in Larsen's novel pronounced it a "death by misadventure." "Misadventure" was a tantalizing word that lingered with me in a circuitous way that led finally to this novel—*A Death in Harlem*. But rather than directly resurrect *Passing*'s characters Clare Kendry and Irene Redfield, I've reimagined them into a more complex story. Here, they emerge as Vera Wright Scott and Olivia Frelon. However, for those who will take delight in *Passing*'s echoes, there will be allusions. Of course the ways of white folk have a place here as well. In fact, some might read my Hughes Wellington as a version of the always available and overly interested Carl Van Vechten; but take care—fiction composes more from landscape than from memory.

So, if you recognize, or feel the brush of memory as you read *A Death in Harlem*, enjoy the moment; but don't give its origin too much sway. This is a fiction. As a guide, I'd suggest you let Harlem's first colored policeman, Weldon Thomas, lead you into this mystery, with my assurance that he will indeed bring you out again safely. Somebody has certainly died in Harlem. And despite insistent whispers from the known world, there is so much more to be told. My advice is, listen to the book. It talks.

A DEATH IN HARLEM

PART I

The Fall

1

Weldon Haynie Thomas

IN LATE MIDWINTER OF 1927, WHEN THAT LADY THEY THOUGHT WAS white jumped, or fell, or got pushed out the window of the Hotel Theresa, Harlem's first colored policeman was assigned the night watch.

Slender tributaries of blood from her broken body soaked the snow and matched the color of her evening gown. Where her head hit between the pavement and the street, steaming vermilion paths sliced through the snowy drifts that had blown up against the curb. As the night edged toward day, her body, the blood, and patches of frozen snow—seemed a crystallized etching that the streetlamp selectively illuminated.

Officer Weldon Thomas later recalled it had been one of those days when he got that feeling. It was like a push or nudge. Something wanted attention. There was no use in sitting around trying to figure out what it was about beforehand, no matter how hard he tried. He would have no idea whatever it was until it was over and done with. Months would pass before he could say with clear-eyed certainty that the dead lady was what triggered that December morning's mo-nition. He pushed his chair back from the kitchen table in the rooms he let from Darnell Zenobia and shook his head. "Umph. So that's what it was."

When he was a boy, the old lady who lived in the brownstone's basement apartment told his mother that he had the "mo-nition . . . He's gonna know things before they happen." Weldon had put his head down on the table. The cracks in the wood surface looked like a branch creek. His tiny finger followed their routes. She was small and wiry and her appearance didn't match the strong gravelly voice she directed at him. "Boy, I see you." She tittered. "You go on with tracing out my river." Weldon wanted to ask his mother how the lady knew there were rivers on her table. He met her bleary eyes with his bright ones. "Sweet boy," she said. "There ain't no hiding the kind of seeing you got." He tried to read her eyes. Their blur of bright specks looked like a map. She spoke over him to his mother. "Mrs. Thomas, your boy got a kind of mo-nition that don't show more than what it wants." She put both hands on the table to push herself up. Weldon's mother put the warm bag of rolls on the lady's table and reached into her coat pocket for a case quarter.

"When's this thing you say he got gonna show itself?"

"I just said it ain't nothing he can see." She sucked her teeth. "Sth. You listening at all? It's about what he's gonna know." She paused, searching for the words to say it. "It's more like, well, it's like he's gonna know he don't know something that could use knowing." His mother leaned toward her, trying not to show her own frustration with the old lady's circular speech. "But here's what you need to understand." She leaned in. "You got you a sensitive boy. The kind of boy where knowing there's something he don't know will bother him mightily unless you find him something to do that can sidestep this thing."

"How do I do that? Just tell me. We'll do for our boy."

"That's clear. You here aren't you? You came down here; you knocked politely and too, you brought me these just-made rolls." She opened the bag and let the yeasty scent escape. After a while she said, "Here's what. You gonna have to give him things to know about. Things sure and certain. Things that he can learn and go back and learn some more. So he don't frustrate hisownself." The two women and the boy sat still in the quiet. Even now Weldon remembered the quiet, the river-shaped ridges on the tabletop, and the smell of oven-fresh rolls as if they always went together. Not long afterwards, his mother took to bringing him to the Harlem Branch Library on 135th. Books could offer him a focus, she thought. And too, she never heard of anybody getting in trouble over some reading.

December 1927

By the time the awards program upstairs started, it was late. It seems like the ones amongst my people that got to be the élite—e-lights, my moms calls them—haven't any better a handle on the clock than regular coloreds. I'd finished patrolling the lobby, keeping the outside crowds outside and under some manner of control. Earlier on in the night, you couldn't tell which set of folks was more trouble than the others—the ones coming into the banquet or the ones outside looking them over. I knew when I got assigned to this affair that my real job would be to stand around and look like a first colored policeman ought to look. I've got to represent the race no different than the siditty folks prancing their fine selves through the Hotel Theresa lobby.

By the time I decided it was okay to take myself to the chair between the shifty-eyed bellhop and the grand staircase, it wasn't a good fifteen minutes before all hell broke loose.

I'd chosen the straight-backed chair so nobody could think I was goofing off by sitting even though I was still officially on duty. There were others, all plush and soft, with deep tufts and edged up with fringe and velvet; but they weren't appropriate. I chose a chair that was as near to being business-like as the lobby had available. It faced the grand staircase, so anybody could see I was more than ready to be attentive. When I sat down good and had my book out and turned to the right page, the bellhop decided he wanted to conversate and find out about being a police. Seemed like he was thinking he could just carry himself down to the station house and exchange the uniform he had on for a cop's uniform. Like I wasn't the only one who got selected, tested, interviewed, and inspected and only after all that became the experiment in colored police. There was no kind of line waiting for me. I was the line—its beginning, and if I didn't turn out right, its end.

Me, I was trying to get into my book. Anybody who knows me knows that Weldon Haynie Thomas always has a book. Moms says, "That boy always has got some book about his person," like me and my person are different. Other kids stop whatever reading they do with their McGuffies. I didn't know it then, but reading was the key to the whole business.

I like to use the words from my books. That's one of the things you get from reading, I tell folks who try to call me on what they call my high-talking ways. The ones who are always asking me where do I think I live, up in Sugar Hill? A book doesn't cost a thing but the effort to carry yourself down to the library. And at the library, they are sincerely happy to see you show up, unlike some places my people have taken a fancy to—like this particular hotel that doesn't even let overnight rooms to coloreds but will be more than happy to take their money for a fancy banquet long as they are disappeared from "the public areas" by daybreak. At the library, you don't have to worry about who you know, or who might drop a black ball into somebody's bowl and keep you out. By the way, whichever one of us thought up that nonsense (or copied it from white folks) needs to do some rethinking about the symbolics of the matter.

On this particular night, I'd opened the book to my favorite page and was just about settled into it when the kid decides he wants to make small talk. I tell him "no it's not a police manual" and "no I didn't need for him to hold on to it while I took a necessary." That's what he called it. It made me wonder who had raised him up not to be able to say the word "toilet." He either had some strange home training or none at all. I couldn't tell which.

Still and all, it didn't look like he was going to let me get back to my reading. He starts going on with some story that would show me how much he knew about these affairs and the whys and wherefores of when "our folks" can be up in the hotel and when we couldn't; but I wasn't about to get in a conversation right there about race can dos and can'ts.

That's not to say that things aren't changing to some degree. Nobody coulda bet on this development here that a uniformed officer of the law of Harlem, New York, could be colored. And too, even this kid is a sign of race progress. Between the both of us, it could look like uplift come uptown. So it wasn't going to be me who would ruin the potential evolution of the race.

I was thinking on all these things while I tried to settle into the chair. It wasn't particularly comfortable. I'm a big guy—not stocky, but not what anybody could call thin either. Straight-backed furniture seems to be made for littler butts than mine. Still and all, this one chair amongst all of them in the lobby would keep me looking alert and vigilant. I understood symbolics.

I came knowing it was going to be a long and drawn-out affair. The clock on the lobby wall verified it. Seemed like each swing of the pendulum took longer to get to the other side. Added to all this, a bleak and blistering freeze had taken hold. "Long and cold as a witch's tit," my daddy woulda said.

COME TO THINK ON IT, THE NIGHT MISS OLIVIA DIED WAS THE SAME kind of dry brittle cold the night my daddy put that too big jacket on me and the flannel cap with the flaps that come down over my ears. Moms wouldn't let me go out before she wrapped a scarf around my neck enough times to strangle me and then pulled some of it up over my face to my nose. She always said "cover your mouth" when it's cold. But soon as we get outside, Daddy took it off, did one loose loop at my neck, and let the rest lay down the front of my jacket. He grabbed hold to my hand. That was warm enough for me. I don't remember if I asked him where we were going. It didn't much matter since I was with my daddy. We came back home dragging a scraggly Christmas tree. Mr. Chasen had it propped up against the side window of his grocery store. I got to choose it when Daddy asked me which one we should bring home.

"That's your decision?" Daddy asked.

"Yes sir! That one is my preferential."

"Preference," Daddy said.

He never teased me about my words, just helped me get them right. He always said getting things right was the hardest and best thing that anybody could do. I remember that to this day. It didn't make me feel bad at all that he fixed my words. He could fix about anything, except when it came to hisownself. That took me a long time to understand. It was a conundrum. Everything was not as it seemed. The puzzle mattered.

On that night when we was standing outside the grocery, I looked from my daddy and then over to the tree that was already lit up with lights and colored with the paper chains we pasted together at school. Chasen didn't have Christmas, so we kids felt like we were doing something generous when we left extra pieces of chains from our school art class draped on his trees.

Daddy turned to Mr. Chasen. "This the one my son choose," he told the grocer. Daddy said "son" like it mattered. Daddy pulled the tree with one hand and held mine in his other. There was a soft snow, just enough to change the streets from just dark and wet to dark with a feather-light promise of winter. And, it was freezing. Frigid, in fact. In the distance glimmered the bleary light of an alley barrel meeting where men who didn't have a place to stay got together. Daddy said there were rules for these gatherings, that these men wasn't bums. They had ways if not means.

There's rules for an alley barrel group. You had to take time during the day to follow behind the coal trucks, and when the coal man wheeled the full barrel back behind the store or apartment building to fill up the bins, you get just a few minutes to pick up some of whatever falls in the street and pocket it real quick before he comes back from his dump. Whatever coal you get is your ticket into the alley. Sometimes you got several pieces, other times just one or two. Didn't matter, you just had to contribute. It put me in mind of that folk story we read in school, "Stone Soup."

By the time we got down to the alley, we didn't stop much more than time for my daddy to give a polite nod to the group all huddled around the barrel. The fire inside was bright and hot and sparks were flitting up into the air like fireworks do in July. They stopped talking and watched us. I held my daddy's hand tighter, but I didn't say nothing. One of the men spoke up.

"All y'all look at that right there." It was the man with no gloves and no hat that was the one talking. "Y'all look what we got right here." The rest of them moved a bit so they could see us. "What you got here is a real man. He done got his boy a Christmas tree." Their soft grumbling sounded smooth and warm. Then he said it again. "Don't none of y'all miss this right here. It's a real man right here by us tonight and he got his boy with him. This a real man." I felt his voice as warm as fire. Now sure, it coulda been some heat from the fire barrel; but I bet it wasn't. My daddy didn't say a thing. Me neither. And I never asked him how come he knew the rules.

Miss my daddy. God rest his soul. Don't know why he had to die like he did. Don't know now whether I remember it on its own or I remember it because it was the first time I put together that feeling I get when something is going to happen.

Any other day I woulda been hanging out with my friends or finishing up my chores down to the grocery. But for some reason I stayed home with Moms. Annoying her. I didn't want to be there. I was hot and edgy and I was mad all day long.

I can get mad quick. Which they don't know about down to the station house. My temper comes out in the same way that I always can find something to say; but still and all I'm nobody's fool. When Reverend Charleston told me to apply for this police job, that they were going to take one of us to experiment with, he knew me enough to sit me down and give me a good talking to. "Boy you keeps to yourself, keep what you hear to yourself, keep your person to yourself."

I said "yessir," like I was supposed to. Reverend Charleston was close to preachifying.

"Keep things close. Don't go mouthin off or sharing what you think about the race oughta do and ought not to do. These folks, they your work not your people. Don't let them get inside your head. Not one iota. Because the truth is, they don't give a rat's ass about what you think about something." My eyes got big when Reverend Charleston said "rat's ass," but I was smart enough not to say anything about it. He stopped for a minute and breathed out deep and long. Like he wasn't even standing there in the church vestibule with his hands on my shoulder but some-place else. He came back, though, just soon enough before I had to figure whether to reach up and put my hand up on top of his. His hands felt heavy. He squeezed my shoulders. Now Reverend Charleston, he had some of the biggest hands I'd ever seen. But I didn't think for one second, If he don't let me go now, this is going to hurt. Instead I felt grateful for his laying his hands on me. And safe.

I said, "Yes sir." But I was really thinking about looking up the word "iota" in the big dictionary at the Harlem Branch Library. I didn't know you could use it like that. Like "one iota."

On that day Daddy died, Moms could tell I was not in a good mood and she kept on telling me, "Go on and get on out of here, it's another day the Lord has made and you don't need to be wasting it acting all ugly around here."

But I was sitting right in the same place I had been sitting all morn-ing when the two men came to the door to tell us about the man who had gone and jumped from the Willis Avenue Bridge. Or maybe he fell. "Ma'am," the first stranger spoke up. "I seen the whole thing. He just stood up there on the top railing, took off this cap here, and threw it behind him. Then he fell over into the water, all the while shouting something fierce and pitiful. Hollerin straight on till he hit the river." The man's eyes watered, the other man just stood there like he didn't have a thing to add until it looked like his friend had said all he could. Then he spoke what they had come to say.

"Mrs. Thomas, ma'am, I'm real sorry to bring this news to you and yours, but one of the mens that works on the bridge with your, with Mr. Thomas, founded the cap we got right here an we seen these initials sewed right there into the lining, 'M. T.,' an so somebody said shouldn't one of us go over to that family and find out was he at home and maybe it wasn't him. And that's why I am so sorry to be standing here on your doorstep on this day."

I looked at the cap and knew right away that it was my daddy's. It went quiet for what seemed a long time. And then there came a sound like I hope to God never to have to hear again. It was long and slow and seemed like it worked its way up from her insides till it came out of my mother's mouth. A queer high sound that shattered the heart of everyone left standing in the room. Me too. Broke it full on.

So because it was me at home waiting for something that I didn't know what it was going to be, it was me who went down to the morgue with Moms and held on to her hand while she looked to Daddy's body laid out on a metal table with just a sheet over him. It was wet—damp from his river-soaked clothes. Moms looked down to the end of him. First it was him by the bootstrap that had lost its buckle and then it was him because of the mismatched buttons on his waistcoat, dark blue and olive green, and finally it was him because of the wedding band that was her own daddy's—the one he gave them just before they headed up to New York.

"Yes," she whispered. "This is my Maurice." And the only reason I was there to hear her say it was because of that feeling that kept me home that day. The first time it happened—when the trolley hit the little girl and the car behind swerved to get out of its way and was headed for her mama before I pulled the lady out of its path—I almost didn't recognize it until afterwards. But with my daddy, when I got the chance to think on it some, and to remember the feel of it all, I got the sense I needed to pay attention.

ON THAT NIGHT WHEN EVERYTHING HAPPENED MY ATTENTION WAS going back and forth between the folks who watched the coming in and those that were the featured attraction, and the hotel bellhop. The staircase and balconies were crowded with guests pretending to stop and look around when truth was they wanted a breather before they got up to the banquet floor. It's not like folk don't take some pride in my being their colored policeman. But that respect didn't carry over to my people—the watchers not the watched—not giving me the eye when I told them to "back off some now" when they got a bit close to the society folk.

It wasn't like these folks hadn't come there all shimmery and glittering fully intending to be the spectacle they turned out to be. Most all of them woulda been disappointed if nobody was lined up to watch them come into the hotel like they was the main attraction at the Savoy. Shoot. I couldn't help but to stare myself at the fur coats striding by one after another with ladies' little heads snuggled down inside them peeping out to see if anybody had noticed them. But understanding the urge didn't mean I shouldn't have grabbed hold of that lady's hand when she reached across the rope toward a woman with a honey-gold fox wrapped around her neck. It was my duty to tell her to keep her hands to herself. These folks were there to be looked at, not to be stroked. Except for their egos.

"It's no way I'm trying to touch on her," the crowd lady said in a huffy tone back to me. "I just wanted to brush something off a her coat."

I was polite but firm in my response. "Yes ma'am; but could you just step back some?" I had her back under some control and it woulda stayed that way if the society lady didn't let off with that high-pitched screech.

"Puh-leeze!" she squealed in a voice that had to be as irritating to the gent that came with her as it was to me.

"Oh no you didn't say that. I know you didn't just call for no po-lice?" the crowd lady asked, her hands on her hips so I know she's about to go off. At that she calls the lady in the fur coat a "high-class hussy bitch" and like that wasn't enough she went on and said, "And you can take that fake dead animal head from off your neck and shove it right down to where it might bite at some company it can recognize."

Now this is the kinda stuff that I'm supposed to keep from happening so I whispered to her that she and I both could tell when folks just been misraised and how we need to let them just go on about their business. That just about ended it till the crowd lady told me, starting out in a nice quiet-like voice, "You sure is right young man. And I thanks you for having enough mannerisms to come correct with me." But then she shook loose of my hand and shouted loud enough for everybody to hear, "Home training shows on a hussy or a ho." Folks busted out laughing. Thank goodness the vacuum of the revolving doors sucked the uppity lady inside to the hotel lobby. No telling what can happen when two ladies goes at it.

At the beginning of the evening that was as close as it came to things turning out. But it didn't stay that way.

In the lobby, everybody had gone up to the banquet, and like I said, I wasn't having a whole lot of success staying with my book given the way the bellhop kept up with wanting a conversation. I finally put it away. It wasn't like I didn't know the page I was on by heart. It's the one that goes,

> It is a peculiar sensation, . . . this sense of always looking at one's self through the eyes of others . . . One ever feels his two-ness, . . . two souls, two thoughts, two unreconciled strivings; two warring ideals in one dark body.

And right as I was saying my favorite words from it to myself—"unreconciled" and "one ever feels"—and had started to stand with the intention of going over to try to be more sociable to the boy, he had something to say to me.

"Feels what?"

"Nothing," I said, walking over to where he was. "It's just some words from the book I was reading." But he wouldn't let it go.

"What doesn't one never feel?" By this time I was feeling like it was my responsibility to point out that he had his words a bit mixed up.

"It's not one 'never feels.' The book says 'one ever feels.'" It wasn't more than a few seconds that had passed, while he was thinking up what to say back to me, when things turned out.

First off, neither of us said a single solitary word. We didn't have to. The noise coming from above us was enough to unsettle us both. We looked up at the ceiling, then across to each other. We knew without saying a blessed word that something was gone terribly wrong.

2

Harlem Night

SHE KNEW IT WAS GOING TO BE A LONG NIGHT. BUT THIS STRETCHED past what she would tolerate. Earlene Kinsdale's pique was nothing new. No matter how far our people come, we can't get this issue of time together. Being late and being colored go together like cane sugar and butter on white bread. Not that she ordinarily indulges in those things; but her girl LaVerne would occasionally sneak some on a tea tray just to let her know she remembers the old ways.

The program of the Ninth Annual Opportunity Awards Banquet had already consumed most of the evening. Earlene was bored. It wasn't like she was there to win anything, but there were the rumors about who would win the grand prize and by that time anything about Olivia Frelon was of interest despite the fact that she hated the bitch. So she sat through two awards and didn't even comment on the ill-fitting dress of Sylvia Wallace Hutchins, the mousy woman receiving the poetry award. Earlene could tell by Miss Hutchins's demeanor, waiting on the stage and having stepped back to make room for the "grande" prize-winner, that she was piqued at the apparent grandstanding of the night's big awardee. She wasn't the only guest who was irritated. Earlene had already shared—with anyone near enough to hear—her opinion that it made no sense whatsoever that a short story should be the top award. At some point she expressed her exasperation or said, "Oh dear Lord." Grace

15

Milner discreetly kicked her and whispered "Earlene Kinsdale, remember yourself!"

By now anyone with a bit of discernment could tell that both Mrs. Hutchins and the nonfiction essay winner, Professor Shedrick Lyons, were displeased. Dr. Johnson was on his third announcement. This time he went on and on with something outrageously effusive like, "Ladies and gentlemen, our newest authoress, a new member of our talented community, the beautiful, the enchanting, the exquisitely talented Miss Olivia Frelon." Earlene smirked, and of course Grace kicked at her again while Dr. Johnson swept his arm to the side, ready to usher Olivia to the stage. The audience was trying to help move things along. Their applause grew louder and more sustained, as if its sheer force would usher forth the winner.

Finally, the draperies did open. But it absolutely wasn't "the lovely" Olivia Frelon who came out. Instead, a hysterical Mrs. Wilhelmina Tilden, who was decidedly unlike the intended awardee in either appearance or manner, staggered awkwardly into the room. To a person the applause quieted, paused by her untidy apparition. Without any attention whatsoever to her unbecoming dishevelment she rushed past the front tables and onto the raised platform at the front of the dais. Her piercing shriek trailed across the room until it was finally amplified for the entire ballroom. She literally snatched the microphone out of the hands of the unsettled Dr. Johnson. That conduct alone would have been quite enough to shock everyone into silence. But it was her blubbering, scandalously ungrammatical cry—and in front of the wait staff at that—that caused the room to descend into total chaos.

"She dead! She dead!" Wilhelmina Tilden sobbed. "She done fell out the window!"

Earlene Kinsdale immediately grabbed her couture evening bag and ran for the door, all the while thinking, "Good gracious! She should have said 'has fallen.'"

The noise expanded like a rumbling roll of thunder. But it was queer. Like thunder on a snow day. And different. But not unusual kind of different—different like trouble.

Before we had time to think about what it could be, the bellhop and I saw a swarm of people come trampling down the mezzanine staircase. Not one of them was taking their time to glide down the velvety carpets to show themselves off. Nobody glanced into the mirrored walls to see how swell they looked. They were stumbling and pushing and shoving. Waiters and folks from the kitchen, aprons on and off, cooks' hats falling by the wayside, were all mixed in with the guests. Fur coats got dragged and pearls bounced up and down the ample bosoms of the society ladies with nobody at all mouthing a word of complaint about the class mixing. That's how I knew it was serious.

I started up the stairs trying to figure out what in the hell had happened. Folks were screaming like they had left their class and color behind. I could make out some of them saying something like, "She fell!" and, "The window!" One tuxedoed gent looked over and saw me running up the stairs that he was running down from. He grabbed ahold of me and said, "Officer, not that way! Down here! Outside!" The only thing I heard clearly was, "There's no way she could have survived!" I just got to figuring things out when the revolving doors spun me around and smacked me outside.

The air that had been breezy and brisk had turned into a fierce cold that nearly took my breath away. One thing I remember is how it didn't take much more than folks being shoved or pulled or pushed out into the night air at first all shouting and screaming at the top of their lungs and then almost as quick as they got turned out everything went quiet as dark. Something was laying stretched out in the snow so I pushed through the crowd. It was a lady laid out across the sidewalk. A white lady. Damn! I thought. This was trouble coming and going.

One thing absolutely true was that she was dead. I could tell that right away. I went in close to check for her breath and a pulse, but she was full-on gone. All those folks who weren't invited to the affair, anticipating that it would be worth the discomfort of the frigid night to be able to tell friends about the fur coats, the fashionable limousines, the famous faces, and the haughtiness of the Sugar Hill crowd were gone. Now it was just the banquet folks, the servers, busboys, and some cooks, alongside the guests, who got shocked into forming a silent vigil around the dead lady. All of them, and me too. The truth was that at first, I couldn't think of much more than, "Why'd it have to be a white lady laid out dead up here in Harlem on my watch night?"

WHILE STREAMS OF WARM BLOOD POOLED UNDER AND AROUND HER, films of steamy condensation floated above, like what happened when you breathed out into the cold air. But this was no breath. It was her life that seeped out. The back of her head was pressed in a way that fit over the angles of the curbstone. Her blood spilled out in steamy mists, melting icy white crystals and etching a winding path that sloped down towards the iron grate at the cross street. A river of red slipped from her body, fell over the curb, splattered into the gutter, and wound its way down and into the city sewer.

3

Bound North Blues

ON A LATE-IN-THE-WEEK'S DAY, TWO GIRLS, NEARLY BUT NOT QUITE women, disembarked from the bound north train. One of them got on the train the very same way she left—rushed and without a thought other than her next step. Her eyes had already gone dim. She was skittish and had an easy loveliness that stood book-open for a kind word or a resting place. Both of them, the skittish one and the one with some polish, looked like they could use a good bath and a change of clothing. And in fact, one of them did take the time before she left the station to freshen up and exchange her journey-worn black dress for a freshly packed one. It was a bit threadbare in places not obvious to an unpracticed glance but only a lingering eye would notice. None did.

The other one eventually changed too. But hers was into a bright bird-yellow dress that told everything anybody needed to know. She was already far past the fix of a loving welcome. She'd only managed her way onto the train by a cousin's good graces who gave her a shoebox with deviled eggs, fatback, and white bread and told her she had to get outta town before that man or his wife came looking for her. The one in black had the means to hail a taxi. Maisie James waited until somebody offered something that sounded better than the nothing she already had.

YOUNG WYCKOMB DEBAUN CLIMBED THE DARK, WINDING STAIRCASE with practiced ease, reached behind the hydrant for the key, and let himself in. Maisie was already in bed. "Expecting me, sweet shakes?" he asked as he climbed on top of the blankets and nuzzled the back of her neck. He still couldn't fathom how her hair could be so soft and welcoming there, just like it was between her legs. The thought of it made him slip his knee between her legs, trying to nudge them apart. The blanket covered her. He tugged at it to pull it down, but Maisie moaned and grabbed at its tattered edges, pulling them back to cover her.

"No baby, no! Stop!" Then she whispered, "Not now."

"I told you before not to tell me no." Wyck tried to sound implacable, like his father did whenever he took that tone. With a fierce kind of seriousness, he whispered, "You can't say no to this baby." He reached between her legs and forcibly pushed them apart. He hadn't turned on the light, but he could tell from the feel of it that her slip was already wet. "See. You're all ready."

"Micky, stop! Something's happened. Please just stop." Her pleading made him want her even more, but there was something in her voice that made him reach for the lamp and turn it on. A pale yellow glow flooded the small room and its grim streaks of light stretched listlessly across the bed. He tried to discern exactly what it was he was seeing. Something was wrong. The sheets were wet but dark. The bottom of her slip was stained with an off-color clamminess. Maisie looked dry and shriveled, not all hot and ready for him. Then there was the smell. Like metal . . . bitter and sharp at the same time. And fresh. Like blood.

"Awwwwww no! No!" he screamed at her. "This ain't nothing normal. What is this? What the hell is this?"

"It's not my fault," she pleaded. "Please. I didn't know! It's gone. I lost it. We lost our baby."

Wyckomb blanched before he regained that authoritative demeanor that he desperately prayed would change the ugly scenario evolving in front of him. He punched the bed near to her cheek. She clenched with a familiar fear. Not that he would have noticed. He never did. "Oh uh-uh. No siree. There's no 'we' here. Who told you to say that? You worthless whore crazy nigger bitch. What's the matter with you?"

Maisie was whimpering and weak. Her energy was spent. She'd barely made it back to the bed when she heard his key turning in the lock.

"Don't even try that." His growl was as much anger as fear. "There isn't any 'us' and no kind of 'our.' Not with your kind there isn't." Maisie looked up, too tired to even show any shock of a now understood awareness. He saw he was getting to her so his tirade continued with an assured and privileged intensity. "You know as well as me that this thing here is nothing more than playtime and a few dollars. We were good. We saw some pictures. I let you ride in my car. It was a good time. And here you go and ruin it doing . . . doing . . . whatever the hell this here is." He looked around, the stench and stain blurring in his head. "I can't do this anymore. I can't have a part in anything like this. It wasn't supposed to be like this." He got up from the bed wiping his hands across the sheets. "Look at this. Look at you. It's . . . you're disgusting." She grabbed her knees and shrank into the shadow at the edge of the bed. But when he didn't come toward her, when he didn't even reach out to smack her, she was even more frightened. "I'm out of here. This is way past over." He did raise his hand, but the dank pitifulness bundled up on the bed was far too sordid for his refined upbringing. Or the energy he'd have had to exert in a corrective slap.

The door slammed shut and she could hear his pounding down the stairs. It took her last bit of strength, but Maisie didn't know what else to do but to follow him. She stumbled down the stairs and out the door. The night was thick with sleet, and because she couldn't see where he'd gone she ran into the street. It didn't even matter she still had nothing on but the slip. Micky was the hope she had for something different. Even when different hurt. So she stared into the dark night until the white lights of his coupe turned the corner. He was going too fast, and if she didn't stop him now he would drive right past her. So she ran toward the lights waving for him to stop, screaming, "Please, Micky. Please. Just stop. Stop!" Of course he saw her. And that made it even more urgent that he get away. So Wyckomb deBaun pressed the accelerator to the floor and Maisie took the full force of the automobile's right fender. Startled with the intent as well as the surety of his response, she tried to grab on to the smooth metal. But there was nothing to hold on to. The automobile's swipe came with such intensity that it lifted her slightly off her feet. She fell with a thud and rolled over twice before her body stopped at the curb just above the gutter. By the time the car took the corner some blocks down where a crowd of glitterati and others were gathered around the scene at the Hotel Theresa, the speeding yellow coupe was of little interest to anyone except the colored cop who looked up and, noticing the driver, shook his head with disgust at the white boys who used his streets and his people for their carelessness.

MOST EVERYBODY WHO HAD ANYTHING TO SAY ALREADY TALKED ABOUT Maisie like she was somebody who didn't do us any favors. It was one thing that she was available to strangers, but quite another that some of them were white men. Some whispered that they heard there were women too. That changed everything. She was not proper company during the day and folks suspected how she spent most nights. Out late, skirt up, legs wide open, waiting for pay or love. Likely both. She wanted the love and needed the money. Poor thing even thought that the stuttering towheaded white boy that drove his fancy yellow car into Harlem every weekend and went up to her rooms like he belonged there would make the difference she was waiting for. He did, but not like she expected.

Maisie's death—not nearly as quick or easy as the one who got off the train with her and then went out the window—was slow and should have been painful. She lay against the gutter cold and confused and bleeding from where the car slammed into her. What was left of their lives, hers and the baby's, spilled out, messy and sad, slippery and alone. There was no circling crowd to cover her or to speak a prayerful "Lord have mercy." The bitter cold and painful slam of the automobile nearly finished her off. She lay on a side street waiting for a hurt that never came. Instead a deep still quiet crept into the spaces left vacant from her emptied-out lives. Both of them. Because there is grace, a dark and easy peace washed into and filled each crevice left from sorrows fixed to flesh. Her soul slipped over with an embrace so gentle and so fully compassionate she wished she could have stayed within it. And in that thick moment voices older than she could know gathered to sing her across. Maisie James and her babygirl—neither with lives long enough to earn a sigh—earned the company of an ancient and necessary chorus of voices.

4

Political Parties

"I DON'T SEE WHY WE HAVE TO HOST THE MAYOR'S HOLIDAY PARTY."
Mavis deBaun's whimpers were edging toward a full-force whine. "It
ruins the carpets, there are more Jews than I can count, and I had to call
half the staff back."

Vice Mayor Victor deBaun turned to leave their upstairs sitting room
but not before he checked his image in the mirror above the fireplace. His
square jaw and slightly gray temples gave him a decided dignity. When
he turned away from the glass, he gestured his butler toward the cabinet
and nodded in the direction of his wife. Other than that subtle instruction, he walked toward the parlor's doors with barely a pause. "I expect
you to conduct yourself with appropriate decorum."

Mavis tried to recapture her bearing, especially since Burleigh and the
upstairs girl were both there. "But why should it be our affair?" she said
with an affected authority. "Everyone knows that these holiday gatherings
are done by the mayor and his wife. Why must we take on their task?"

His irritation was palpable. "You can't be serious." He turned back to
the rooms he'd just exited trying to control his growing rage. His wife
was now leaning, but still with an arguable gracefulness, against the fireplace pilasters. He knew it was a pose chosen to steady her as much as for
its dramatic effect. "I can't believe that after all these years of strategiz-
ing for my taking the mayoral seat, it isn't evident why this is a brilliant

23

opportunity." Mavis turned away. His admonishments grew closer to a tirade: "Try to get this through your head, darling." Nothing in his delivery felt endearing. "People have to see us in the role if we are to have it. All the talk now is about the mayor's philandering. And that's our open door. One more chorus-girl scandal and his seat will be handed to me with instructions to restore civility and dignity to the office. Your only job is to make sure neither you nor that delinquent son of yours interferes with my potential." Mavis pressed her hand against her lips as if she needed help in keeping silent. It didn't work.

"He's our son. Ours!" A forlorn wail betrayed her despair. "Wyck? Wyckomb? Burleigh! Where is my boy? You must send him to accompany me downstairs. It's only proper I should have an escort. Where is he? Where's our son?" Burleigh closed the doors to the second-floor family parlor and left Mavis with a small glass of the tincture that usually calmed her.

There was no answer from their son because at that very minute Wyckomb deBaun was driving his yellow coupe with frightened abandon back down to Manhattan. It didn't even matter that there was a phalanx of folks gathered outside at the corner of 125th and 7th. He took the corner without slowing down or even noticing whatever it was that was splayed out at the edge of the curb. He swerved around the gathering. One of the cops looked up, but his speeding car was less important than the dead lady.

"It appears the young master is out for the evening, ma'am," Burleigh said quietly as his gloved hands eased the door closed. Mavis gathered her resolve, took a last glimpse in the mirror, and walked toward the landing. By the time that she reached the bottom of the staircase there was no residue of the earlier unpleasantness. She was as good as her husband knew she could be.

"Darlings, how lovely of you to come," she told one couple, limply offering a bejeweled hand while turning toward another to say, "How delightful it is to see you again. How is your little one?" She smiled wanly but had already turned towards another couple: "We're charmed that you would grace our home this evening." When she saw the police commissioner's wife chatting in a circle of first-tier women gathered by the fireplace, she slowly made her way over to the group of them. By the time she reached the clutch of society mavens she was in fine form, having been sufficiently indulged with numerous greetings and congratulations on a superb affair—and her prescriptive tincture had its effects. "My dears," she said charmingly to the gathering of women, "you look absolutely stunning in this firelight. It does become you so!" Her greeting seemed sincere. "Now," she clasped the arm of the woman closest to her and said in what was intended to be an intimate whisper but was actually overly loud, "you must tell me the latest stories." She waved her free hand across the room in a way that allowed her rings and bangles to pick up the fire-light and glisten with a not-unwanted effect. "I haven't caught up on any of the news."

While the women chatted, the enigmatic Hughes Wellington, Esq., entered, handing his coat and top hat to the butler. DeBaun rushed over to greet the man everyone knew must appear at an affair if it is to be marked as top-notch. "Wellington! So glad you could make it."

"Absolutely my pleasure, Victor. I came straight away after a brief stop at a banquet in Harlem."

"Oh, so you've been up there again, eh?" He tried to mask his curiosity. "I'm sure it was—ahem—an engaging and fancy affair, by their stan-dards." The coloreds were certainly worth a good conversation, but no matter his own curiosities, he'd never want to be particularly close to any of them. Wellington noticed his attitude but ignored it.

"It was an awards banquet for literary arts, attended by all their best people."

"No doubt, no doubt," deBaun assured him, leading him away from the vestibule and ushering him into the salon. "I know Mavis will want to hear all about it." He looked around, but his glistening wife was already at his side, closely followed by the group of women who had seen Wellington's arrival. He was the prize guest of the night, and the glow that surrounded him easily quieted Mavis deBaun's own discomforts with the duties of being a reluctant host. Wellington fell into the entertaining mode everyone always enjoyed, especially when he engaged the ladies with stories of uptown. Both deBauns were delighted with the liveliness of the repartee, and Mavis didn't even notice when Burleigh discreetly approached the vice mayor informing him the police commissioner had an urgent visitor The party was in full swing and the commissioner wasn't of particular interest to many, especially with Hughes Wellington holding forth on the "occasion" he'd left in Harlem.

But a short time later, when a police officer in full uniform showed up in the parlor—in plain view of anyone turned in that direction—and announced without any effort at all to be discreet, "I come for the commissioner," everyone was immediately attentive—even leaving the cluster around Wellington to get closer to whatever this new entertaining interlude might produce. The developing drama in the vestibule seemed more interesting than their own conversations, especially as they had become redundant. Commissioner Leach took full advantage of the guests' interests and effected a rather dramatic turn away from their peering to read the note the officer handed to him.

The commissioner took the opportunity for the attention now universally directed toward him. He opened the officer's note, took out his reading glasses, and read it through, then turned back to face the group, slowly folding the paper and placing it into a pocket while holding on to (and baiting) everyone's mounting interest. "Honored hosts and fellow guests, please accept my sincere apologies for the necessities of my professional work having at all interrupted these superb festivities. I'm afraid it does call for some explanation." It was clear that he had everyone's attention and Leach was perfectly willing to indulge it. "My office had become aware of a death in Harlem that, well . . . at first glance seemed to be one of our own!" He waited until people realized that he must be speaking of a white person. A few turned to look at Wellington, some with a bit of an accusatory mien. Leach continued his explanation. "At first review, it also seemed to be a lady of considerable means." Those in attendance responded with a collective gasp. The commissioner used the moment to his advantage. But deBaun was beginning to show some annoyance. His plan for the evening had not included much attention past a gentlemanly welcome to the police commissioner. Whatever his professional title, he was still not quite in the social stratum that should command the attention of an audience of his guests. But Leach chose to take advantage of the moment. "Not to worry. I have just been informed that all is safe and well. I can assure you that any concerns we may have had can be placed aside from our interests." An audible sigh greeted his assurance, as he had anticipated. Leach paused just a moment before he added, "However, I must say there was indeed a death in Harlem." He allowed just a bit of conversation to scatter through the room before he said, "but . . . she was not one of us." The gathering let out a collective sigh of relief. "Instead, it seemed one of these colored gals who seemed to be, umm, what is it . . . what do they call it when they look like us but are truly of the Negro persuasion?"

"Pasted." Mavis deBaun filled in the word. Victor hoped that the slight slur in her speech would escape notice.

"Of course, that's the lingo. Thank you most kindly, Mavis. You always have a way with these unusual terms. It was a gal who was—or at least could have been, had she been in our good company—pasted." There was an appropriate gasp. "Let me tell you, I've seen some of these folks, and frankly, it's a bit unnerving. These people can look as white as any one of us." The pronouncement had its effect, especially on the women. A few fans fluttered nervously. "But do rest easy," the commissioner continued, "it has turned out to be a colored gal that seems somehow to have jumped, or fallen, and died. Whichever it may be. My staff tells me that it made quite a spectacle over at the Hotel Theresa. Seems she was a real looker." The men standing nearest him laughed. As smaller conversations emerged in the chatter that followed the announcement, the host finally regained control of his affair.

"Friends," deBaun addressed the crowd, "I must say, we hadn't expected the commissioner to contribute to our entertainment this evening." His guests returned his successful attempt to lighten the mood with a hearty chuckle. "But I can invite you all into the gallery, where you will find the extraordinary Madame Maria Jeritza here with her accompanist, ready to share some of the season's best for us as a private concert." Waves of appreciative and impressed sounds filled the halls. There was even some quietly gloved applause at the unexpected treat. And, except for one guest, everyone eagerly followed their host, who had taken his wife firmly by the arm and led the company into the gallery. Few paid much attention to the fact that Hughes Wellington, his face blanched, retired to the cloakroom, removed his coat, hat, and cane from the racks, and left the event with extraordinary dispatch just as Madame Jeritza finished the plaintive Rossetti hymn: "What can I give Him, poor as I am? Give my heart."

5

The Ninth Annual Opportunity Awards Banquet

MRS. EARLENE KINSDALE EXPLAINED TO ANYONE WHO WOULD LISTEN that Olivia Frelon came to the affair fully intending to be a spectacle. So it followed quite logically that everything Olivia did that night, from her dramatic entrance to her rather unconventional departure, was a performance. The organization clearly anticipated the gathering of Harlemites outside the hotel, and Earlene was quick to affirm it. "Why ever do you think we arranged to have the carpet in front of the door with the sides roped off? Those people were, well, they were our conversation starters."

Not wanting to miss Olivia and Vera's entrance, Earlene quickly found Grace Milner and escorted her toward the ballroom stairs. But not without taking a moment to catch a glimpse of herself in the mirror. Even Grace commented on how the glow of her topaz skin was elegantly accentuated by her bronze chiffon gown. Earlene loved how the fabric shimmered when she moved. She especially liked the tiers that flowed from the dropped waist. Each was intricately trimmed with rhinestones and glass beads and, because Grace sometimes does not have quite the eye for detail and missed the effect, she was considerate enough to point out to her friend the hand-sewn embroidery's delicate pattern of crystal leaves and blossoms.

Earlene wouldn't be able to recall what her friend Grace was wearing, although she remarked later that she was nearly certain it was quite nice. However, she did remember Grace's remark on how the shading of her fox nicely complemented both her gown and her coloring. In fact, it was that compliment that led Earlene to take her friend Grace's arm so that they could walk into the ballroom together.

Earlene Kinsdale wasn't the only one who matched skin, gown, and wrap. It was something of a trend. Or at least an acknowledgment that variations of skin tone could be made more palatable with a selective array of accoutrements. Dresses of chocolate satin went stunningly with minks slipped seductively across polished ebony shoulders. There was some talk that the ladies with a darker coloration need not have been given so much attention; but this was the creativity of the Harlem glitterati on display. The men, of course, did not have this burden. Their duty to lighten the race would come from their associations with appropriately hued women; or, if not correctly colored, at least well-heeled.

At the banquet table, the guests—Mr. and Mrs. Eugene (Grace) Milner, Vera Scott (whose husband was unexpectedly called away), Myra and Augustus Wood, and Earlene Kinsdale (the widow of Edgar Kinsdale)—settled into gossipy conversations about what it was like to have to nudge their way through crowds of the "Harlem regulars." Grace Milner exclaimed, "And what about the one who said, 'Them's those uppity Negroes'?" She shuddered at the recollection. "Why in heaven's name can't our people do better with grammar and proper form?" The table nodded in full agreement and shared harrowing tales of making it into the hotel past the threat of the gathered onlookers. After several attempts to break through the ladies' chatter, Augustus Wood finally had their attention. "You had to have seen him. An absolutely pitiful fellow in threadbare mittens—not gloves, but mittens!"

"No!" Grace replied, appropriately impressed with the fellow's odd choice of outerwear.

"And had the nerve to thrust his filthy hand right out in front of us."

The table sucked in their breath with a collective gasp. His wife reached across to pat Earlene's wrist. Their conversation moved on to how fortuitous it was that our Officer Thomas was there to intervene and how perfectly gallant he was.

"Well yes, dear, I agree," Augustus commented, "but do recall that despite the good officer's best efforts, he couldn't control the man's filthy mouth."

"Gracious!" Earlene exclaimed. "Whatever did he say?"

"He said," and here Myra and Augustus spoke in tandem, "'Ain't just one of y'all cain't spare a nickel?'"

"No!" All the guests pulled away from the table, as if the language might have a taint; or perhaps that the audacity of the request had merit.

"I assure you it happened exactly as I am telling it," Augustus continued, fully appreciating the attention his conversation earned. He sat forward in his chair and leaned in toward the table guests, who shuddered with appropriate disdain. He was encouraged with their response and continued, "And as if that weren't enough, he addressed me quite directly and accused me of acting as if I could not hear him. I assure you that I heard him well enough to make sure he didn't come within a hair's breadth of my Myra."

"Well my dear, truth to tell"—and here Myra reached over and patted his hand—"Officer Thomas assisted us in that regard." Augustus cut his eyes at his wife, and their uncomfortable pause gave Earlene an opportunity to interrupt with a bit of her own, far more interesting reality.

"Well it was, I daresay, equally providential that you were able to have your husband there as your escort, if only for that event." She reminded them all she was "recently" widowed. "Even though Dr. Scott isn't here with us tonight"—she nodded at the empty chair next to Vera—"it's because your husband seems to be, shall we say, 'otherwise engaged.' But my darling Edgar is dead and gone!" Before Vera Scott could comment Earlene continued, taking a hanky from her bag to dab her eyes. She let out a long sigh. "In fact, after I entered the lobby, it took a moment before I could find appropriate company; but then I saw you, sweet Grace." What Earlene did not share was that she selected Grace's company because her friend would not easily compete with her for attention. "At first Grace tried to be naughty and pretend she didn't hear me hailing her. You remember dear," she turned to Mrs. Milner, "it was when that quite unfortunately garbed woman walked past us and I explained to you how some people seem to just forget to look in the mirror before they leave the house."

"I remember, Earlene. Your voice does carry, sweetheart." Grace had used the potentially embarrassing moment to whisper that Olivia Frelon was probably already upstairs with Vera Scott. She knew Earlene wouldn't want to miss her. They anticipated correctly that Olivia would have wanted to make an entrance.

Vera Scott momentarily excused herself from the table while Grace asked, "Do you think that the two of them settled their tiff?" But Earlene wasn't quite ready to shift the attention away from herself.

"Do you think it bothers me one whit whether Vera and Olivia settle whatever seems to have happened between them? Now"—she focused on moving the attention back to herself—"about my evening bag. Custom, of course." She unclasped it to reveal the hand-stitched inside label.

Earlier, when Earlene Kinsdale and Grace Milner entered the banquet, it wasn't at all difficult to find Olivia Frelon. Neither was it unexpected that her gown was stunningly inappropriate. It was as if she had never heard the admonition that nice girls don't wear red. Earlene was standing near the group's assigned table and tried to get Grace to notice the vigorous exchange between Hughes Wellington and Olivia. "Look at them! Just because their coloring is similar is no reason to command the floor!" The color was flaring on Olivia's cheeks and Wellington appeared overly attentive. Earlene started to tell Grace that there was no way the woman deserved that much attention from the man, but then the headwaiter walked through striking the dinner bells. The occasion was called.

For an event that was already running late, Dr. Charles Johnson's timing was exquisite. Earlene whispered a challenge to the table to count his malapropisms. His velvety baritone was so beguiling that most were willing to forgive his florid style.

"Ladies and gentlemen, please accord me your gracious and kind attention and allow me to welcome you to the Ninth Annual Opportunity Awards Writing Contest. As you all know, I have been duly accorded the complete honor of being your humble master of these august and splendiferous ceremonies. And for those who have not yet had the opportunity to be led to my acquaintance, I am Doctor. Charles. Spurgeon. Johnson, Junior. The Second. Esquire." Earlene couldn't help but giggle when he said each element of his name as if it were an independent clause. When he paused Earlene asked Grace if she thought he had written "pause for applause" right there on his notes. Grace kicked her. Again.

"Thank you, kind friends. Thank you! What an extraordinarily appropriate welcome you have given me! I acknowledge you with gratitude and opprobrium. To you—my fellow denizens of the race—and, of course, to our greatly honored and distinctive guests, those of you from the other equally prolific branch of the brotherhood of men." There was a hearty round of applause so that the five white folks in attendance would feel their gratitude and pleasure.

"I am inordinately grateful to have been elected your esteemed president of this venerable organization, The. Negro. Welfare. League." He pronounced the name of the organization with such flair (and carefully placed caesuras) that it too received the congregants' applause. "And of course, with this joyous opportunity for leadership that I shall unselfishly and unflinchingly provide, I am also the editor in chief of our national organ, the Op-por-tun-i-ty Magazine, *In*-corporated." He emphasized the first syllable. Dr. Johnson allowed a substantial applause to build. It was a performative tour de force.

"So you will of course, dear friends and guests, understand and appreciate the destination of my request to you. If I might take this intimate license, you are undoubtedly the most extraordinary and resplendently attired audience that has had the fortune to gather for this gilded 'opportunity.'" Here he smiled when he got a few chuckles, but it was clear he had anticipated more. "You have ostentatiously displayed every dimension of the gift of sartorial attire for this revered occasion." Grace kicked Earlene again, and it nearly caused her to choke. But Johnson didn't miss a beat. "It is my most delightful assignment to request that you kindly stand for the entrance of our panel of judges, who, with flair, finesse, and rectitude, brought their inestimable talents of discernment and equanimity in evaluating the many and manifold entries in our benighted competition."

"Gracious," Earlene declared to everyone who might have been listening. "You'd think he was standing at an altar during the reading of Revelations."

Earlier in the evening, Miss Silk, the Harlem librarian, excused herself from a front table so that she could receive the secret list of winners and have time to write out their titles and names. She was known to craft the cards in her most elegantly executed script, and she always encouraged them to frame them. Most winners had already ordered the frames. In front of the gathering, Dr. Johnson dramatically broke each of Miss Silk's freshly waxed seals and slid out the enclosed announcement with as great a flourish as he could muster.

First came the poetry prize. The plan was that the society's secretary, Mrs. Wilhelmina Tilden, would escort the winner from the private room where the awardees had all surreptitiously gathered (even though just about everyone knew they were there). Nevertheless, respect was extended for the occasion's rituals.

At first, everything was in order. Sylvia Wallace Hutchins came out to accept her plaque and read her winning entry. Mrs. Hutchins was a perfectly uplifted Negro. Her dainty features didn't protrude. And although she could not be called bright (her skin was a bit too deeply toned), her thin hair was appropriately waved and gathered into a neat chignon. She was even attired in a fashionable dress (for a poetess): a dove-gray silk with its understated holiday flair displayed in a lace collar and cuffs. In fact, it contrasted quite dramatically with the purple and gold costume worn by Zora Hurston, whose feathered headdress obscured the view of those seated behind her. As it was designed to do. Miss Hutchins's entry was a sonnet titled, "Ode to the Darkened Ones," which ended in the extraordinary couplet:

> Our fate will find our color thus entwined
> A prideful race allegiance to our kind!

Dr. Shedrick Lyons's nonfiction prize was similarly well received, even though Dr. Johnson's rather detailed review of its major arguments was unnecessary. The essay argued that only the physically strongest and most mentally acute of those captured from dark Africa successfully survived the harrowing passage on slave ships and America's cruel plantation system. And therefore those who survived into this century were exemplars of the best of the race—its most mentally fit, physically superior, and spiritually refined. It seemed entirely plausible. So the applause for Professor Lyons's award was not inappropriate and only circumstantially related to the fact that the evening was finally coming to a close.

Dr. Johnson broke the seal of the last envelope, held the card aloft, and announced, "Our final award is the most coveted. The judges have declared the winner of the fiction category to be . . ." He slipped the card dramatically from the envelope: "Miss Olivia Frelon wins the Ninth Annual Op-por-tun-i-ty Award for Creative Fiction for her story 'Sanctuary.'" Gasps of surprise came from the audience, many of whom stood to welcome her to the dais. Most clapped and clapped. But after a while—CPT notwithstanding—everyone felt the awkwardness of the pause when Dr. Johnson's dramatically extended arm in ceremonial welcome just hung there and Olivia failed to sweep elegantly into the room. He repeated a version of his announcement, this time saying, "And to culminate our splendid evening of effulgence and excellence, I now present to you, ladies and gentlemen of our esteemed community, the winner of the award for creative short fiction—in this, the Ninth Annual Op-por-tun-i-ty Magazine Writing Awards—Miss Olivia Frelon. Authoress extraordinaire." He slowly drew his words out, but not for their performative value. Some wondered whether Olivia was delayed in the ladies' parlor. If this was the case, her timing was extraordinarily ill-considered.

But finally, the curtain did part. To everyone's surprise it was not an elegant Olivia Frelon who emerged. Instead it was Wilhelmina Tilden, and she was a fright! Her slightly lovely ball gown was indecorously bunched into her fists. And her scream—which started from one end of the dais and which was eventually magnified by the microphone Dr. Johnson unwillingly relinquished—was something terrible indeed.

Everything froze. And it wasn't simply because Mrs. Tilden had displayed appallingly bad grammar. It wasn't long at all before the horror of the moment took its effect and some started screaming and fainting into the arms of their escorts—or onto the floor for those who were ill positioned. Mrs. Tilden and Mrs. Morris (the organization's treasurer) grabbed each other's forearms and stood together on the dais hollering in high-pitched unison. Some, the annoying and pushy Zora Hurston among them, squeezed into the small waiting room and leaned, rather dangerously, from its wide-open window. Others, including Earlene Kinsdale, rushed to the exit and down the grand staircase. They were the first to see the body. Even though bearing witness is a part of racial duty, the entire scene was, quite frankly, heartbreaking.

Olivia Frelon had fallen flat on her back. The amount of blood was a clear indication of the severity of her injury. The evening's snow, falling a bit more heavily now, was already forming a gossamer coverlet over her that exaggerated the effect of her pale coloring's striking contrast to the gown splayed out around her. Earlene's thoughts raced. Given who Olivia was, and the rumors that were already circulating, she knew immediately that there would be questions. So the first thing she did after she got a good look at the body was to look around and ask, rather loudly given the solemnity of the moment, "Where's Vera?"

6

Misadventure?

SWEAT POURED DOWN MY FACE. IT HAPPENS WHEN I'M NERVOUS, NO matter whether it's midsummer or a witch-tit night like this one. But it's not like I don't have good reason to sweat. Cars full of police and detectives coming up here from downtown and my folks—police and community—getting antsy. And they should be! It's a white lady laid out dead on one of my streets and I'm right here in the mix of it. Here I'm thinking I just wanted to be a cop. Not the Negro cop. Not the colored cop. Not the one assigned when my folks misbehaved or our kids went truant. And especially not this cop here assigned to po-lice the élites. But that's exactly where I'm finding myself. When the chief assigned me here, he wasn't expecting much more than pickpockets and purse snatchers. Not neither one of us would have anticipated a dead lady.

By the time the detectives and all showed up, I had enough info to begin to put things together; but the white officers pushed me away like I wasn't one of them. If they'd listened I could've told them who she was, what it seemed like had happened, and other details. But my information don't have the same value like what they collect. First thing one tells me is, "Step away from the body." It didn't matter one bit that all of them need me right where I am for all the reasons I got this job in the first place. With this kinda messiness and two sets of folks not knowing and certainly not trusting each other, it's not going to take much to get

36

to trouble. So I got to moving through the crowd and asking politely, "If you please, would all y'all move on back now?" Then one of them downtown fools got out a bullhorn and shouted, "You peoples!" so loud that the insult of the address got up under my own skin and left me feeling every kind of way but helpful.

I wanted to snatch the horn out his hands, but I did not want to be the precipitating factor. So I go up to the officer and try to talk to him like we was on the same team. "Look man," I tell him. "We still need folks' names and addresses. Some of 'em could be witnesses."

He looks me over like he wants some time to be the one that thought this on his own like he shoulda done. "Yeah, okay son. Why don't you get us some names from your people." I ignore the insult of address. He puts that bull up to his mouth an gets to shouting again. "Okay. We wants names and addresses. Line up and get your particulars in order." I looked at him like he was the natural-born fool he was. With that nonsense, I didn't have any choice but to snatch the horn from him. I kinda knew that he wouldn't have enough nerve to take it back. So I say what he shoulda said. And I didn't use the horn to say it.

"Hey folks, you could help me out if you would share your names with me before you leave the scene. You ladies and gentlemen could be official witnesses, and this would be a mighty big help to me." Then I turned to the white cop. "What's your name?" I could see he was still trying to figure out how the bullhorn ended up in my hands instead a his.

"Officer O'Malley."

"Okay O'Malley," I said, "that's the way you and me"—and I put us together so he could remember we was on the same team—"that's the way you and me gonna get some cooperation. Folks here be willing to help out; but you gotta come correct." I gave him back the bullhorn and walked away. A detective was standing over by the patrol cars, and before I could go about the business of organizing folks, he called out loud as he could, "Hey boy!" and gestured to where he was. It took about everything I had to keep straight and tall. I could tell without much looking that everybody was kind of waiting to see what he did as much as me. I decided to act the way I shoulda been treated.

The truth was, everybody out there was still kind of stunned with what all had happened. It didn't take much to figure out that the police thought it was a white woman dead on the street, and that all by itself could turn into a whole lot of trouble. This was Harlem. And whether it was a white woman or a white-looking woman dead up in here, it was going to be somebody's bad news.

I was headed over to the fool that called me "boy" when I saw Mr. Shannon from our church, one of our deacons. I recognized him first because he had him some of what Moms calls his "arthuritis" that makes him wobble kinda back and forth when he walks. I called him by his proper name hoping it would signal to some of the white cops not to mess with him. "Mr. Shannon! Mr. Shannon, sir? What can I help you with?" He tilted his head toward the body and lifted up his arm just a bit—and that's when I could see it was a fresh table linen from up on the banquet level. It was clear what he was fixing to do, and I already felt regret that I had not been that attentive to what was called for on this occasion. So I just said real quiet like, "Thank you, sir. Thank you, Mr. Shannon. Let me give you some help with that." I could see outta the corner of my eye the white detective getting irritated, but he didn't interrupt. The two of us went over to the dead lady and spread the linen over her body. They'd already photographed the scene so it wasn't going to hurt none for her to be covered up. Nobody needed that kind of display, and whoever she was, nobody deserved this on their passing. One of the white cops started to say something about it was evidence but decided he wanted her covered up too. It probably felt right to him that the lady wasn't lying there in plain view anymore.

"Ain't nobody should have to die like that . . ." Mr. Shannon shook his head real pitiful-like. "A spectacle for everbody to come take they own peep at. Shame. Pretty gal. Shame." I took my time to help Mr. Shannon lay the corners straight and give him some time to adjust his bad knee before I made my way over to the detectives.

No matter how fine these folks were who were up here tonight, or how long they had been upstanding Harlem Heights Negroes, this one wasn't gonna be swept up and over like it was just another dead colored gal. This thing was going to attract a mess of attention. I started taking a few notes myself, not because I was trying to look official or nothing. There was going to be a report due on the captain's desk by the duty cop. And that would be me.

It was just when I turned to go back inside and make a few observations in my notes that a kid—a boy no more than ten or eleven—came from around the corner, tugged at my jacket, and asked if I was the officer he should talk to because he had seen the whole thing.

"Uh-huh, sure you did, son," I said. Lots of kids get it in their minds that they can do police business. Like that bellhop earlier on tonight. But I was decent to him and told him that the detectives already had their list of grown-ups who they want to talk to waiting inside. The boy wasn't nearly dressed for the weather, and too, he didn't look old enough to be out on this time of night. He was talking a mile a minute not like he was ready to just scoot like I politely asked him to do.

"Man, I tell you. I ain't never seen no cars like those Cunninghams that done drove up here tonight! And there was more furs and feathers than you find in . . . in church on Easter Sunday! An for damn sure I ain't never seed people like this! Not back in Stump Sound. No siree! That's where we moved up from, from Stump Sound. Wait'll I tell my gang down home what I done seen up in here tonight!" The kid's eyes glistened with excitement, and I got to thinking that maybe he did see something, but it didn't make me ready to send him into the lobby to the detectives. He was too young, and a bit too eager. I already had my notebook out so I told him he could tell me what he saw.

"Okay son. Take a breath, slow down some. I can take your statement right here." I turned it over to a fresh page and asked him what his name was and where did he live. "Now just tell me exactly what did you see from first to last?" I figured it wouldn't hurt to do this one interview; I could do it real quick and then send the kid home where he belonged.

"Everbody was so excited and acting all crazy and fainting all over the place an nobody even seen me, so, ummm . . . after I got me a good look at the dead lady, I went up the stairs to see where they had all come from." It was right then I realized what the kid was saying.

"Wait just a minute. You mean you was up there where she fell from?"

"Well, ummm, yeah. I mean it was getting kinda thick around the body and all so I just . . . well I just kinda thought . . . I figured I'd get me a chance to see it." I already knew from practice and the section in the manual about interviewing witnesses that when folks changed things in the middle of a sentence some kind of prevarication was going on. But the boy didn't miss a beat. "And good goodness was it worth it bein up there! All them tables covered with candles all lit up and silvery—you think that silver was the real deal?—anyway, there was crystal glasses too with silver all around the tops of them, but had some ladies' lipsticks messing them up. It was all so light and bright and sparkly, like Christmas done come and set down right damn smack in the middle of the Hotel Theresa."

"Okay boy, let's take things one at a time first . . ." But he was still caught in the story.

"Did I tell you about the food? Do Jesus, there was food enough for all a Harlem up in there. And googobs of dessert. I only had one—well, maybe a couple pieces of the cake cause for sure wasn't nobody going to be coming back for dessert after what they seen down there and too, I took one of these. Just one." The kid opened his palm and revealed a slender silver cigarette case. "There was lots of 'em still at the tables. But I just got me one. I swear." I think that's when he saw I wasn't looking none too happy and he tried to backtrack some. "It was like a memento souvenir," he said, sounding defensive. I snatched the case out of the kid's hand before he could wrap his fingers around it again.

Damn! Why'd the kid have to go and take this? Here I am trying to protect the kid from an official interrogation, but knowing that he had been up on the floor where it happened was a problem. The cigarette case would absolutely bring him the wrong kind of attention from the white detectives, and this kid did not need to get to know city police. I was trying to think of what the boy said, and what I was going to do with this upstart from someplace called Stump Sound. Sounds like somebody's ghost story.

That's when I decided I needed to put a stop to that potentiality. I made my move sudden because I was trying to scare him, so when I stooped down, I grabbed him tight by one of his shoulders and talked real quiet.

"Young man!"

"Yeah?" He looked at me straight in the eye and that's when I knew he wasn't a boy that could be easily cowed.

"Let's you and me try that just one more time. Young man!"

"Yes sir?"

"Now that's what I consider respectable. So now that I have your proper attention, I want you to listen to me right here and now. You do exactly like I say. Don't you even think of doing a thing but what I am telling you to do. Do I make myself clear?"

"Yes sir, Officer."

"Good answer, boy." I noticed he was looking kind of fearful like and that's how I knew I had him where I wanted. So I kept my quiet tone. It was better than hollerin. Folks pay attention when you whisper. "Now here's what you gonna do. First, you gonna scat right back home. Now. And you not going to stop anyplace anytime or anywhere. You listening son?"

"Yes sir."

"Good. Second. You are not going to say a blessed word about where you've been or what you've seen, and not a single thing about tonight and the banquet and the accident here. Nothing. Not to nobody. I don't care if it is your best bud or your dog or somebody else's stray. You hear me?"

"Yeah." He looked kind of disheartened at this, and that was when I knew I was right about his plans to tell his friends and all. So I had to be real convincing. I put both my hands on his arms and held him real firm so he couldn't move one way or the other. "I mean yes sir. I hear you." The kid was gutsy. "But can I have my case back? By rights that was mines. You ain't got to keep my silver box." I was a bit taken aback at his nerve; but I was also more than ready for this foolishness. So I slipped into my I can talk the talk just like you can voice. I snatched the neck of his thin jacket.

"Boy you ain't getting this is you? You want me to treat you like some of these fools that steal stuff and carry you on over to the station house? Cause I can do that with no problem whatsoever. That what you want?"

"No sir, I sure don't." It seemed like he finally figured out he was not the boss in this situation.

"So the onliest right thing for you right now is for you to get yourself on outta here before I decide that that's exactly what I'm going to do with your pitiful butt."

"Hey, boss man!" A detective with a thick wool coat and hat pushed down over his ears stuck his head out of the hotel. I turned toward him, not a little disappointed that the boy had likely heard this.

"Hold on. I'll be right there." The detective noticed the kid.

"Is that another witness for us?"

"No. He ain't for us." I figured if I talked like he expected me to he'd be more willing to believe me. So I laid it on a bit more heavily. "He ain't nothin y'all be needin. Just a neighborhood kid anglin to see what all the commotion was about." I turned around to give the boy a shove, but the kid was sufficiently impressed with what I had told him and took the opportunity to follow my advice and skedaddle. I slipped the cigarette case into my pocket.

The detective flipped his notepad closed and said, "Well good. Soon as the M. E. removes the body we're done here. Get rid of the rest of your people in here, and make sure we talked or got a contact for everybody who could be material. You got that?" I nodded but didn't answer him right out. It didn't matter. He kept talking like I had. "The spectacle is over. Tell them to go on home."

Makes sense to me, I'm thinking. Soon as you finished bossing folks around, that's when I get my badge back.

The detective came out and was walking toward his car when I caught the door to go inside the hotel. Mr. Shannon was on the other side and crooked his finger at me. I went over to thank him for his courtesy earlier in the night, but he spoke before I had a chance to express my appreciation.

"I seen you with that nice young man. I didn't have time to thank him—do you know his name?" I told him what he gave me for my notebook—LT Mitchell. Not initials, just LT was his given name. "Well, your young LT was so hepful to us tonight. We didn't have no idea we would be needing any extra kitchen boys for this here affair. But when all those peoples showed up—some of 'em without they reservations—an we had to prepare extra plates and even set up some more tables. It just shows to go you that no matter how high up and mighty they done got, folks can still ack like somebody misraised them to show up unexpected without risvipping."

I tried to say something, but Mr. Shannon was all wound up. "That boy was jus as hepful as he could be, come and stayed right there and with a willing spirit too, jus like it says in the good book—'let a willing spirit sustain me.' It do your heart good to see young folks like that."

"Mr. Shannon, sir, you mean 'right there' when? When everything happened and all the commotion began?"

"Oh uh uh. He was waitin right at the kitchen door right when we started for the night aksing if we would need any extra hep—so polite too! He said something like he could use the extra money, but he'd work for free just for the chance to see colored folks dressed up!" Mr. Shannon chuckled at the memory. "Yes sir. Your LT was quite hepful mos all of the night. Polite, ready to do whatever somebody aksed."

"Excuse me, Mr. Shannon. Just checking what I heard you say. Did you say 'most of the night'?"

"Deed I did. Most all night. Least ways right up till when the awards started. Dessert trays had almost all gone out, so we told the boy he could get on home. Seein him jus now, well . . . I guess he did stick around." Mr. Shannon shook his head sadly. "Poor lad got more to see than he planned for . . . more than anybody shoulda had to see."

Now this was something I did not want to hear. I flipped open my notebook and circled the kid's name thinking that the last thing I want to do is go bother that boy's mama and tell her I got police questions for folks that just come up from someplace called Stump Sound.

OUTSIDE, FLASHES FROM CAMERAS OF THE POLICE PHOTOGRAPHERS and a whole bunch of reporters who had descended on the scene broke through the blanketing snow. Their illuminations seemed like lightning in a winter storm. The lobby where, just a few hours back (but it seemed like more), Weldon and the bellhop struggled to have a conversation was now buzzing with urgent conversations. Weldon went back outside to check one more time. The mortuary van was removing the body, and clusters of cops, blowing into their hands to keep warm, stomped around the few cars that were left. He turned back towards the hotel just as a fancy yellow roadster came barreling up the street and took the corner like it wasn't slick and like there wasn't a bunch of folks standing around. Weldon could see that it was a white boy at the wheel. Nothing new in that. Weekends brought them down from Manhattan to play in Harlem's bars and nightspots. The coroner dropped the cloth that Mr. Shannon had placed over the body out in the street. Bloodstains stretched across the fabric like blossoms. The medical examiner was the last to leave. Weldon heard him say that, in his judgment and by what he could tell by the position of the body, it wasn't likely she jumped and landed like that. That stuck in his mind, because if that turned out to be true, things wouldn't wrap up as quick as they would if it was a misadventure, which is what he had been thinking. In his notebook he wrote those very words, a summary of sorts of the night's event. Except that nothing in this frigid night was finished. Not with the bodies, not with Harlem, and not with its first colored policeman.

7

The Morning After

WYCKOMB FRANCIS CORNELIUS DEBAUN PULLED THE CAR INTO THE back carriage house. The house lights flooded outside and he could see crowds of shadowy figures through the windows. But the carriage entry was in the back alley way and none of these fine folks would be seen near a back door, so he managed to get the car garaged without attracting any attention. He walked around to the coupe's passenger side. It was dented. Worse, there were stains. He wanted desperately to just leave it as it was, go inside, and begin the forgetting. But he knew that, at the very least, he had to get rid of her blood. He grabbed a rag the chauffeur used to buff the cars. The snow and slush on the fenders allowed him to get it sufficiently wet to rub out the stains. He gave the area a final swipe, stuffed the rag in the incinerator, and entered the house through the service entrance. He'd thought he hadn't attracted any notice, but the downstairs help quickly passed word to Burleigh, who passed it on to the vice mayor that young Wyckomb was now home and, even better, had requested his tuxedo in preparation to join his parents' guests. It was, in fact, not long before he did exactly that.

"Good evening, Father. I assume everyone you wanted to be here has come?" Wyckomb hoped his demeanor reflected nothing out of the ordinary. His mother was already rushing over to greet him, but his father's irritation was palpable.

"It's nice of you to make it," Victor replied icily.

"I ran into a, well, I had a bit of a scrape with the car. Minor mishap. Some bodywork, I'm afraid. But, I'm here now and ready to act as the heir apparent. Whom should I chat up?" Wyckomb looked across the rooms where Manhattan's finest were talking, eating, admiring the home's fine furnishings, and gossiping about the absent mayor. Mavis reached the two of them and grasped her son's arm. Her words were slightly slurred, but it was evident she was relieved.

"Darling boy, you're finally here. I have the nicest young ladies who have asked after you, and you've been too, too naughty to keep us waiting!" She gestured much less deftly than she intended to a clutch of young women who stood by the piano. "There's the Strandberg girl. The one in blue velvet. She's been asking for you all evening." Wyckomb glanced at his father.

"We'll discuss your car tomorrow. Since you asked, I believe it would be of most help to me for you to keep your mother entertained. And son," Victor clasped him firmly on the shoulder, "I am glad you are here." He didn't remark that the boy looked rather flushed, but it crossed his mind.

"Yeah, sure Dad. I am too." Wyckomb deBaun took his mother's arm and allowed her to lead him over to meet the daughter of the newest member of the charity luncheon committee. He moved from one group of glittering guests to the next. They fawned over him and made him feel quite swell. It was easy to let go of the unpleasantness down in Harlem. But by day's light, or at least by midmorning when he was summoned to his father's downstairs office, the afterglow of the party was also falling away. The dry, cold light of a wintry day matched the mood in the vice mayor's study. Wyckomb waited for his father to speak.

The vice mayor, rather too deliberately, continued to occupy himself with the papers on his desk. He regretted it when he finally looked up and directly at him. His face showed a controlled fury Wyckomb had seen only once before. It was the time when Victor had to come up to Rhinebeck to get his son reinstated in the school that took upper-class boys with "challenges," whether it was a physical and mental disability like a stutter or a socially unacceptable habit, away from the city and off the hands of their parents. The deBaun heir had both. But after he was caught visiting the girls in Rhinebeck and bringing them back to the dormitories, and especially after it was discovered that he wasn't treating them very well, it took every bit of deBaun's stature—and a not immodest donation to the school's development funds—to keep Wyckomb's place. This time, the boy's habits would bring trouble to Victor's own ambitions. And he was not willing to risk this.

"What did you hit?"

"Sir?" Wyckomb answered quietly, unsure of what to offer.

Victor's voice exploded across the office. "What the fuck did you hit?"

"It, it was d-d-d-dark and I'm n-n-n-not sure. Probably ju-ju-ju-just a d-d-dog or something, I tried to clean it off . . ."

"Goddamnit! What kind of fool do you think I am? If it was harmless, you would have left it for somebody else to clean up. So let's not dawdle. Here's the fucking truth. You hit somebody. You tried to hide it, and I have to guess that you have been as unsuccessful with that as you have been with anything else in your pitiful excuse for a life. This latest mishap, I couldn't even hear from you. The chauffeur told Burleigh that damage to the car included blood and scraps of fabric."

Wyckomb groaned and his skin turned pale. He wanted to sit down, but he knew better. He wanted to run to his mother. He clenched his hands into a fist, wishing there were a wall or somebody to hit. But since there wasn't, he jammed them into his pockets and said, without looking up, "I d-d-d-d-don't know what t-t-t-t-to say."

"Don't say a damned thing. Just shut up and listen. Is that clear?" His son nodded. "Understand this. This moment will begin and end what anybody ever says about any of this." His voice was tight and forced. "I am tired of cleaning up after you. In fact . . ." he looked over at his son until the boy's eyes looked up and met his, "in fact, I am tired of you. Do I make myself clear?" Wyck shifted his weight from one foot to the other and nodded. But his father's statement wasn't quite correct. The chauffeur had already told the kitchen girl. When Linny Lou left—just before dawn—she watched Royce expertly glide the yellow coupe out from the carriage house.

"Hey Royce. Don't guess I can sneak a quick ride uptown?" He placed his fingers over his lips.

"Gal, you ain't seen none of me, an you ain't seen hide nor tail of this here automobile."

"What you talking 'bout, Royce? I'se standing here just like you is."

"There's some mess up in this house today. My onliest job is to

47

disappear this here car." He gestured his head back toward it, and that was when Linny saw the damaged fender. "An your job is not to have seen none of this. Now get on wit your biness like you was goin to before you didn't seen none of me."

Linny took a long, curious look at the car, said a quick prayer for whatever had happened (which was sure to be no good knowing her white folks), and started down the long driveway. She trudged through the freshly deep snow and up the long blocks until she got to the trolley stop. She thought she might get home in time to change out of her uniform for church. Somebody surely needed some praying for today.

A few hours later, inside the vice mayor's expansive home office, Wyckomb deBaun was feeling the full force of his father's fury.

"The car has been taken care of. As far as you or I know, sometime last night it was stolen. I've already reported that to the police. Now, two things will disappear: you and it. I have spoken to your mother, who will tell you how you will proceed." He was quiet for the longest time, until it was obvious their encounter had concluded. "Now get the hell out of here."

"Dad. Father. S-S-S-Sir, I'm sorry. I'm so s-s-s-ssorry. I . . ."

He didn't get a chance to finish. His father turned away from him. But he did respond.

"That, my boy, may be the most accurate observation you've made in your lifetime." The leather desk chair swung around until it left him faced away from his son. Wyckomb didn't waste a moment leaving the office. Burleigh was waiting discreetly in the vestibule and directed him to his mother.

"Madam is in her chambers, sir. I believe that she is expecting you."

Wyckomb paused outside his mother's door, trying to gain some veneer of composure. It wasn't forthcoming; the encounter with his father had its effect. Finally he just knocked. He barely heard her raspy whisper, "Come in, Wyckomb. There are things we must arrange."

8

Downtown—
Upper East

HUGHES WELLINGTON SPENT THE NEXT MORNING IN HIS PRIVATE GAL-
lery. His lean fingers traced the spiraled locks of Carpeaux's *Negresse
Captive*. He brushed the sculpture's full ivory lips with an almost loving
gesture and called her by the name he'd given to her when he acquired
the piece. "Well Josephine. What have we gotten ourselves into?"

The telephone buzzed and Meade, his butler, announced the arrival
of a private detective. He glanced back once at the ornate chamber, as if
to check that each treasure was safely in place. They were. African masks
bulged defiantly from the walls. The now twenty-three masks (counting
the ones recently discovered in the Belgian Congo) were vibrant and
robust. Grassy collars swept the wall space beneath some of them. Those
with glass beads sparkled in their eclectic array. Other masks, including
significant Benin and Yoruba specimens, mixed exotic woods and metals
of different hues—bronze, blond, and ebony. They reminded Wellington
of the American Negro's many colors. He closed their curtained tapestry
with ritual solemnity, as if they were a precious rendering of his last duch-
ess. The busts were never covered. Josephine's white marble figure was
mounted on an obsidian base, others were enclosed in glass. His collec-
tions of elaborately carved Ashanti royal stools, including the prized gold

stool procured directly from the Asantehene's palace in Kumasi, were strategically placed beneath Ghanaian tapestries. Because of their delicate beading, the Ndebele pieces were encased. But the wooden pieces, especially the columned totems, all stood free. Their deeply carved edifices flanked the walls like caryatids. The buzzer rang again, and Wellington pressed the latch inside the bookcase that held yellowed manuscripts from the libraries of Timbuktu. The case moved quietly into the wall and revealed a door that allowed him passage into his study.

He looked back out of habit, seeing only the richly paneled wall of bookcases that were customary in homes like his. To the unpracticed eye, there was no evidence of a hidden room. Wellington strode purposefully across the study, opened its door, crossed the marbled checkerboard tiles in the entry, and entered the drawing room where Sanders Campbell sat, nervously waiting for his audience with the famed Manhattan entrepreneur.

"I assume you've had the opportunity for a first assessment of the situation in Harlem?" Wellington's question nearly preceded him into the room. Sanders Campbell rose to greet his distinguished host so quickly that he nearly toppled the slender chair where he'd been waiting.

"Good morning, sir. Mr. Wellington. Pleased to make your acquaintance." He extended his hand for a welcome. Wellington used it to hand him a notepad and asked him to join him in his study.

Campbell was unhappy with the opening of the meeting. Especially since it was more common for abject and troubled clients to come to his small flat in the village. He was not used to being summoned. Meeting the enigmatic Wellington left him ill at ease.

"Sit down. Let's get straight to business," Wellington directed.

"Yes, sir. Thank you." Campbell sat at an office chair and Wellington took his seat behind his desk and leaned forward, emphasizing the distance between them.

The only thing he knew about Hughes Wellington was what everyone else had heard. He was somewhat of an iconoclast, a businessman, a philanthropist, a global traveler, and, oddly, a lover of all things Negro. He was known for showing up at affairs given by Harlem's upper class, if they could be called that. They liked having him there as much (it was rumored) as he liked going. It was difficult to guess his age, although most saw him as mature and distinguished, but not nearly close to elderly.

His money assured his full acceptance into the city's social register. New York's élite agreed that someone of his obvious wealth could indulge whatever habits he wanted—even if some were inexplicably attached to the coloreds.

In fact, there were even a few who shared Wellington's fetish for the Negro and who enjoyed sharing rumors about his weekend forays into the lairs of their resident exotics. Their habits earned them more invitations to social events, being they were the ones with all the best stories to tell. Exciting, lurid sometimes, and slightly exaggerated stories circulated about how Wellington spent time talking with colored musicians, shared their drinks, danced a mean swing with some of their women, but always returned home—alone—before questions could be raised.

His idiosyncrasies were balanced by a well-cultivated public role. Wellington exercised power and influence in the city. He'd appeared on Manhattan's social scene just towards the end of the war buttressed by a substantial fortune rumored to have its sources in a Brazilian enterprise. His investments blossomed into a significant global wealth. His eager hangers-on were told that he'd always planned to reside in New York. What he didn't share was that he would not do so until his wealth and reputation could assure him entrance into the very top social circles. So he waited, building his empire and even planting stories of his success in important publications so that his reputation would precede him.

When he finally arrived in the city, brokers competed to find a Central Park–facing home for what was then an unknown client with an extraordinary set of requirements: a detached Upper East dwelling with more square footage than many of them could easily pull from their listings. The twenty-thousand-square-foot freestanding, seven-story mansion on the corner of Fifth and Eighty-Second overlooked the park as well as the Metropolitan Museum. It didn't hurt at all that the area was known as Millionaire's Row and boasted tobacco heirs and steel magnates among its residents. It was a perfect landing for Wellington, especially after his required renovations.

With such a pedigree, who cared if he associated with Negroes? Wellington was at least selective enough to be useful for those who had the responsibility of governing the city—the mayor and the police commissioner among them. So he hobnobbed with bankers, politicians, and corporate executives and frequented their parties and complimented their wives. His eccentricities and his business interests were always meticulously balanced. When the colored gal jumped, was pushed, or fell from the Hotel Theresa, nobody was surprised to hear that Wellington had been there. The fact that he was already at the mayor's annual holiday affair before the tragic event actually verified the presumption that, despite his rather extraordinary interests, he exercised the good judgment expected from those of his race and class.

When Wellington had arrived at the Opportunity affair, he took time to make himself available to each of the important guests, and also to hold what others later reported as an "intense" conversation with the beautiful Olivia Frelon. Detective records indicated that Frelon actually went to the affair with the hopes of being introduced to Wellington. Given her own strategic moves into the top echelons of Harlem's élites, no one was surprised that she wanted to sidle up to the most important person at this gathering of their best and brightest.

Campbell was uneasy because there was a long pause, which he was polite enough not to interrupt, before Wellington spoke to the detective.

"I want you to find out what happened in Harlem last night."

"Oh, you mean the gal what fell out the window? Sure, heard all about it."

"You will notice, sir, that I did not ask what you may or may not have heard," Wellington replied with an edge in his voice. "My instructions to you are to investigate the matter. Is this within your capabilities?"

"Sure thing! Those people are known for talking amongst themselves. I've got sources who will give me the inside scoop."

"If by 'inside scoop' you mean what happened, whom it happened to, and how, we are in accord. I want every detail you can find out about the situation of the deceased. Follow the police investigation, talk with the people who knew her . . ." Campbell was writing down everything the man said. "Is this something I need to spell out for you?"

"Oh no, sir. I mean yes sir, I sure do. This is routine. Get at it from all angles. I got you covered."

"Let me be clear, Mr. Campbell. This is not about me. I have no need to be 'covered' by you. However, you are to find out whatever you can about the deceased and any official investigation regarding her death. You will keep me informed of any and everyone who is involved; what they are thinking, what they are thinking about thinking about, and what they have changed their minds on regarding any dimension of this matter. That means an update from you when you have news, and an explanation when you do not." Wellington paused. "Am I understood?"

"I'm on it, sir. Right away. I'll head right down to the police headquarters, or maybe the morgue, or—do you know if they took the body to the hospital first?" Wellington raised his eyebrows.

"Perhaps you are not the man to do this if you think I am a source for your investigation," he said sharply.

Campbell realized his mistake. "Oh of course not, sir. Just wanted you to see I've already several notions on this. That came out wrong. I meant to let you know this could get complicated."

"I see," Wellington replied. He silently buzzed for Meade. The butler was already at the door with Campbell's coat and hat, but the detective hadn't noticed his entry.

"Sir, I'm the man to take this case on. Me and my staff " (there was in actuality only a secretary, his sister Ida Belle, who came in part-time while her husband was at work, which was fine, as long as she was home and had dinner on the table by the time he returned), "we stay abreast of the latest in investigations. Did you know that most of your criminal types can be fingered by their head shape?" Meade came up behind him and tapped him on the shoulder. Campbell turned to see his coat held open for him and understood his departure was imminent. Before the detective could express his thanks, Sanders found himself standing outside beneath the glass and iron portico that framed the intricate ironwork of the mansion's doors.

After the detective left Meade asked if there was anything that needed the staff's attention. Wellington's mumbled "That will be all" was really unnecessary. As soon as he heard the double doors click, Wellington pressed the latch, waited for the paneled bookcase to slide open, and retreated through the private gallery's hidden door. Despite the early hour he nursed a scotch and soda while he wandered through his exhibits, each one a museum-quality piece that documented and traced the evolution of African and European arts reflecting the history of the Negro.

The collection was growing along with his satisfaction with it. He would soon have to call the tradesmen back to create additional space. He already planned the conversations he and his assistant, Ellie Howard, could have about the addition. He smiled with satisfaction, thinking back on how he had rescued her from that "lady's assistant" job in Harlem. Before that she was a secretary at one of those magazines for the striving class of coloreds where, as far as he was concerned, her talents were wasted. He did worry over how she would react when he told her about what happened down there. Her being in a job away from her people is a delicate situation. He would need to tell her in a way that wouldn't get her too worked up and maybe make her think about working in Harlem again.

Wellington sat down in one of the upholstered divans. His collection room calmed him, and even chased away some of the shadows of the night before.

OF COURSE WELLINGTON HAD NO IDEA THAT ELLIE WOULD HAVE HEARD the entire story of the death in Harlem from Weldon Thomas earlier that morning. Weldon knew the horror this would hold for her and immediately after he left the hotel, he made his way downtown and waited until Ellie came out to meet the morning paperboy. It was near daybreak anyway by the time the body was removed and the last bystanders had moved on. Weldon knew Ellie's habit of meeting the boy and she wasn't at all surprised to see him waiting there. She smiled brightly, but the look on his face told her something was wrong, so she invited him for coffee and scones in the staff's hearth room. By the time they were sitting at the long trestle table, she was already nervous, trying to figure out what kind of news this was going to be. Nobody was up yet except cook, who had grown used to seeing the young policeman and approved of his interest in Miss Ellie. She just hoped their hiring a colored girl had not brought Harlem's problems along with her.

Weldon slipped his arm around Ellie's waist and held her gently, anticipating the effect the news would have on her when he said, "Baby Girl" (that was his affectionate name for her, because he always claimed she seemed too young and pretty to have the high-class smarts she did). "Baby Girl, it was an accident uptown last night and somebody died. It hurts me to have to tell you this, but it was that lady you used to work for . . . Miss Frelon." Ellie gasped. The look on his face betrayed the truth of the matter and she collapsed into his embrace. How could something have happened to Miss Olivia? She'd given Ellie the chance to leave the smug offices of the *Crisis Magazine*. At first the magazine's executive office seemed a secure and fortuitous start for her career. But Jessie, the assistant editor, had an argumentative relationship with the magazine's editor and Ellie often found herself pinned between the renowned scholar's exasperating temper and Jessie's clear-sighted ambition. Miss Fauset wanted to be a writer. But Dr. Du Bois needed a typist and his was a race man's magazine and a race man's organization. The tension between the two was uncomfortable for Ellie, so when the magazine received an advertisement for an assistant to a lady new to the city she interviewed for it herself. She'd felt somewhat deceitful, but it was increasingly clear that she had to leave the magazine.

Olivia Frelon's beautiful home and her social needs afforded Ellie some dimension of a professional situation. It may not have been quite as challenging as she'd wished, but since Miss Frelon left for a European buying trip soon after hiring her, Ellie was hopeful that an opportunity to travel with Miss Frelon might eventually be possible. But while she was on the Continent, finding furnishings for her home and purchasing a wardrobe that would be appropriate for Hamilton Heights society, the magazine that once employed Ellie ran an advertisement for a position for an art librarian in Manhattan. It wasn't ordinary that Negroes would be candidates for something like this, but its publication in the *Crisis* was a signal that the job would be open to her. It was exactly what her Fisk degree in art history had prepared her to do.

Olivia Frelon returned from Europe so excited and eager to open her home to Harlem society that Ellie's announcement of her new position was only a brief disappointment. Mamie Walker, the girl that Ellie hired while she was away, seemed perfectly suited for the kind of assistance she needed. There was nothing more important than her entrée into the correct social circles, and Olivia Frelon easily bonded with Mamie once she saw how well Ellie had trained her.

Miss Frelon's generous response to her leaving endeared her to Ellie even more. But Weldon's horrible news seemed like punishment. Miss Frelon hardly had time to enjoy the success of her social ambitions. She hadn't even been in the city for a full year. She was gone? Fallen from a window? Nothing made sense. "Weldon, this can't be true. My Miss Olivia dead? What could possibly have happened?"

9

Harlem, In Between

EVERY KIND OF BODY CAN FIND SOMEPLACE HERE. SOMEBODY'S ARMS, somebody's interest, somebody's joys, somebody's blues.

North was balm and promise. Nowadays folks still coming on up, pulling themselves along for the promise despite the peril. Toting emptied shoeboxes and shaking off red dirt for a deep brown loamy soil that never stretched far or wide enough to remind them of the lands they came to forget. Welcomed with a press of flesh and warm hugs that didn't mind how close it had got up on the train. "How you been, sweetheart?" "How you been?" Then the chiding. "You sure enough took your time. I sent for you back a year full a yesterdays." But forgiving too was in the offering. These folks intended to stay and those welcoming them would make room.

But the cold had its challenges. Thick living was a hazard, and a fierce winter and the unrelenting consumption thinned out the newcomers and even some who had been here awhile. Come summertime, letters from home were carried proud and careful on the shoulders of children and men, no matter how frail the winter had left them. The heft of home was prideful. It was as common as property ever got when they fell and split red and juicy into the streets. Nobody saw its broken flesh as omen.

Congregations of Episcopal and AME and Baptist and street-corner fly-by-night and window-paned, storefront, fire-baptized folks flowed out from Sunday services to hazard a mingle with Saturday all-nighters. Street sleepers woke just in time to greet the dressed to impress and remark on how good they were for the race and weren't they fine, while their children, much too interested in their unruly colors, got tugged away from the unchurched, unwashed, and unsaved.

There were coughs and contagion and christenings and community. Schooling and socializing and speechifying. Men did race talk. Women did race work. There was death and dying and births and new trainloads arrived and belched out folks and fire, iron and grit. Families scrambled out the narrow doors, looked up at dreams deferred and saw the station's vaulted star-studded ceiling like heaven and believed as surely as Jesus saves that they were finally home to Harlem. They wrote home, stuffing letters with coins or maybe even a dollar that promised more than they could deliver. Some believed in the promise enough to board the trains themselves, nearly holding on to their breath until the colored porter removed the Colored Only placard and grinned at the applause. For sure and certain they were up-north Negroes now.

Like on that late Monday morning when the two girls disembarked, neither one taking notice of the other but who likely met again in that region past this one. Their deaths matched in finality if not finesse.

ON THE MIDWINTER'S NIGHT OF A BANQUET UP IN HARLEM AND A soiree down in midtown, the remains of one lightly held-on-to shadow of a life etched its way through the snow and ran down the sidewalks, slipped over a curb and down into the grates.

It wasn't the only life spilled that night.

There was the shooting down on 136th that left plenty of blood to puddle and flow.

And the bruised and bloodied lip that asked wasn't there going to be something for the children this Christmas. She leaned against the sink trying to rinse it in the trickle of rusty water spilled from the faucet.

A girl's womanhood came in and frightened her when it stained her party dress. She ran to a washroom to scrub away her coming-of-age.

A born-too-soon babygirl flushed like the waste that came with it. And there was the angry white boy who jumped into his roadster and sped away despite Maisie's standing there pitiful and pleading. The snow and sleet claimed her before she went down when his fender tore into the girl's frail body.

A funeral in Harlem, as fine as they come, would be planned for the woman who fell from the window. She went with sprays of flowers, sweet singing, fine words, and a congregation of refined tears.

For the other one, it was quiet when, some weeks later, the stack of caskets in the storage shed worked its way down to her pine box. The already weary gravediggers stopped at a sun-sprayed spot on Hart Island where Maisie James would find a resting place. Two men, burly and bundled for the cold and their task, readied themselves to attack the ground. There was no way for the cold or dry winter dirt to let the gravediggers do a quick job of it. But with the first swing and sink of the ax, they found the soil softened just enough for a real deep-down burial. They tossed their pickaxes, stunned with the ease they felt from the giving ground, and quickly took to their shovels, knowing that somehow in this moment of in-between, they could dig deep. And they did. In part looking for the miracle of it, in full hoping for the splendor.

PART II

After the Fall

10

The Thirtieth
Precinct—Harlem

CAPTAIN CARTER HARRISON LEANED OVER THE CLUTTER ON RYAN Fitzpatrick's desk. "Hey Ryan. Sorry to take you away from all this work you got piled up here. But you supposed to have something there for me. You got that CPT yet?"

In the case notes, Harrison noted that "CPT" was critical to getting information on the colored society lady's death back in December. He put his lead detective on tracking down this witness. This case could mean folks start picking sides. But as long as it was inside Harlem, he was fine with it. Coloreds divided between themselves was no problem. Light ones up in the Heights and the rest of the folks down hill didn't faze him much. Just so long as it wasn't a race conflict. Still, he had to keep the case moving. There was some word that Wellington was interested in it, which would mean city bigwigs could decide they were interested as well. But Harrison was having a hard time with this one. Usually the race stuff was about black or white. The fact that he couldn't tell the dead gal was colored by just looking at her was discomfiting. Colored women were brown. Not just ordinary crayon-colored brown, but different shades. Which was okay by him. Some were dark and shiny like autumn chestnuts, others were more like, well, sort of like a walnut shell. But nobody was supposed to have any trouble telling they were colored. And Fitzpatrick was giving his captain exactly nothing to dispel the oddities that were mounting up.

Fitzpatrick looked up from his seat. His face was blotchy with embarrassment. He could hear the suppressed guffaws from the dicks in the rest of the room.

"Ummm, not yet sir. But working on it. Close, too. I can feel it."

"Son, I ain't never solved a case by feeling nothing; but if that's how you operate, let's just say I need to be feeling what you feeling. I got the chief and the DA after me on this one. Which means you got me and the chief and the DA on your ass. And none of us give a fuck about what you might be feeling. We need this CPT down here yesterday. Is there anything about that you don't understand?"

"Yes sir. I mean no sir. I'm close, I can tell." Ryan slapped his hand down on the papers that were now underneath the captain's coffee cup. Of course it fell over and spilled its contents onto the desk. He tried to blot it up with the papers from his desk.

"Guess whatever you working on ain't so important after all," the chief said.

"Oh I got copies. Believe me. These are . . ." He held out the soggy papers toward the captain. "These are replaceable "

"Uh-huh. That's real good to know. Keep that in mind, son. You and them papers got something in common." The laughter in the room was now audible, but Fitzpatrick was too flustered to respond. He dumped the papers in the wastebasket and headed out of the room to scour the station house for Officer Weldon Thomas. He found him just inside the entry lobby, swallowed hard, and asked if he might talk to Weldon privately. The two men walked to a small windowless area near the end of the hall.

"Umm, hey Weldon, how you doing, my man?" Weldon knew that this could not be a casual greeting; station-house folks usually just pretended he was invisible.

"What you want, Ryan?" he asked, deliberately using his first name, which he knew white folks hated.

"Truth is, I need to know something you people know."

"You people?" Weldon repeated. He may as well enjoy this while he could. "Which people you got in mind, Ryan? Us cops?"

"Awww no, man. You know. You people, you col—you nig . . . You

62

Negro people. You know. The your colored people you people." Weldon let the nonsense settle.

"Uh-huh." Weldon paused long enough for the detective to get even more uncomfortable. "And what do I know about my people that you people want to know?"

Fitzpatrick knew he was being played, but he also remembered what the captain said about his being dispensable. So he swallowed his pride and asked if his people, or maybe even Weldon, knew where he could find this CPT.

"Did you check my report?"

"Your report?"

"Yeah. From the night Miss Frelon died. Cause you know I turned in my duty report alongside everybody else's what was there that night."

"Umm, no. I didn't see them in the file. I mean we got everything we needed from the detective's notes."

"So you didn't check to see if CPT was in my report?"

"Sheesh, man. Sorry. Just didn't think about that."

"You didn't think to check, or you didn't think mine was worth checking? Which one of those scenarios are we discussing, because I need to be sure if what I know is what you want to know."

"Aww, man. I'm sorry. But I just gotta answer to the captain. He's coming down hard. Do a fellow cop a favor, please. And I'ma tell people to get your report next time. Can't say they'll be typed up with carbons and all. But I'ma do what I can." He thought about slapping Officer Thomas on the back as a show of camaraderie but thought better of it when he saw Weldon draw back away from him. Instead, he let his upraised hand wipe some sweat from under his cap.

Weldon gave him a look that showed his disdain. It was as far as he would go in letting these folks know how he felt about anything. Nobody had had a blessed thing to ask of him since the night of Miss Frelon's death. There wasn't any problem in ignoring the report he'd so meticulously prepared. Nobody was going to ask him about that night even though he was the duty cop. And up until this point, not one of the "official investigators" was the least bit interested in his assessments even though for a good while, until the precinct got the call and sent over the first patrol cars, he'd been the only cop on the scene. So when Fitzpatrick pulled him aside to ask him what part of Harlem he should go to to find CPT, Weldon met his inquiry with cool detachment.

Ryan asked again. "Man, just keep it on the down low. Between us. Where do I need to go?" Weldon waited long enough for Ryan to do one more nervous glance around, to see if anybody was watching him converse with the colored cop. And then he called him again by his first name.

"Ryan?"

"Yeah man, let me have it." Once again, Weldon suppressed an urge.

"Ryan, come real close now." Fitzpatrick leaned in, with obvious discomfort. "Well, since we's fellow cops an all, I guess I could tell just you." As irritated as Fitzpatrick could have been, he remembered the stakes. He opened his notebook and had his pen primed over a blank page. "Now write this down like I say it: that CPT 'tain't nobody at all. What it means is 'colored people's time.' C for colored, P for people, T for time. Get it? 'Colored People's Time.' It means things was running late."

Fitzpatrick paused for a moment, realizing that he had been played. He backed away from their intimate stance, slipped his pencil and pad into his back pocket, and worked to regain his composure. "Okay. Got it. Sure, man. I got this. In fact, you know, I had already figured that part out. Just got to check out everything, you know. Wanted to verify facts with our own colored expert." He gave Weldon a not-quite-playful-enough jab to his shoulder. "Every little thing we find, we got to track it down. Nail it to the wall. Keep it real, man. Thanks. And don't you worry. I won't tell anybody you told this to me. Race secret and all. I'm down with that."

I'll just bet you are, Thomas thought as he watched Ryan rush down the hallway to share his newly acquired racial knowledge with the captain.

Captain Harrison was at his desk going over the mortuary photos. This gal had been a real looker. He studied the photographs over and over. She had on real good clothes. Top-of-the-line fabric. The label on the dress was Italian. A swath of the silk and velvet fell from where it had been bagged on the coroner's side table. She was clearly a stunner—or was, before the fall that nearly flattened her head. Harrison couldn't get over the idea that if he had passed her in the streets, he would have spoken politely, even tipped his cap with a "Hello, ma'am" like she was white, not knowing she was just a colored gal in a good dress. He looked up at Ryan, either irritated that the cop had interrupted his thoughts or concerned that he might have given himself away. Perhaps both were true. "What you got for me, boy? I want this one moved outta here soon as we can."

11

Rumor, Gossip, and Innuendo

IN THE WEEKS FOLLOWING OLIVIA FRELON'S DEATH, THE TALK BEGAN kindly enough—with baleful sighs about the heartbreak of it all and tidbits from news stories. Downtown papers focused on interviews with whites who attended the event, even as they noted that attempts to get a comment from Hughes Wellington, Esq., had been unsuccessful. And then came the editorial about the efforts of Harlem's "striving class" coming to this "not fully unexpected" tragedy. "Despite their best efforts," the editorial read, "copycat affairs cannot replicate the elegant refinement of the classes they emulate. Those qualities are inbred, rather than imitated. It renders these piteous efforts ultimately and instead, tragically colored." The Negro Welfare League held a passionate conversation considering a response, but afterwards agreed that the less public attention directed toward their set in the days following the event, the better.

Harlem's *Amsterdam News* published numerous interviews. In one way or another, attendees or spectators reflected an effort to distance themselves from the "tragic victim": "Well, she hadn't been a part of our set for long" or "Nobody knew her people" or "I hear her house was among the more notable of our set—but I never set foot in the place myself."

This last comment was Earlene Kinsdale's, who was still smarting from not having been one of the ladies invited to tea when Olivia first arrived in Harlem. But as is often the case when sordid affairs hit the élite, folks scrambled as far away from the attention as they could get and made sure not to be caught being overly solicitous to those unfortunate enough to be involved. After all, someone had to maintain the dignity of the race.

For that reason, the Dr. Reynolds and Mrs. Vera Scott received fewer expressions of concern than might have been expected upon the occasion of the loss of Vera's dear friend. Olivia had been a frequent guest in the Scott home and many recalled the two had arrived at the banquet together and some added the tidbit that they might very well have been quarreling. There was no surfeit of gossip about their relationship. But until things "died down," the Women's Auxiliary of the Negro Welfare League was considerate enough to leave the Scott family alone, not wanting to intrude at an indelicate moment and, of course, not wanting to be tainted by association.

Despite the fact that Olivia had died a little more than a fortnight ago, the auxiliary determined that the tragedy should not preclude their scheduled meeting. It was held in the ostentatiously appointed Hamilton Heights apartment of Earlene Kinsdale.

After appropriate gushing over the elegant appointments, the silk drapery, the walls filled with exotic, titillating, and confusing canvases, and the remodeled vestibule and music room, the talk settled on who knew what about the affair. The majority held the opinion that Miss Frelon had stumbled, perhaps on the lengthy train of her pleated silk gown, which, it had finally to be said, was just a bit too dramatic for the occasion anyway. Earlene shared what many should have been thinking. "After all, sisters dear" (they always used these terms of kinship and endearment with each other), "did any of you wear a dress with a train?" Without missing a beat, or waiting for the less informed to offer their judgment, she answered her own question: "Of course not. Each and every one of us has more sophisticated tastes than poor Olivia displayed. Our set knows better." One of the club women—a newer member— attempted to insert that she'd heard Olivia's gown was likely in fashion in Europe, but she was appropriately ignored. As hostess, Earlene felt perfectly entitled to dominate the table talk: "And then consider the chance of her train being caught up in the elements . . ." Diana

Bingham's "absolutely" settled the matter and led them to agree that Olivia Frelon's ensemble was poorly considered.

Earlene was delighted to be at the center of things again. It had been quite a while since she could claim that role. In fact, ever since Olivia arrived in Harlem she suffered the imbalance of the attentions that were directed to "our Miss Frelon." Her final pronouncement left little to the imagination. "The fact that we now know she was there to win a prize . . . Well, one might reasonably wonder what she did to earn it." One of the elderly members of the group gasped, but Earlene quickly shut down the pretense of shock. "Oh Eula, please! This is 1928. People do things to get things. And don't say you don't know this. I recall your own trip to the Continent in the last few years. I happen to know you went quite prepared to, shall we say, explore your options?" Eula got up and dabbed a hanky to her cheeks, explaining that she was just feeling "a bit damp . . . it's rather close in here."

Grace Milner suggested maybe Olivia didn't fall at all. "After all, ladies, who knows but that she might have jumped?" To Earlene's dismay, the attention shifted to Grace. "We all have commented on the fact that there was a decided enigma to her."

Olivia's mysterious past was certainly a puzzle that prompted quite a bit of chatter about where she was before her arrival in Harlem and started life (in the postmortem phrasing of the *Amsterdam News*) as a "light and bright" Harlem socialite. She had always been pretty close-mouthed when people asked, with overly polite curiosity, "Who are your people, sweetheart?" or "Where did you say you went to school?" or "Your church home was . . . ?" Since Olivia didn't respond to these genteel inquiries, it wasn't at all unreasonable to suspect that perhaps she harbored a deeply embarrassing secret. In fact, it seemed perfectly logical to consider that somebody found it out and, in a desperation over the loss of her now elegant life in ruin, she jumped from the banquet floor before the sordid news came to light.

"But what could have been terrible enough to make her jump?" Myra asked. And then she shared that she had it on good authority—having heard it at church—that there was a girl who looked just like her that grew up on Chicago's South Side, but, when her father died, her white aunts took her back across the color line. She was married as a white woman—which Olivia easily could have done—and lived on the North

67

Shore. But when their baby came and its color came in a bit dusky, she was banned from her husband's estate. That's when she came to New York. "There was an estate?" Joanne Sharpe asked, intrigued by the potential.

"Well, my dear," Chloe Woolf looked over the rims of her bifocals at the young member who dared to inquire after her story, and haughtily replied, "if there were such a marriage you can be well assured that it would have been a marriage of stature and class. Which suggests, arguably I do concede, that there was an estate."

As the afternoon advanced, there was plenty more to be said. Mrs. Woolf's opinions were always given appropriate deference. She gave the young Miss Sharpe an imperious look before offering her assessment of the matter. "So of course then, when this white man discovered her perfidy—how he had carried her into the homes of the most distinguished white citizens, let her be waited on hand and foot by their staffs, and seated right next to those respectable hardworking white folks at their own dinner tables—he tossed her out without a penny to her name! Little wonder she would shield that unpleasant history." But that doesn't explain how she had so much money, Joanne thought. She wasn't the only one keeping opinions to herself.

Millicent Henderson did not share she believed that Olivia was from New Orleans and that she had taken on a whole slew of affectations to hide the fact. She was pretty certain of this because her own people hailed from deep in the bayou and she could recognize the lilting tones of a Creole accent anywhere, even when it was disguised. But Mrs. Henderson didn't share this with the group because her own story that she came from a line of free coloreds in Wilmington was a fiction.

"The poor dear," Charlotte Woods offered as if the story had somehow moved from speculation to fact. "So it seems that when she came to Harlem, she was, in effect, coming back to her people, all the while bearing fateful memories of a secret life." Mrs. Woods willingly took up the edges of the imagined narrative. "Why else would she be so circumspect about her past, even after we've all so kindly and frequently inquired after it? You know, I am going to call on some of my contacts in Chicago to see if they might know her."

"Oh Charlotte," Madeleine Drane exclaimed, "we can always count on you to do some research."

"My absolute pleasure," Mrs. Woods replied serenely.

Up to this moment Earlene Kinsdale had been silent, taking in the gossip as if it were all a delectable treat prepared especially to assuage her feelings of being ousted from Vera Scott's inner circle. After all, ever since the spring fete when Vera decided that Olivia was a far more complementary pairing than she was, Earlene took the snub quite personally. She'd always suspected that Vera might be color struck, and given her ridiculous attention to the new girl at the spring affair, it was potentially apparent to everyone else as well. Remembering the occasion still made her shudder. It was frankly unbecoming the way she rushed over to grab the Frelon woman as soon as she came into the parlors reserved for the auxiliary's event. It was, at the very least, overly interested. Not to mention that just before Olivia swept grandly into the room, disrupting the clutches of women who were talking about things far less interesting than she promised to be, she and Vera had been the center of attention, and everyone was trying to sidle their way into their conversational circle.

Earlene Kinsdale and Vera Scott had been best of friends and companions for years, beginning with college. They were overjoyed when they met again as adults in New York. But none of this seemed to matter when Vera glanced over her shoulder, noticed the "new girl," and immediately displayed an overabundant interest in the interloper.

OLIVIA'S ARRIVAL IN NEW YORK WAS SUDDEN: ONE DAY IN THE EARLY spring she just appeared at the league's annual spring fête, selectively handing out cards elegantly embossed with her name and address— Miss Olivia Frelon of 898 St. Nicholas—and informing the delighted recipients that she would be "at home" on Thursday "after two," which everyone knew was an invitation to visit. There had been talk all season about how the grandest house in the Heights had been sold. That gossip soon yielded to fervent speculation about the large shipping containers that were carted into the house. A woman who was obviously a secretary stood at the door with reading glasses and a checklist. Ellie Howard could be heard directing the workmen to various rooms in the house. In fact, whoever engaged Ellie in her position as household manager got exactly the same story: a "Miss Olivia Frelon" would be in residence in midspring, but she was currently "on the Continent" overseeing the purchase of appropriate furnishings for the home. Drapery makers and designers hustled in and out and the goings-on took up weeks of curious speculation. No one had been inside, but you wouldn't have known it for the numbers of "I can tell you on good authority" about a certain piece of furniture or color of a room or divan. But then came the spring event when Olivia herself, along with her elegant response cards, turned up. Not everyone, including not Earlene Kinsdale, received the coveted invitation.

Olivia had the wherewithal to be discriminatingly selective with her newly printed cards. By the end of the spring soiree, the women clustered excitedly to ask who got a card. They gushed over the lovely magnolia blossom embossed on the design, and wondered how so-and-so deserved one while they didn't. The tactic, if it might be called that, had the desired effect, and, eventually, an invitation to tea or an "at home" at Miss Frelon's became a token that had all the markings of a new social stratum. All of this was especially irritating to Earlene Kinsdale, who—before Olivia's arrival and ever since the days she and Vera had been roommates at Howard University—had been Vera Scott's best friend.

Although it was poor taste to speak ill of the dead, Earlene remembered the snub and was frankly pleased with the restored position of leadership in her group. She looked around her newly decorated parlor with satisfaction. In fact, her seemingly simple question, inserted just as the conversation lulled, "Speaking of Reynolds and Vera" (in fact, nobody, up to that point, had been speaking of the two together). But since the momentum was decidedly in her favor she quite easily directed the conversation towards her own objective. She had the room's attention, so she began again. "Speaking of Reynolds" (this time she strategically left out Vera's name), "does anyone know whether Olivia was seeing anyone?" As intended, the question caused the conversation to take a considerable turn. The sliver of its tantalizing opening necessitated serious and sustained engagement with intriguing rumors that had been circulating since last summer regarding Vera's husband, Dr. Reynolds Scott, and Miss Frelon.

Earlene smiled with a quiet satisfaction. Of course, her intervention was at Vera's expense, but then, perhaps, she thought, it was time for someone else to learn what it was like to be on the outside looking in.

12

Indictment

ON THE LAST FRIDAY IN JANUARY THE DISTRICT ATTORNEY ANNOUNCED that he had enough information to ask a grand jury for a bill of indictment. Members of the auxiliary who'd spent their meeting gossiping about Olivia had no idea the order was pending.

The unresolved issue from their meeting was what, if anything, would be appropriate for them to do about the unhappy circumstance of Olivia's death. Fortuitously, an anonymous donor stepped forward with funds that were more than sufficient to cover her burial. The poor dear had been in the county morgue longer than was proper for any members of their set, even those as tenuously attached as Olivia, and the auxiliary's members were supremely well suited to a task that called for ritual, pomp, and ceremony—especially if their own funds would not be called upon for the costs related to the occasion. So the auxiliary committee arranged her funeral service. By happenstance, they scheduled her service for the same day that the grand jury convened to receive testimony from several witnesses, including Officer Weldon Haynie Thomas and Mrs. Earlene Kinsdale.

Weldon was not surprised at all to receive the summons. He saw the way the case was going the day Chief Harrison told Weldon to stop interviewing people. When Weldon asked who should get his interview notes, the chief chuckled, cuffed him on the shoulder, and said, "That's okay, boy. Turns out your 'death by misadventure' idea didn't make the cut. But it sure gave folks in the DA's office a good chuckle. Don't get me wrong. Nobody blamed you for wanting it to be an accident. These your people. But all the important evidence already been turned over."

Weldon was used to this disrespect; but with regard to this matter he was far more interested in determining who was the focus. There would inevitably be a person of interest.

On the day of Olivia's funeral, or—depending on your standing in the matter—upon the occasion of the grand jury hearing, Weldon took his notes to court. He knew it might get somewhat argumentative, given that his report from the night it happened did suggest it was an accident. "Death by misadventure" still merited consideration.

But he also considered Hughes Wellington reasonably suspicious. In a way, Weldon hoped it was Wellington and that way his people could stay out of it. But in another way, he knew what a setback that would be for Ellie, who was really proud of the job she had with the man. He sat outside the courtroom with an attentive but nervous formality.

Inside the chambers, and despite the January chill, the room was stuffy and warm. The radiators hissed with a fierce insistence. Lyndon Smith, the DA, ruled the room and his opening statement revealed the focus. In it he claimed that the state had sufficient evidence to indict Mrs. Vera Scott for the crime of murder. He promised evidence that would indicate both motive and opportunity to want and to carry out the death of Olivia Frelon, her tragic victim. He declared that as distasteful as it is, "This woman willfully premeditated the demise of her former friend, and you will see clearly that her jealous passions are consistent with a shade indelibly writ on her dark heart. We will unmask the sinister soul that led to this despicable act."

Since this matter of color was difficult to put out of his mind, he figured that meant it would matter to the jury as well. So he decided to use the oddity of these white-looking colored ladies as an indication that both the victim and the perpetrator were ill-fated. He brought along a photograph of Olivia and warned them not to be fooled.

At the conclusion of his statement, the DA asked that Officer Thomas be invited in. Weldon strode purposefully into the courtroom, but only his walk was confident. His high cheekbones glistened from the sudden warmth of the room, and this made his dark eyes intense and brooding. Inside, he was in tremendous turmoil. He keenly felt his professional responsibility as a state witness. He also knew that this proceeding could cause a significant upheaval amongst some of his people.

"Yes, sir. I was the first officer on the scene." Smith moved quickly through the preliminary identification to the essential element of Thomas's testimony. The informality of the grand jury process dispensed with a lot of the regimen found in a trial court. He asked him to describe what he saw.

"Well, the captain, he told me to monitor the club affair—it was an annual thing, an awards dinner—I was to keep the wrong people out of the event."

"Officer Thomas, it was a colored event, is that right?"

"Yes sir, there was mostly colored there."

"So who would be the wrong people? This was Harlem, wasn't it?" A smattering of titters rippled through the jury. Weldon interrupted.

"Well, it would be the ones who weren't invited. Those that were invited were all gussied up. Fur coats, tuxedos, and the like. You could pretty much tell who the onlookers were." A few jurors raised their eyebrows when he noted the fur and tuxedos, but there were no interruptions.

"Thank you, officer, for that background. Now tell the jury where you were when the event that brings us here today occurred?"

"Well, um, since my assignment for the first part of the affair was over . . . I was, well I was actually downstairs in the hotel lobby reading. I didn't have to be on duty again until it was time for them to leave."

"Excuse me, did you say you were reading, Officer Thomas?" His emphasis on the "you" and "reading" brought another slight titter from the jury box.

"I did."

"I see. Had your racing pages with you."

"No, sir. It was a book. By Professor Dr. Du Bois. An eminent scholar."

The DA cleared his throat and asked Weldon to stick with just answering his questions. He commented, "I guess we'll have to step carefully with you. You being about books instead of bookies." The laughter was more pronounced, but Weldon didn't respond. The DA continued, "What happened later that night?"

"Well, first I heard shouts and a lot of screaming. By the time I got to the staircase, people were stampeding down like it was a fire or something. But then I heard somebody yell that a lady went out the window."

"Explain." He turned away from his witness—a posture he'd learned would direct attention away from himself. The jurors looked intently at Weldon.

"Well, given what I was hearing, I turned around from the stairs and carried myself outside. A lady was lying on the ground with a lot of blood around her head, and she was just . . . well, she looked dead."

"I see. And then . . . ?"

"Like I said, I thought she was dead. The back of her head hit the curb, but still I knelt down to see if she had a pulse. Wasn't one to find. I made sure that somebody called an ambulance and the station house—I mean the station house and then the ambulance—and then I took out my pad and started to take notes."

"And in all of this activity, did you see a Mrs. Vera Scott at any time?"

Thomas swallowed hard. That was the insight he'd been waiting for. Now he could see which way this was going to go. He tried to recall if there was anything that would have directed him to think suspiciously of Mrs. Scott. The pity was, he could. He remembered her demeanor. Everybody he talked to noticed it. The DA, who clearly already knew everything that Weldon did, was waiting for his answer.

"Yes, sir. She come out of the hotel and walked over to the body."

"Forgive me, Officer Thomas, but I thought you said people were 'running.'"

"Yes, sir. I did say that. But Mrs. Scott was more walking than running. And there was another lady with her."

"And that would be . . . ?"

Weldon looked through the notebook he had brought with him to the stand. He already knew the answer, but just wanted to assert a bit of authority by taking his time. "A Mrs. Edgar Kinsdale."

"Thank you, Officer Thomas. What else can you tell us about Mrs. Scott's demeanor—that word means about how she was acting—other than she strolled rather than ran to the body?"

Weldon took the opportunity the DA offered. "No, sir. I did not say 'stroll.' I did say she was walking. She was moving at a more deliberate-like pace than the others. Most of these folks, especially the ladies, were unsettled and sobbing. Mrs. Scott's demeanor was comparatively more benign." The DA turned and faced the officer.

"Was what?"

"More benign."

"I guess that's one of your reading words. For us ordinary folks, is it that you mean she was calmer?"

"Well, in this context it means more like temperate. But yes, 'calmer' would work too."

The DA cleared his throat. "Let me make certain we understand your"—he cleared his throat with a little cough—"your context. You are, in fact, testifying that Mrs. Scott was, if we were to liken her to the others around her, 'calm.' Is that correct?"

"Yes, I guess."

"Can you state that more directly, officer? We'd like to know your assessment of the situation." Weldon didn't bother to note this was the first time his assessment seemed to matter.

"Yes. Mrs. Scott was—in comparison to others around her—calm."

"I see. Is there anything else in your notes the jurors should know?"

Weldon knew what the man was going for. "There is." After he didn't volunteer more, the DA asked, "And that would be?"

"Well, when she—"

"She who, Officer Thomas?"

"When Mrs. Scott got up to the body, she just sorta blurted out a question."

"I see. And what was it that she 'blurted out'?"

"Is she dead?"

"Is she dead?" He paused for effect. "Let's see if I have this correct. Mrs. Vera Scott walked calmly, in a temperate manner, up to a bloody and disfigured body of someone she knew well and simply asked, 'Is she dead?'" He let the words settle before he continued, eliciting from Thomas a meticulous reconstruction of the scene, asking him to include anything that might have looked awry, given the circumstances.

"Well, there was the handkerchief in her hand. I noticed it because with her falling and everything I thought it interesting that she could hold on to it." Smith went over to his table and brought up an envelope. He reached inside and withdrew a delicate white cloth that he placed with a dramatic motion in front of Thomas.

"Have you seen this before?"

"Yes, sir."

"Where was that?"

"It was in the right hand of the deceased—Miss Frelon."

"But are you certain this is the same one, officer? From what I've seen, ladies carry these things all the time and they all pretty much look the same. In fact," Smith volunteered as he examined the item more closely, "it's nearly like the one I purchased for my wife." The jury tittered.

"Well, it seems identical to the one I saw in her right hand."

Smith took the hanky and asked if Weldon had seen the initials on it. He replied that "with it being stuffed into her hand" he wasn't sure what it said. But "the embroidery around the edges seems like it matches the one I saw that night."

"Well, let's see if you can read it now. Here," Smith opened the cloth and pointed to one of its edges, "tell the jury what you see."

"Letters. A *V* followed by an *S. V. S.*"

Smith turned to face the jury. "'V. S.' as in Vera Scott." Weldon slumped some in the witness chair, fully aware this meant it would be his people on trial. Smith went back to his desk and brought forward another envelope.

"Officer Thomas, is this the picture of the deceased as you first saw her?" Smith pulled a glossy image from an envelope and dramatically placed it onto the ledge of the witness stand. Thomas didn't need to see a photo. The scene was fixed in his mind. If required, he could recite its details: the shape of the blood pool, the amount of splatter, the clothes she wore, and the way the scene assaulted the fresh snow. But Weldon responded to the question as asked.

"Yes sir. Yes it is." The DA passed it around the jury. Smith waited for its impact to settle and asked again, "Now, just to clarify matters for the jury, this Vera Scott saw what we are all looking at today, and it is your testimony that everyone around her was crying and upset, and she seemed, let me see if I can find your words . . ." He dramatically flipped the pages of his pad, as if Weldon hadn't just testified to this matter. He paused dramatically on one page, "'temperate and calm.' Is that correct, officer?" Weldon replied that it was and Smith thanked him and released him from questioning. As he walked outside the courtroom door, he held it open for the lady who got up from the bench outside as the bailiff called her name. It was Earlene Kinsdale. She didn't speak to him, and she was obviously a bit flustered to be seen by someone who knew her. But now, understanding the impact of his own testimony, Weldon knew she would be on the DA's list.

After preliminary identifications and establishing that she had been at the dinner and seated at the same table as the deceased, Smith asked Mrs. Kinsdale, "And who were the others, ma'am?" She replied there was an empty seat for Dr. Scott, who was not in attendance, and Miss Frelon, who had left to wait in a side room to wait for an award "she was supposed to have received, although goodness knows how she was qualified . . ." and that in attendance were "Mrs. Vera Scott, Mrs. Grace Milner and the Woods, Myra and her husband . . ." she looked puzzled for a moment, because she couldn't recall his name.

"Not to worry, ma'am," Smith replied. He asked Mrs. Kinsdale to explain what happened after the realization that an accident had taken place. She told the jury that some of the party's guests headed toward the waiting room to look out the window, including the aggressive Zora Hurston. Miss Hurston's patron, Fannie Hurst, left the room as soon as she saw that the event had gone bad and thought better of her presence. Earlene said that she considered rushing to the window herself, "But I thought it might be more helpful if I went outside. After all, the poor dear was already gone. I mean . . . Well, it seemed quite reasonable that one would not have been able to be of much help from the window's ledge." She shuddered and lowered her head. "It was a horror." She looked directly at the jurors. "An absolute horror." She thought it would be an appropriate moment to reach into her bag for a hanky to dab her cheeks. So she did.

When the district attorney asked her whether she got close enough to the body to see if there was anything in her hands. Mrs. Kinsdale looked at him with some disdain.

"Young man," she said, "may I remind you there was a bloody body on the street and people were simply traumatized. That horror commanded my full attention." The jury noted her tone, and there was a bit of throat clearing in the courtroom.

"Perhaps then," Smith continued, "you can tell the court whether you've seen this before." He presented the handkerchief to Earlene.

She reached once again into her bag, this time for her reading glasses.

She unfolded them and examined it carefully before saying, "It does, shall I say, 'resemble' the one that Vera Scott showed off at one of our club meetings. She said it was Belgian lace and that Reynolds had presented it to her during their honeymoon on the Continent. But of course some of us knew better and were certain it had come from the linens counter at Macy's." Again the jury tittered.

"So is it your testimony that it belongs to Vera Scott?"

"It is my testimony," Earlene said carefully, "that it appears to be Mrs. Scott's handkerchief." Then she asked, "Where did you get it?"

"Ma'am, I'll ask the questions," Smith replied icily.

Earlene added that last bit of information to give herself a moment to process the stunning realization that Vera was of interest to these proceedings. But there were, quite frankly, things that didn't quite add up about Vera's conduct. Vera might have been more of a fool than she'd assumed.

It wasn't as if Earlene was not somewhat relieved to understand their interest in Vera. Frankly, she had been dreading the event ever since she received the summons. So on the day she was asked to appear, Earlene just got dressed as if she were going to the funeral along with everyone else. But she instructed her driver to head downtown for the courtroom in Manhattan and to wait for her outside so he might drive her back to the Harlem church for the funeral services. That's why her dress for the occasion was so somber. Well, somber by her standards. It was black, but the cut would have made it as appropriate for a cocktail party as for a funeral. One could not sacrifice fashion. She crossed her legs so that people in the jury might notice her footwear. Her black suede pumps fastened with a red velvet bow. A slight touch of drama was never fully inappropriate.

The DA indicated that he had just a few additional questions. Earlene was more than ready to follow the lead he'd given her.

"Mrs. Kinsdale, do you know how the window in the waiting room came to be open on such a chilly winter's night?"

"The window?" she replied with obvious pique. "You want me to tell you something about a window? Why would I know anything about that? Ask me something else."

"Ma'am, my question is, do you know how it came to be open?"

"As I just said, I don't know a single thing about any windows. I suspect, though, it was open because someone was directed to lift it."

She rolled her eyes, but he ignored her sarcasm. "Well, might I ask if you recall the weather that night?"

"Now that's something I can answer. It was absolutely frigid." She looked at the jury. "I know because," and here she sighed dramatically, "I had my LaVerne bring out the full-length fox for the first time that season. It's always such a task." She said this as if she had not planned to wear the coat regardless of the weather.

"Your LaVerne?" the DA asked.

"Yes. My day maid, LaVerne, ummm, well I just call her LaVerne." Some of the female members of the jury looked at each other with puzzlement, and Earlene noted their surprise, with not a little pleasure. The DA directed them back to the matter at hand.

"Was it snowing?"

"Well, not at first, but by the time I got outside and saw poor dear Olivia all splattered onto the sidewalk, I do recall it was snowing then."

"So on an 'absolutely frigid' night when it was snowing, would it be reasonable, in your judgment, for a woman like yourself, one with your cultivated sensibilities, to open a window?"

"Well, now that you say it in that way I suppose it would be somewhat unusual. But then again, she might just have been a bit overly warm. It happens." She glanced over to the women on the jury, suspecting that one of them might offer a sympathetic nod. But they sat stoically, looking at the district attorney to see his next move.

Earlene had already begun to gather up her coat, gloves, and purse, thinking she was about to be dismissed, when Smith told her he had "just one more question, if you would be so kind, madam." She shot him an exasperated glance as she sat back down. "My apologies for keeping you, ma'am, but I understood you were in the ballroom when Mrs. Scott and Miss Frelon came into the affair. Is that so?"

"Well, yes, yes it is true." For the first time she was actually grateful for the chatty exchange she'd had with one of the detectives the night of the tragedy. Having been sworn in and everything, it would be her duty to be perfectly honest about the matter. It was out of her hands the way things were going. She settled back into the witness chair.

"Would you please be so kind as to recap for the jury what you told our lead detective regarding their interaction? If it would be helpful, I can refresh your memory with notes from your interview."

"That won't be necessary. I am perfectly capable of recalling what I told your detective. They were exchanging words."

"And who would 'they' be, Mrs. Kinsdale?"

"Olivia and Vera. Their exchange was rather heated. Olivia was weeping and Vera was being rather sharp with her."

"Ma'am, I believe you also noted something you overheard Mrs. Scott say to Miss Frelon?"

"I did. I told the detective that Mrs. Scott was saying something like, 'I won't tolerate it one minute more.' She said, 'It has to stop.' I must admit I was taken aback some by her tone. I mean, we were in public and their set-to was entirely inappropriate. And . . ." she reached up to pat her impeccably coiffed updo. Of course, not a strand was out of place. ". . . and their voices were raised." She shook her head disapprovingly.

"I see. And what did her comment 'It has to stop' mean to you, Mrs. Kinsdale?"

"Well, considering she wasn't seen again until after dinner . . ." She stopped, and put her fingers briefly up to her lips, for what had to be dramatic effect. "Oh goodness, I don't think I mentioned that before. Is that a problem?" She batted her eyelashes at the DA, who was momentarily taken aback with her sudden warmth of personality.

"Um. No ma'am. No it isn't. Please just go right ahead. She wasn't seen until when, Mrs. Kinsdale?"

Earlene testified that she was sorry to be the one to say this. But after all, it was the truth of the matter. "Well, Vera came back to the table after dinner just about the time Olivia was called out to receive the award."

"You mean she was missing until then?"

"Well, I guess you could say that. But it wasn't as if anyone went looking for her. Vera is known to be, well, Vera Scott could take things seriously." She looked over at the jury as if she were explaining this just to them. "We all thought that she wanted to patch things up with Olivia, given the unpleasantness at the beginning of the night."

"So she wasn't seen during the evening?"

"Well, not by me."

"And did anyone at your table comment on this?"

"Well . . . there was some talk at the table regarding the matter. Grace . . ."

"That would be Mrs. Grace Milner?"

"Yes, Grace said she thought Vera and Olivia had finally had it out about Reynolds."

"What would 'had it out about Reynolds' have meant to you, Mrs. Kinsdale?"

That was when Earlene Kinsdale reluctantly—or at least she said it was reluctantly—explained to the court the rumors regarding an affair between Miss Frelon and Dr. Scott. Some jurors leaned forward, waiting for the chatty Mrs. Kinsdale to tell more. She kept saying, "I'm so, so sorry to have to say this . . ." at the beginning of almost every sentence, which had the effect of making everything she said have that much more weight. And when she told them that Vera had even shared her suspicions directly with her, at a "private tea party" just a few days before the dinner, Lyndon Smith knew he could dismiss her. His case was made. He did, however, want to put a bit more of the personality of the two women into the record, so he asked, "If you will kindly indulge just one more question. How would you describe the relationship between the two women before that night?"

"Oh they were the best of friends. They told us all the time of their shopping trips to Manhattan and their intimate teas at the Astor." As soon as she said it, her eyes widened and once again she put a gloved hand up to her mouth and looked stricken. Smith took the bait.

"Mrs. Kinsdale?"

"Oh do call me Earlene." She was feeling more at ease now that she knew the questions were coming to a close.

"Thank you, but the court does require formality, so Mrs. Kinsdale, is it your testimony that Mrs. Vera Scott was known for frequenting establishments generally reserved for others?" Of course he meant white people, and of course she could not deny that was the case. "So your testimony is that she was practiced in taking fraudulent advantage of her unusual outward coloring without the knowledge of those who may have sat with her in those tearooms or shopped in those exclusive ladies' establishments?" Earlene, quite regretfully, had to admit that was the fact of the matter.

Smith thanked her for her perspective on the character of Mrs. Scott and dismissed her. Earlene left quickly, thinking how fortunate it was that things went so smoothly and rather quickly at that. She might still have an opportunity to make the funeral. After all, it being one of their affairs, it was not improbable that the services may be somewhat late getting started.

13

Obsequies

AT THE MONTHLY MEETING OF THE WOMEN'S AUXILIARY, BETWEEN the main course and dessert, Myra Wood, Millicent Henderson, and Eula Ann Pettis were selected to the funerary committee. These were women with an abiding appreciation for pomp and ceremony, and who would assure that the funds would be disbursed in a way that would honor the anonymous benefactor. The bequest was timely. Discreet inquiries made regarding what all understood were well-endowed bank accounts of the deceased were met with a statement that Olivia's accounts were closed and unavailable.

Their first decision was that Mason & Sons would have the body. Mason's had a long tradition of serving color-struck Harlem élites. Everybody knew that black people turned darker in death, and the ladies felt obligated to honor the appearance Olivia had so carefully cultivated while she was alive.

Mr. Mason sent a limousine to collect the committee. The car was his most recent acquisition, a Cunningham, and the ladies made a point of telling the driver to motor slowly and to take the longer route so that their friends and neighbors might appreciate their fine accommodation. By the time they arrived, Mason was waiting outside under the midnight-blue canopy that extended from the doors of his business down to the street—an accommodation to prevent the delicate hairdos from succumbing to the city's weather. Just the deceased were going home. Not their hair.

It would have been difficult for anyone not to be moved by Mason's carefully crafted displays of grief-inducing pathos. The walls were draped with sheer black curtains that framed hand-painted vignettes of weeping angels and lambs with ivory, black, and even cinnamon-colored wool following gloomy garden paths. Each scene finished with a finely executed vista of a horizon brightened with a glimmer of golden light. After the ladies took in the full effect, Mason ushered them into his office's plush seats.

Mrs. Pettis was the first to speak. "We must plan a beautiful funeral for Miss Frelon. Everyone must notice how generously our league extends our Christian devotion."

Mason nodded approvingly. "Well then, the first thing we must do is select the casket. I know that it will task your delicate sensitivities. But that selection will guide us in our arrangement of the service." None of the ladies noticed him press a button under the right-hand drawer, but he had, and it brought a formally attired attendant to the door, who silently extended his arm. His gloved hand gestured toward an ornately carved door at the end of a hallway. Upon entering the casket "chamber" the ladies could not help but gasp at the display. At least a score of caskets were elevated on miniature pairs of columns of different heights. There was a series of wooden coffins with different stains, and others with velvety-flocked fabrics. Some were not quite as luxurious as others. "These are not much more than wooden boxes, painted to improve their appearance," Mr. Mason said dismissively as he led them quickly down one aisle. They turned a corner and paused in front of one nestled in the niche. Its pearlescent exterior nearly shimmered against the ebony drapes that fell behind it. They immediately agreed it would be their choice for Olivia. Mason congratulated them on their exquisite taste, but cautioned that their business was not yet finished; they had yet to select her final garment.

The room just adjacent to the casket chamber looked like an elegantly appointed closet. Beautiful dresses hung from satin hangers. They could have been evening gowns except that they had no backs, tailored instead to be discreetly tucked around the form of the deceased. Mrs. Wood, who directed the debutante balls for the league, chose the gown. "Silver," she announced to the others as she reached for a hanger that held a gossamer gown of iridescent lamé. By the time they left Mason's, Olivia Frelon's funeral was destined to become the year's first not-to-be-missed social event.

On the blustery day of the ceremony, Harlem's Seventh Avenue was lined with mourners watching for the glass carriage. Olivia's body had already been installed in the church. Torchères stood at either side of her coffin. Mounds of gardenias and lilies formed a fragrant cushion around her casket.

Mason's craftsmanship was evident to those who had seen her lying on the street. The morticians had perfectly reshaped her head and their beauticians styled her hair, removing any lingering traces of dried blood. Her bronzed curls were loosened from their usual updo and were arranged to form a golden crown circling her face. The strategic coiffure also helped to mask the necessities in the restoration of her skull, but nobody thought of this when they looked down at her to appreciate her nearly ethereal beauty. Mrs. Nanella Mason had taken personal responsibility in applying the makeup herself. Other than what seemed a soft sweep of blush (but was actually several layers of No. 10 foundation), her face bore no hint of the dusky tone that a mortician lesser practiced in the necessities of race-based funeral care might have presented. Olivia lay against a delicately embroidered pillow. She held an antique silver cross that dangled from a chain of pearls. A miniature bouquet of lilacs, roses, and brilliant white gardenias was tucked in her clasped hands. She was as exquisite as she was pitiable.

The crowds quieted as the coach approached. It was topped with a massive floral bouquet of lilies, gardenias, roses, and lilacs whose scents cut through the wintry air. Intricate iron-work gilded the roof lines and everyone appreciated the majesty of the massive white horses that pulled the ornately carved carriage. Velvet drapes and a gilded yet delicate tracery of flowered borders framed its wide windows so that the bier designed to hold the coffin was dramatically displayed to full effect. The crowds gasped as it passed by. The horse's high-stepping prance showed off feathered plumes of lavender, silver, and white, as well as the flowing black ribbons braided into their manes.

Mesdames Wood, Henderson, and Pettis, accompanied by their Omada spouses, rode in the first coach. It was the first Harlem had seen of the new Silver–Knightstown coach. Next came officers of the Negro Welfare League, and then members and friends who had secured enough of a role in the services to be counted among the guests who earned chauffeured rides. The ladies spent a good amount of time determining who would ride in which cars. This detail called for significant diplomacy. After placing themselves first, the committee carefully weighed the order for those selected.

The procession arrived at Mother Bethel AME Church. Its grand front stairs were lined with morticians and funeral directors from all the best Harlem establishments. Dressed in formal attire—morning coats, top hats, striped trousers, and white gloves—they made a striking photograph for the newspapers and were not an insignificant draw for those waiting for pageantry. The church was packed to capacity. Miss Frelon was not known amongst ordinary folks, so Mason's careful attention to detail assured the more than respectable gathering. The announcement of "Obsequies for the Late Olivia Frelon" published in the *Amsterdam News* ran with two important "notices" outlined in thick black boxes. The first indicated that in lieu of the traditional wake, Miss Frelon's casket would be open in the church for two and a quarter hours in the morning prior to the services. The funeral directors deliberated some over the time frame and finally decided that the "quarter hour" would better contribute to the desired effect. The notice respectfully asked the community to kindly understand that because of its unique "qualities," her bier would have to be guarded at all times. The guards wore tuxedos. The casket's "unique quality" referenced in the newspaper was the surprise of a custom-designed glass cover. Rather than a piece of flat glass, placed atop the casket to deter a casual (or intentional) touch, this special-order cover actually mirrored the casket's size and shape and was inverted over the outer edge so that mourners could look but not touch.

The second black box that the paper printed indicated that because of the number of guests expected only the very first in line could be allowed into the sanctuary for the funeral service. After reading the announcements, the numbers of Harlemites who determined to be among those first and fortunate few increased exponentially.

Consequently, a virtual parade of newly discovered mourners passed the casket during the assigned time for the wake and then strategically took seats in the pews rather than take the chance they might not be allowed back inside. As a result of the strategic management of the wake, an overflowing congregation escaped the day's overcast skies to celebrate the promise of rest pronounced in the call to worship: "I am the way, the truth, and the light . . ." Reverend Charleston took the parable of the prodigal son as his text. By the time he finished welcoming Olivia into the loving arms of the colored community and then sending her on to her Jesus, everyone felt as if they had a personal stake in Olivia's salvation.

"IT WAS A SPLENDID FUNERAL." MYRA UNBUTTONED HER GLOVES AND placed them on the hall table as she led her guests into her drawing room. The dusk-dark was threatening to claim the room, but her girl came in to stoke the fire and turn on the lamps. An increasingly ferocious swirl of snow outside reduced the streetlamps to a dim glow, but inside a warm flood of amber light recast the room's shadows and displaced its chill.

"Oh yes, most splendid, and most extraordinary," Eula Ann agreed, joining Myra and Millicent on the divan where they sat together. "And just everyone was there. I noticed even Mr. Wellington at the back of the church. He seemed quite moved. The presence of a gentleman like him"—they all knew she meant a gentleman who was white—"was quite satisfying." The ladies agreed, but it was clear they were fully exhausted. Myra's girl brought them tea and a bottle of spirits, and the clubwomen sat quietly for a while, letting the emotions of the day settle.

"Poor Vera," Eula volunteered. "It breaks my heart that she had to miss Olivia's services." She looked out of the drawing-room window and watched the wintry sun battle the early night sky. The darkness won and the ladies let it settle across their conversation.

"But it was good that Reynolds came," Myra noted. "He was brave to stand in for our sweet Vera. Thank goodness he has taken some days away from work to be with his wife and daughters. Olivia's death was such a shock." Then she whispered, "I hear her recovery is a bit challenged."

"But of course," Millicent was irritated and just tired enough to interrupt their uncritical rehearsal of the events, "that's just the issue, isn't it? I mean, why can't we say it at least among us? The man who has always been so dedicated to his practice has had lots of unusual absences as of late. We know what we've heard. Do any of you believe it?" Millicent's intervention halted their selective obituary.

"Of course not!" Myra seemed adamant. "Not a man of Reynolds's pedigree. She continued almost conspiratorially, "And not" she paused for effect "*entre nous* Kyria, a man pledged to the Omada. We know the unfaltering fidelity they promise."

"A promise ain't worth diddly if you cain't hold on to it!" Eula Ann let her speech slip into the vernacular as if that would better convey the seriousness of her point. "I don't know what you all have heard, but somebody caused Brother Reynolds's secretary to have to ask Dr. Battle to be on call for him during all those afternoons and evenings and other occasions when he was supposed to be carrying out his Hippocratic Oath." The other two women placed their teacups back on the tray, and Eula had their full attention. "And let me tell you something else," she continued after a generous bite of tea cake. "Kyria Ethel was getting mighty weary of her husband having to take up for Dr. Scott and drop whatever he was doing so Reynolds could do . . ." The ladies paused over their teacups, shocked at the implication Eula seemed about to voice. But she recovered the bearings of her class and did not complete the thought.

Millicent acknowledged, "I have to admit that I've wondered about Reynolds. It's too disappointing to believe he would betray Kyria Vera like that. But I agree with you, Eula. It was becoming increasingly difficult to accept his excuses. I can't tell you the number of times we were together and he'd take a phone call, and then make that same old tired excuse."

"Don't I know it!" Myra said. And then, dropping the register of her own voice and imitating Reynolds's carefully hypercorrect speech, "Vera, my dear, and honored guests, you will please excuse this most unfortunate turn of events, but I find myself called away to stand at the side of one of our fellow travelers in this mortal world. I cannot deny the calling, although I deeply regret my necessary leave-taking."

"I bet her 'calling' could not be denied!" Millicent exclaimed as the ladies dissolved into a hilarity more a consequence of their exhaustion (and the whiskey) than their taking any delight in Kyria Vera's sad predicament.

"So who really knew Olivia?" Myra asked the question none of them could answer.

"Frankly, despite what we've heard, I think that Vera turned out to be less than fond of her after she really got to know her. But at first they couldn't be pulled apart," Millicent volunteered. "Olivia sort of sucked the air out of a room when she arrived. I know that I had to remind my darling Hal to whom he should be paying attention whenever that . . . that . . ." The two women gasped, hopeful that their refined friend was not going to say that word, "well, whenever that Olivia was around." The ladies breathed a sigh of relief; grateful their friend's circumspect nature had taken control.

"Well, can I just say that you weren't alone in that!" Eula Ann volunteered. "She was obviously a beautiful creature, but . . ."

"You don't do her justice, Eula Ann," Millicent said. "I mean, you saw her in that casket. She looked nearly ethereal. Myra, you were so right to choose that silver garment for her, but it really didn't matter. Whatever we would have put on her, she couldn't be anything other than exquisite. Thank God she didn't come after my Hal, or your John"—she looked at Eula—"or your Augustus . . ." she nodded toward Myra but didn't finish her thought. She didn't need to. Each of them knew that a woman like Olivia was dangerous, and that her attentions could render an Omada oath—or a marriage vow—as nonbinding as a childhood temperance pledge.

They settled into the evening's silence, lulled by its quiet and their tea (with just enough whiskey to ward off the night's chill). They had no idea of the tempest about to beset their carefully refined community. The firelight's glow and the sitting room's gentle hospitality were deceptive. Outside, what had seemed to be the beginnings of a winter blizzard calmed and the blustery winds retreated into the depths of an indigo sky as if the next day's events—when Vera Scott was arrested, taken from her home, and brought to a holding cell in the police station house— would be cataclysm enough.

14

Arrested

BY THE TIME OLIVIA FRELON DIED, REYNOLDS HAD COME TO HIS senses about the damage he was doing to his family. For some time he'd been trying to win back his wife and rescue their family from the consequences of his betrayal. But Vera's silence was frightening. The shutters she drew around herself encased them all. The enormity of his loss brought Reynolds's failures into focus.

He'd been overly attentive to his practice and especially to the escape offered in Olinda—the name he'd given to the flat above his offices. Reynolds read about a Brazilian city by the same name in one of his atlases. Olinda meant "O beautiful" in Portuguese. The flat became an indulgent retreat from marriage. But now he was desperate to atone for his infidelity. He tried every way he could to make his presence matter again. But his daughters had their own routines and Vera retreated to her rooms as if she were the only resident.

After Olivia's death and despite her husband's effort to revive their marriage, Vera's depression reached a perilous nadir. He berated himself for not having accompanied her to the banquet. But, afraid of her answer, he never asked her directly about what happened. When Earlene Kinsdale brought her home she gave him a look that indicated his wife's dangerously fragile state. He barely reacted to Earlene's stunning news about Olivia Frelon's death.

The weeks afterwards were extraordinary. Their home was like a tomb—the family's silences overwhelmed. Reynolds considered a Mediterranean cruise to give them a space for some healing. Sooner or later he knew he'd have to confess; but for now he could only concentrate on trying to keep her attached to their family. In fact, he was reviewing their itinerary on the very morning that his nurse uncharacteristically burst into his office reporting that their day maid, Sadie Mathis, was on the phone hysterically reporting that the "po-lice" had come into their home and arrested Mrs. Scott, charging her with Olivia Frelon's murder. Folders with beguiling images of Amalfi went flying across his desktop as Reynolds rushed out the door. Without notice or explanation to waiting patients, Dr. Reynolds Scott desperately hurried home to Harlem.

VERA'S QUIETLY CONTROLLED BEAUTY SEEMED OUT OF PLACE IN THE police station. She tried to maintain some degree of composure, but the station house was filled with folks she would ordinarily avoid. If she were to encounter them at all, it would have been when they were targeted for social philanthropy. The lot of them seemed perfectly suited to the goals of her uplift society. But here she was, mixed in with men who were unkempt, stained, sooty, and loudly belligerent, and women who seemed not much different. Although her sobbing quieted, her tears streamed down her alabaster cheeks, smudging the luminescent powder and the subtle hint of rouge she had applied with her morning toilet. Officer Thomas guided her towards the desk sergeant, a burly man with a handlebar mustache who exercised control over the raucous melee in a loud, gravelly voice. "This is Mrs. Scott," Thomas explained.

The sergeant checked his log, but he had actually waited all morning for her appearance, anticipating the attention it would likely attract. "So it is." He glanced at her dismissively, but not with disinterest. An increasingly unruly crowd of reporters threatened at any minute to fall past the glass doors and spill into the station's waiting room where his massive desk sat elevated. He shouted toward the door: "Youse keep outta here, you know yer place. Get on back into the press room. The show's over. At least for now. And you," he looked down at Vera, who shrank from his ruddy display of authority, "you go to police court this afternoon. Officer, get this gal booked and take her to holding."

Weldon had not spoken to Mrs. Scott on the way in to the station. He sat glumly in the front seat of the police car, listening to her sobs, hoping he could just do this job and get back to his beat. He was used to his people asking for him, saying that if they were going to be arrested, they wanted the best—they wanted the colored cop. But this assignment was nothing like those moments of misplaced braggadocio. Thomas was trying to think of a way to keep from being in the photos that would certainly hit evening newsstands. Earlier in his career he thought that being photographed was a good thing, something that allowed neighbors a certain pride in being identified with one of the city's finest. "You got it working there, Big T. Taxpayers giving you folding money for sitting on your ass all day" or "Thomas don't take no shit off us cause he ain't gotta take none off the white man. Ain't anything badder than a colored man with a billy club." But over time he realized that being easily recognized was more curse than blessing. His uniform did not always earn respect. White cops would not hesitate to take an interest in him when they noticed his uniform. There was that time over on Lenox when an argument at a rent party spilled out onto the street. When he tried to get folks back into the flat, a couple of uniforms came up behind him: "You'd think a coon cop would know better than to take up with a bunch like this." The paunchy one walked over to Thomas and feigned a friendly slap on his neck, just below his jaw. "You go on home now like a good boy and we'll take good care of your friends here. I'm sure that with the public drinking, a noise ord, illegal gambling, and disturbing the peace they should be home by the time the watermelon's ripe." He and his friend guffawed over their witticism. It was better, Officer Thomas had decided, to stay out of the picture. But this morning the press was already there, packing the small lobby and outside stairs and forming a cacophonous corridor that descended from the station house doors to the icy street below. Even the relative disarray of the station house seemed a respite from the circus outside.

Weldon stayed with Mrs. Scott while she was fingerprinted, and he escorted her to the women's holding cell. Up to that moment he had been quietly official, but he could not help but feel sorry for her. "Ma'am?" Vera didn't even look up at him. He thought, though, that he might have her attention because he noticed a slight tensing of her arm when he spoke. "Ma'am? I'm sure you won't be here long. Dr. Scott will get you the best lawyer there is and you'll be bailed out of here in no time at all. So try to settle yourself down, find you a corner in here. Not one of these women will even think of giving you a bit of trouble. They know to mind their own business." He raised his voice to direct that remark toward the holding cell, as if an instruction to the women inside who stood in small groups or who sat alone with their backs glumly pressed against the walls of iron bars. "Just try to settle down. Your people will have somebody here for you soon."

His words would have been reassuring had she heard them. But Vera had already disappeared to her quiet place. She slumped down onto a corner of a bench in the midst of the wretched and wronged, and nothing much distinguished her from them. There were white women and colored, hues as various as the whole of the city gathered from separate boroughs and districts and mixed together in the iron cage that fixed the room's center. They looked like her, and, except for her clothing, she could easily have changed places with any of the women (well, with any of the white women) in the pit. Her sable skirts rustled quietly as she tucked them into the space between the bench and bars.

Mindlessly, she reached for the Belgian lace hanky that was still tucked into the sleeve of her blouse and wiped at the ink from the fingerprinting that stained her long, ivory fingers. When she looked down at it and realized it was from the same set she used on the night of the fateful banquet, she dropped it, leaving it to the grimy floor of the holding cell. It was identical to the one she'd shoved at Olivia who stood trembling before her with what had to be a pretense of outrage when Vera accused her of having an affair with her husband. She remembered stuffing the hanky into one of Olivia's open, pleading hands with the curt instruction, "Wipe your eyes, bitch. Your tears don't mean a thing to me. This is over. This ends tonight." In retrospect, perhaps she was just a bit overwrought.

15

The Omada

REYNOLDS WAS GRATEFUL THAT KENAN MONTGOMERY MADE TIME FOR a meeting. But the wait left him even more unsettled than he was when he entered the doctor's home and was directed to a chair outside his private office. Eventually the elderly doctor—his "brother" in the Omada fraternity—ushered him in and graciously offered him a seat as if the visit were an everyday courtesy. But both men's postures betrayed the occasion's seriousness. There was no script amongst the Omada for murder. But Reynolds hadn't known where else to go, and Montgomery was, after all, the Omada's "Protos."

Kenan Montgomery was legendary. He was nearly seventy but kept his home office and its accoutrements in pristine condition, as if he were still practicing medicine and would at any moment need one of the thick tomes shelved in the mahogany cabinetry or one of the metallic instruments carefully displayed in the glass cases. Everything about him—his tailored suits and crisp shirts of Egyptian cotton—was carefully manicured. Protos Montgomery was the epitome of class and character.

"Protos" meant that he was the national leader of the society known as Omada. Its members were Negro men of a certain class who were fortunate enough to find a sealed parchment slipped into their college diplomas. By this discreet signal they knew they had been invited to stand for membership in the fraternity. Seven years from the date of their graduation, after careful scrutiny and review of their achievements and conduct, they might be invited to a membership ceremony. But reaching that stage would depend on their successful negotiation of the probationary years. The wax seal in the diploma was an indication of interest, but not a promise of membership.

The founding members had been wise enough to make their procedures just public enough so that young men of the finest black colleges like Fisk, Howard, and Talladega pinned their hopes on a slip of parchment with the wax imprint of the Omada's blue seal. Their discretion upon discovering the seal was the first test. Assuming they made it past their graduation ceremonies without others knowing about their invitation, the scrutiny began. The fortunate few already knew how hard they had to work to earn a place in an intake ceremony whose formality, ritual, and pomp would make their college graduations pale in comparison.

The New York Omada chapter was "Alpha," the first in the nation, installed and chartered by the Honorable Walter J. Givens. Philadelphia's "Beta" was followed quickly by "Gamma" in Chicago. Chapters shared the responsibility of growing the membership, with the goal of chartering new chapters in cities populated by men with appropriate credentials and attention to the highest principles of character, discipline, and selectivity. Only college-educated men from the upper classes of Negro families were eligible. They were watched to see whom they married (they were expected to marry "light"), how their professional careers developed, and which churches they joined (Episcopalian was preferred and Baptist was usually disqualifying). The members evaluated this information along with more subjective assessments. But simple dislike was never expressed plainly. There were other ways to share that judgment, and if the Omada were collectively expert at nothing else, they were masters of signifying—"I hoped his demeanor would become more subdued as his judgment matured, but . . . alas . . ." The candidacy was nullified.

The Omada were particularly attentive to the youth. They cosponsored debutante balls so that selected young men could be groomed in the gentlemanly arts of leadership. The Omada saw this mentoring as part of their charter responsibility to have a vigorous role in the continued betterment of the race. It was a version of what the increasingly famous sociologist Dr. Du Bois called the talented tenth. The top classes would reach down to assist others attain higher levels of education and professional achievement. The difference between the Du Boisian ethic and the Omada's was that members of this group reached across rather than down—selecting those most like themselves. But, as a member of the Omada himself, Dr. Du Bois was not at all uncomfortable with the difference between his published advice and his private conduct. In fact, he worked assiduously to display an indisputable membership amongst the élite.

Montgomery's distinguished leadership of the Alpha chapter followed the sudden death of Protos Walter Givens. Given this unanticipated mantle of leadership, Montgomery felt his responsibility to the legacy quite keenly and now, faced with this situation with the Scotts, he was fully aware that the very foundation of their membership was vulnerable. He looked over at the somber young doctor sitting across from him and could not help but recall what was perhaps the most important ritual of the initiation ceremony, the one that included a dramatic (and briefly painful) snuffing out of candles, during which members pledged undying fidelity, collectively to the brotherhood and individually to each other. Through that ritual Protos Montgomery was honor bound to be of service to Scott. But he was also duty bound to protect the brotherhood's reputation. The Scott affair was a thicket of indiscretions. The Omada could not become a target of salacious gossip. Montgomery's responsibility was to make certain that did not happen.

"I don't think I need to tell you how damaging this could be . . ." Dr. Montgomery was rarely at a loss for words, but he wanted to choose them carefully for this occasion. "You realize of course that we are just about to extend the Delta charter to the Washington, D.C., chapter. News like this . . ."

"Of course, Protos Montgomery, I fully realize the delicacy of this unfortunate matter," Reynolds interrupted Kenan. "That's why I came to you first. I will proceed in whatever way would be best for all of us."

"Undoubtedly." Montgomery shifted upwards in an upholstered leather chair that swiveled behind his desk of Brazilian cherry—a quiet signifier of the yearning he shared with many of his Omada brothers for the racially progressive politics of South America. He folded his hands on his desk.

"It shall be taken as a given that we have the same objectives." Montgomery delivered this judgment in the stilted manner of speech that was characteristic of the members. "Nonetheless, our shared interest will not be enough to guarantee a desirable outcome. So let us move expeditiously to consider what shall best serve us in this vexing matter." The two men talked well past the noon hour. Eventually, the consultation led to Montgomery's prevailing upon one of his many contacts in the Caucasian community to speak with a highly placed criminal attorney, and to secure his services for Vera Scott. By the time they parted, Attorney Davis Edmonds Jr. was already on his way to the precinct house, fully prepared to appeal for Mrs. Scott's bail.

REYNOLDS DESPERATELY CLUTCHED HIS WIFE AS THE TAXI SPED AWAY from the police station. He thought back to last summer, after Vera returned from visiting her parents in Chicago. He'd made it to Grand Central just in time to meet her train as it rolled into the station, bringing an end to her annual vacation with their daughters and her mother. Their reunion was strained. He couldn't make himself hold Vera's adoring face for too long, so he avoided her glances and concentrated on listening to his daughters' happy chatter. He wasn't sure whether the old saying was right, that a guilty man's eyes always betray him. What might Vera see in his eyes? Guilt? Pain? Pity? He certainly didn't want to betray the pleasure he had enjoyed just hours before with one of her closest friends. And what he had been doing with her was as much a surprise to him as it would have been to his wife.

Ever since receiving his blue wax seal inside his Talladega College diploma, Reynolds was well behaved. He rigorously adhered to the script that would assure him an enviable social stature. He was fully aware that the ways and the means to success necessitated the right career and the correctly colored wife and properly managed life. She would need to be not only brilliantly educated and have a family pedigree that modeled upward mobility but also significantly lighter than he was. His own milk-chocolate skin was not a terminal impediment; but it could have been. He'd simply have to ameliorate the unfortunate circumstance of his coloring by a proper marriage.

And then came the blue Omada wax seal! It was difficult not to shout his success for all to hear when the provost distributed the diplomas in the college chapel. His dreams were closer to reality than he had let himself believe was possible. He knew the requisites that would assure his initiation in seven years. Every Talladega man did. He and his classmates talked of little else for four years, and now that he was tapped the briefly disappointing reality was that he could not share this startling news. He looked around to see if he could notice any subtle, celebratory smiles. But either everyone was appropriately circumspect or he was the only one.

Reynolds focused on a mental review of the outlines of his career. He rehearsed this outline as a matter of discipline and habit. He practiced checking off or adding benchmarks and counting the months between one achievement and the next goal. It was a convention of deliberation and focus he would nurture for a lifetime. While waiting for the graduation ceremony to end he was already thinking about his next steps: medical school at Meharry, then a suitable marriage, then a private practice in an important northern city. Everything seemed possible, and after his marriage to Vera Wright, his induction into the Omada, the birth of their daughters, his successful practice, and the enviable standing (and exclusive housing in Sugar Hill) that the Scott family had achieved amongst Harlem's finest colored families, everything felt assured. But there was nothing on the checklist about an affair, and certainly nothing that involved a police investigation and a murder charge. For someone who had managed to orchestrate his life so flawlessly, he was quite suddenly far removed from being a credit to the race. Reynolds had no one to blame but himself. His plans were impeccable. But his philosophy was flawed.

After Talladega, Reynolds Scott easily assumed the necessary values and biases that would mark him for Omada induction. He met Vera after graduating from Meharry and shortly into his internship at Cook County Hospital in Chicago. It was one of the few hospitals in the nation that would accept colored interns, and, even though there were rotations that he was not allowed to join (like obstetrics and gynecology, where the necessary intimate contact with white women patients would have been inappropriate), he learned most of what the white students did. His intelligence and drive placed him near the head of his class.

As busy as he was during this period, he made certain to find time to go to church. He wasn't particularly religious. But it was getting close to the seven years past his graduation and soon his credentials would be assessed. Strategic visits to a select group of churches helped him find a woman suitable to becoming his wife, and, as important, someone who could be an exemplary "Kyria"—an Omada spouse.

He'd listened carefully to how the service staff at Cook County talked about women, especially when they talked about how to meet them. "You go to clubs and bars to get a date, but go to church to get a wife. That's where you find the peaches that still have they fuzz." Reynolds laughed at their crudeness and even joked with them about having no objection to savoring "an overripe peach"; but he knew that Omada-worthy women would not be found at the clubs. "Our kind of people," his Talladega professors reminded him, "have a special obligation to enhance and enlighten."

Reynolds knew that a church with the right congregation might have among its membership qualified young ladies who came from the kind of people his professors commended. So when he saw Vera Wright sitting in the pew ahead of him in the AME church, and when he noticed that the chestnut-colored hair that escaped her neatly rolled chignon was thin and straight despite the humidity and heat in the sanctuary, he made up his mind to meet her. When he learned she was a Howard University graduate and a member of the "first and finest" sorority, he made up his mind to marry her.

They were wed six months later. The invitation itself became a subject of gossip in the area's Negro women's clubs, and those who were among the fortunate replied to their invitations, "Mr. and Mrs. Claude Darcy accept with pleasure the kind invitation of Mr. and Mrs. Lydell Wright to the wedding of their daughter, Vera Grace, to Dr. Reynolds Sullivan Scott of Buffalo, New York." Guests spent an intense few weeks deciding what gifts they might send. The habit of the day was to set aside a room in their homes for a lavish display of the gifts, with the fine china, sterling silver, and especially the crystal having prominence. Discreet, hand-lettered cards indicating the gift's origin would not be completely out of view. A discerning guest would easily notice who sent the sterling-silver tea service as opposed to the one who sent the silver-plated terrine. An invitation to the family's home prior to the nuptials, just to see the array of gifts, would be nearly (but not quite) as coveted as the invitation to the wedding itself. And those who were not on the list of guests could read about it in the fully half a page coverage dedicated to the affair in all the best Negro papers and society magazines. There was extensive coverage of the wedding party of sixteen prominent guests and the series of intricately managed brunches and other soirees that celebrated nuptials. Vera Grace Wright's marriage was the social event of the season, and just the necessary benchmark for the striving Dr. Scott.

Reynolds completed his medical training in the months after his wedding, and the couple moved to New York so that he might begin his career in general medicine. He strategically selected offices that could be considered in Manhattan (albeit at its outermost boundaries and on the west side) for his fledgling practice. Vera had been helpful in securing those leases as well as the bank loan. When she entered the bank's offices, impeccably coiffed and with the quiet assurance of the upper classes, no one even thought to ask if her husband was a colored man. The bankers and realtors only saw a lovely ivory-skinned woman of obvious breeding and class sitting and rushed to be of service. Although he and Vera never spoke of it, both knew why he asked her to handle the real estate encounters. Her demeanor and their plan assured that she would receive only the most solicitous treatment from all the businesspeople she encountered while she finalized arrangements that would assure that her husband would indeed be "Dr. Reynolds Scott, of Manhattan."

In return, Reynolds easily negotiated their purchase of the elegant apartments on Edgecombe Avenue. It was already among the most distinguished Sugar Hill addresses. Soon, if things went according to plan, there would be rumors that he was an Omada brother (leaving his home on every fourth Friday in a tuxedo would assist that speculation), and that would be enough to solidify his reputation among the Negroes who mattered.

The arrival of each of their daughters brought him tremendous happiness, and although Vera initially seemed similarly enraptured, he noticed that with each passing year she seemed less engaged with the girls and with him. She increasingly assigned Sadie to take over their care while she occupied herself with the business of their social life and dedicated her services to the Negro Welfare League's Women's Auxiliary. Reynolds was beginning to think that his own family needed some of the attention Vera expended on the less fortunate. When he was not at his office or the hospital, or spending time with the girls, or escorting Vera to one of their social engagements (and more and more he felt like her escort rather than her husband), Reynolds retreated to the flat above his offices, where he nurtured a new life's plan.

It started out as a mere fascination with Brazil. His Omada brothers stoked the interest, dedicating many of the table topics at their monthly meetings to what they understood as that country's progressive color politics. They conversed admiringly amongst themselves about how the multicolored democracy was a paradise of racial compromise. They collected brochures and maps and pontificated as to how one thing or another would surely be handled differently in what they imagined as Brazil's racial democracy. Unlike their wives, the men were not blessed with creamy, near-white complexions. A few of them were close. But most looked like Reynolds and his Talladega (male) classmates, and many of them came to share a not-so-secret desire that their own darker-toned skin colors might bring them as much purchase as the color of the women they married. They never overtly discussed the ways in which their own biases, preferences, and conduct directed the principles from which their colored prejudices took shape. But they let themselves believe that having struggled with America's racial politics, they were ready to move on to a dream of racial polity. Brazil became the stand-in for this desire and Reynolds nursed that fantasy into a full-fledged longing.

Meanwhile, Vera Scott faded into the periphery. Her husband's imagination was much more colorful than she could be. For him the idea of Brazil developed into a nearly uncontrollable desire for a life that would feel different from one controlled by how light and, for all practical purposes, "white" his wife was. At first it frightened him to realize that he'd actually begun to shrink from her brilliance—not from her intelligence or her accomplishments but from her glistening whiteness, and how it seemed the only thing that mattered was how her color earned them entry to all the best parties and most exclusive societies. He began to nurse a quiet resentment of how she looked, longing for some hint of hue, some more-colorful undertone.

In part, that was the reason he let his attentions wander. He wanted a more colorful life. His affair lasted the summer and well into the fall. He met her whenever he could—after work, for breakfast, and on weekends. He had not realized how perfectly the life of a physician suited itself to an illicit entanglement. Excuses for his absence and tardiness became a matter of course. He begged his wife's pardon, or their guests, with a perfunctory apology indicating that he knew they would well appreciate the moral imperative of a physician's duty.

But now, with Vera's arrest, the terrible consequence of his infidelity nearly paralyzed him with guilt. He'd risked every effort and every achievement that had been so precious. That was why Dr. Scott set aside whatever pride he had left, confessed every intimate and embarrassing detail of his failings, and took up whatever Protos Montgomery advised him to do without question and with deep gratitude for the depth of the brotherhood. The thing he coveted the most was still there for him, even when he fell so short of its principles.

16

Police Court

EVEN AFTER THE HOURS IN THE HOLDING CELL, AND LONG SINCE THE ragged emotions of the morning had exacted their cost, Vera's entry into the police court caused a collective gasp. Most of the onlookers were shocked that this was, as the story quickly spread, a colored woman. Seeing her made the proceedings even more titillating. Newspapermen and photographers moved beyond respectful jostling to full-fledged belligerent shoving in their efforts to get a response from the lawyer and his client, or at the very least a photo of Mrs. Scott.

Edmonds did not acknowledge the newsmen or the cameras when he ushered his client before the judge. But he was not unaware of their presence. He held Vera's arm firmly but respectfully. The gathered press knew that whatever story or images they could get would make the front pages and sell out newsstands. Some came precariously close to falling over the bar that separated them from the judge and the attorneys. Others, still pushing their way through the melee, did not hesitate to trample whoever stood between them, this well-known defense attorney, and his strikingly beautiful client, a colored woman. They would reveal to their papers' readers that she was as white as they come. LOOK AGAIN—SHE'S COLORED!!!! the *Post* pared the story down to its essentials. The judge was secretly pleased with the commotion and cacophony in the courtroom. He knew this case would attract heavy press coverage, and, if he handled it well, it would reflect favorably on him. Just because he was on assignment to police court, he did not have to water down his standards. He had handled high-profile trials, and he knew when to allow limited public outcry, when to demand silence, and just how much latitude to allow. He was, however, decidedly not averse to making it clear that it was his courtroom, and everyone in it was subject to his authority. When he felt that the time was right, when the press had gotten the requisite photos from every angle—shots of the defendant juxtaposed with spectators, clerks, the police—and when the rabble had sufficiently vented, he gaveled the chamber to silence. Attorney Edmonds proceeded with aplomb, unfazed by the chaos the judge's gavel only tenuously held in check. He too was taken with Vera's odd beauty and considered how it might work to his advantage. After the district attorney read the charge of murder and asked the judge for no bail, considering "the seriousness of the charges before us, Your Honor," Edmonds fashioned his response with matter-of-fact assurance. "But of course, Your Honor, this is a woman . . . ," and here he paused for dramatic effect, to ensure that everyone might have an opportunity to take in the loveliness of the pitiful creature before them. Then he continued, speaking rapidly because he didn't want the word "murder" to settle. "This is a woman from whom we have no fear of her doing anything other than following the court's instructions to the letter, and who will be certain to appear before the court on whatever dates shall be determined, to denounce and to fight this ridiculous charge. She is an upstanding member of society . . ." The confident attorney uncharacteristically stumbled but quickly clarified the point, "an upstanding member of Negro society, the mother of two lovely and accomplished young daughters, and her husband is the well-regarded physician Dr. Reynolds Scott . . . of Manhattan." He pronounced those final words with some emphasis, so that it might sink in that this was a family whose reach exceeded the boundaries of Harlem. "Dr. Scott is fully willing, quite able, and deeply desires that the court allow him to take responsibility for his wife. He assures the court, and I do as well, Your Honor (Edmonds instinctively knew that the word of a white man might hold a different kind of sway than that of a Negro), that she will neither flee nor cause any delay whatsoever for the court. Mrs. Scott, as we might expect of a woman of her stature, shall be fully cooperative. If she is anxious at all it is an anxiety to replace the district attorney's spurious allegations with the fact of her innocence."

In truth the judge was moved more by the potential harm that might happen if this colored woman had to wait out a trial date in the notorious tombs. Given his quick assessment of the costs and benefits of the situation before him, he granted what he intentionally meant to be an extraordinarily high bail. Even with his hope that this family, if they were as socially uplifted as their attorney suggested, might be able to make the posting, nobody would be able to accuse his honor of going soft on the coloreds.

Despite the fact that Edmonds gave the answer the judge had hoped for, he was, nevertheless, somewhat surprised that Edmonds did not flinch while thanking him and indicating that his client was fully prepared to post the requisite amount. But neither Edmonds nor his honor knew that Protos Montgomery was underwriting any and all costs associated with this matter.

Reynolds waited outside in a taxi. The attorney appeared at the glass doors only moments before he caught a brief glimpse of his wife, poorly shielded behind the lawyer's briefcase. Reynolds bounded from the cab and dashed through the mob to the top of the stairs. There, the two men buffered Vera as they made their way to the curb. None of the three responded to any of the shouted questions. They tried without success to avoid the shower of blistering flashbulbs pressed loose in rapid succession from their silver housing. The glass crushed in the stampede and littered the snowy steps of the station, the shards mixing into the icy crystals of snow. The white blur of noise and commotion faded when they closed the taxi doors. As soon as they were inside, Edmonds instructed the driver: "101 Edgecombe—Harlem." Dr. Scott trembled with tension and relief as he held Vera tightly in his embrace. The driver, who had figured out who his passengers would be when he saw them coming down the steps of the station, didn't even look back when they piled in behind him. The colored man gripped the shoulders of a white lady, and the white man, who clasped a briefcase close to his chest, stared straight ahead, not indicating any discomfiture with the scene they had just escaped, or with his company in the taxi. But the driver was used to odd fares coming from the station house, so he nodded his assent and took off for the hills of Harlem.

17

The Brothers' Law

THE MOOD AROUND PROTOS MONTGOMERY'S CONFERENCE TABLE WAS somber. Members arrived promptly at six and the evening's shadows had already relinquished to the dark. Their nearly impenetrable gloom seemed appropriate. Dr. Corrigan Battle, who was aware of the agenda, was the last to arrive.

Membership in the Omada was irrevocable. This left the organization with just two options for disciplining its members. Probation—which the local chapter handled—allowed the member to attend meetings but temporarily barred him from the "closed-door" sessions where rituals were observed and the business discussed. He could still participate in the intellectual presentations and the game hour (usually games of chess; bid whist was not an option for this set) or attend the roundtable debate between the elder members, known inter alia as the SOBs—the Society of Old Bulls. After a prescribed period the probationary member was welcomed back into the fold with all rights restored.

Suspension was more severe and required action by the national organization. This sanction meant giving up all rituals and rights. As he traveled to the call meeting, Battle mentally prepared a defense to protect Brother Scott from suspension.

Protos Montgomery did not linger over protocol. The candles on the elaborate candelabra were extinguished and the scroll that verified the group's charter was returned to its velvet cover and slipped back into the cabinetry behind the protos's seat. A dim yellow light from the wall sconces splayed its shadows across the room's paneling. On the table, feathered quills lay in front of each member, tip pointed to the left, ready to be taken up when the member wished to speak. Emergency meetings like this were governed by the "rule of the quill." The members' quills were white, but the one that lay in front of the protos was blue. Just to his right, in easy reach, was an inkstand. A candle in a short wooden holder kept its flame throughout the proceedings. Other than the candle and quills, a silver stamp, blue wax for the seal, and a single sheet of parchment to record the official results of the gathering were the only things on the table.

Montgomery explained to the members, although most had already heard the news, that a grand jury had returned an indictment against Kyria Vera Scott with regard to "the matter we are all following with grave interest and sympathy." His tone shifted slightly. "But this evening, our sacred brotherhood presents us with a difficult and unhappy agenda. And it is because of this circumstance that I formally call upon the membership to share our collective judgment as to whether or not the brotherhood is compelled to undertake a course of action in response to the events unfolding in the public arena."

No one was reluctant to "take up the pen," and the protos was challenged in maintaining order while calling upon brothers who volunteered their assessments. Several shared an intense and self-righteous condemnation of the arrogance and insinuations of the district attorney. But others reluctantly supported the premise that where there's smoke, there's likely fire. Kenan Montgomery struggled to maintain his neutral presentation of the matter.

"You will notice that I have not passed judgment at all about this . . . well, this unpleasantness regarding Kyria Vera and our beloved brother Scott," the protos said with authoritative resolve. "Nevertheless, we cannot ignore the unfortunate circumstance that accompanies today's indictment." There were vigorous nods and some amens from the men seated around the table. The protos paused, remembering that he ought to have acknowledged the deceased. "And let me also say that even though Miss Olivia Frelon is not associated with our membership, I know that your prayers are with this unfortunate young woman. I saw many of you at her services. Good form, gentlemen." Members patted each other's backs or shook hands until Montgomery reclaimed their attention. "However, regarding the matters that are, by charter and contract, our concern, let me assure each of you that the brotherhood has been both loyal and helpful in each stage of this unfolding tragedy. I do not believe I have to remind you that the principles of our brotherhood mean no state court, no religious injunction, nothing but our own standards shall determine our conduct." His emphasis rose dramatically in these last words, and he concluded with a passionate invocation of one of the signature lines from their secret ritual, "*Adelfos nomos*! We" he emphasized, "are our brothers' law." And here, the Omada collectively voiced the invocation, their deep baritones giving emphasis to the Greek phrase *adelfos nomos*, accompanied with a furious tapping of their quills on the table. Protos Montgomery continued with the reminder that they were "not called to convention this evening because of Kyria Vera's unfortunate circumstance." Here he paused again, but merely to emphasize who was not subject to their judgment. The silence suggested consent, so he continued. "However, my brothers, it is the case that we are convened to determine whether there is sufficient reason that this company, under the accords of our charter and constitution, should commence any particular action with regard to Brother Reynolds Scott. So I am asking, at this time, and at this table only, what do you know that the Omada should know?"

After a long and uncomfortable pause, Brother Battle raised his quill and reluctantly volunteered the rest of the story. He told them about the many evenings Brother Scott asked for him to fill in at the hospital. He somberly recalled how he discovered that the "professional" duty he'd been asked to cover was a personal dalliance. His subdued voice penetrated into the darkening shadows of the room. He said that on an occasion late in the fall, Brother Scott had taken him aside and told him that he would no longer be "taking advantage of his goodwill" and that he should expect his schedule to return to normal. He said that it was a contrite and unhappy conversation and that Scott was deeply apologetic—even troubled—about his "indiscretion."

The night's silence quietly overtook the gathering, and the men seemed unwilling to interrupt the pall that had settled over the meeting. The protos finally took up his pen. "I believe that we have reason to institute our procedure for . . ."—you could hear the intake of breaths around the table—". . . probation," he announced to the group. Brother Battle exhaled deeply and sank back into the embrace of the leather chair, folding his arms across his substantial chest. "Please take up your quills." Each member reached for the quill in front of him and held it aloft, waiting for the protos's next instruction. "Those not in agreement shall so indicate." Not a pen dropped, an indication that each was ready to vicariously sign the order agreeing with the protos's determination. There was no actual dipping of pens into inkwells other than the protos's, as experience proved the tapping produced an unfortunate splatter on the immaculate tuxedo shirts they wore on these occasions.

Kenan Montgomery reached for the thin sheet of parchment placed on the table in front of him, took up his pen, dipped it into the official India ink and signed with his characteristic flourish. He then folded the document and let the wax drop until it formed a puddle that would take the seal. He lifted the ornate wood handle of the silver stamp and gravely pressed the seal of the Omada into the quickly congealing wax. The unhappy deed was accomplished and the protos extinguished the candle. Its smoke spiraled into the room's silence.

18

Waiting for Weldon

SADIE MATHIS PUT ON HER SUNDAY-GO-TO-CHURCH OUTFIT, HER GOOD cloth gloves—the ones with little pearl-like buttons at the wrist—and her Sunday coat and galoshes. She took a trolley down from the Scott apartments in the Heights, getting off at the stop nearest Darnell Zenobia's rooming house. Worried that her nerves would make her hesitate, she didn't even pause to take a breath before knocking loudly at the door and spoke straight up when Miss Zenobia answered the door. The imposing woman looked Sadie up and down and declared she didn't have any rooms to let and if this was not her interest to "please go 'head on and tell me right out who you here to see because I got a sweeten 'tata pie in the oven and if the crust burns while you standing here wasting my time you gonna push me past irritated."

Sadie gulped and tried to remember the powerful prayer the HLC group had left her with before giving her the script for the meeting she was about to hold. The HLC, or Household Ladies Circle of St. John the Baptist Church, was formed after Sadie Mathis overheard some of the deaconesses talking about LaVerne Caver and whether or not her place was secure with Mrs. Kinsdale after Edgar Kinsdale's unexpected death last year.

"It's time we looked after our ownselves," Sadie explained to the newly formed group after their opening devotionals. "We can't let somebody outside of this circle mix us all up in their words without us having our own say. And if you ask me, which y'all have actually gone ahead and done by your being here today in this Fellowship Hall, that's a perfectly reasonable mission for a circle of Christian sisterhood." Everybody agreed and expressed enthusiastic appreciation for her leadership. Soon afterwards their monthly meetings became a ritual that began and concluded with extended devotionals and was also filled with helpful hints for dealing with the challenges of their Sugar Hill families. Or gossip. Sometimes there wasn't much difference.

But this Thursday afternoon was solemn. And Sadie was the focus of their sisterhood. They quickly shushed Linny Lou Strasner, who wanted to tell them about what had happened with her white folks and the news in that household about the quick marriage of the young master Wyckomb. She hadn't even had an opportunity to let them know about the family car that they had reported as stolen but that she had seen "clear as I can see you sitting right here next to me," she whispered to her seatmate. "And the fender was all bent up. Like it had hit something hard." The other woman looked interested then, but the two were shushed so the meeting could get back to its agenda. There was more pressing business. After all, the doctor's wife had been arrested and Sadie was so despondent that she almost didn't come. So whatever Linny's story was, it was going to have to wait. They were all focused on how well LaVerne had done, who took it upon herself to go bring Sadie to the Fellowship Hall. LaVerne graciously accepted their thanks. No one even blamed her that Sadie's hair was so carelessly stuffed under a cloche and you could tell it was barely pressed. Instead the women gathered around Sadie and collected her in their circle of warm brown arms. Soft whispers shushed her apologies and folded her into their embrace, each saying a little prayer, pressing down her hair, offering to help her out of her galoshes and get her some hot tea and honey. It was a loving, necessary moment of saving grace.

"Like I said back when we was first coming together like this. As long as everything stays here in this circle I got no problem sharing our confidences with any and all y'all," Sadie declared when they finally sat around the table and while she passed around the liver sausage sandwiches that she'd cut into neat triangles, ends removed, like she did for her people. Under the table, she patted LaVerne's knee, an apology for her reluctance to be pulled away from the house and a thanks for her firm insistence that she would come along to the meeting.

Doris placed a tiny sandwich onto the plate next to her teacup. "That goes without saying, sweetheart. And you know anything you want to say about your person I can match in a minute with something about my Mrs. Millicent. The way she be goin on about whatever she always reading in the newspapers like it's her own personal business got me worried that she done done the thing. She another one standing in need of prayer." Doris took a tiny bite of her sandwich (at the last meeting she'd been admonished for stuffing the whole thing in her mouth). The memory of that embarrassment was probably what prompted her assessment, spoken to no one in particular, that "just a little less sweet pickle relish and these here would be perfect."

"I'll try that next time darling and I thanks you very kindly for your advice," LaVerne replied sweetly, taking the advice as if it were an unencumbered suggestion. Having retrieved Sadie from Edgecombe, she was the acknowledged facilitator for the meeting. "Ladies? Your attentions, please? Ain't no use for us comin together like this if'n we ain't prepared to use our mighty gathering of Christian spirit infested with nothin less than the power of the Holy Spirit itsownself who is ready for us just to reach out and speak His name so we might be of help to each other in times of needs, trials, and tribulations." Amens and yes ma'ams rippled through the gathering. LaVerne asked, "So what should we do?" Once asked for directly, advice poured out across the table, all offered with thoughtful insistence, love, and empowerment. They found blessing in their common commitment. And in a fashion totally unlike that of the households they served, whose meetings were characterized more by talk than by action, by the time they left Sadie had prayers and a plan.

DARNELL ZENOBIA ALWAYS DID HER HOLLERING RIGHT THERE AT THE front door. It was her own form of notice for the called-upon to meet their guest in the shared front parlor, and an informal way of letting her other boarders know that there were visitors in the house. She was certainly large enough for her voice to carry down the two hallways that ran down either side of the front door. She'd place her hands on her ample hips, lift her head back and up, and throw out her voice without particular direction but with correct anticipation that anyone with any sense at all would stop what they were doing to listen. It could be some hot rolls had just come out of the oven. Her deep round alto was as used to singing solos for the choir as it was for calling folks out, both in and outside church. Zenobia was an absolutely beautiful woman with a glistening brown face, eyes that sparkled with an enigmatic appeal, and a broad and confident smile. The fact that there was a lot of her just made her beauty richer and, for many of her boarders, more desirable. But if anyone knew her in any way other than her public management of her boardinghouse, they were wise enough to keep it to themselves. The respect she commanded was absolute.

When Sadie Mathis quietly asked if she might speak with Officer Thomas, the only way to tell it wasn't an ordinary event was that Zenobia's "Officer Weldon Thomas, *you* have a caller!" was shouted with enough emphasis on "you" to indicate the shout was meant for more than Weldon's hearing. Of course Weldon, and everyone else in the rooming house, heard her. Some managed to scurry into the sitting room and find something to do that might make it look as if they had been in there by happenstance at the very moment that Weldon came in to see Sadie sitting nervously on the paisley settee, patting out an imagined wrinkle in her impeccably ironed dress.

Her posture was perfect. Her feet were placed primly together and crossed at the ankles. She wore her Sunday gloves, and it had been rather difficult to keep the gloves from getting soiled while she removed her slushy galoshes. But thankfully the boots were loose enough to slip off when she nudged them at the back heel with the opposite foot. For this occasion, she decided it was more important to keep her gloves clean and dry than to keep to one's propers. Miss Zenobia had already returned to her cooking, not having bothered to do much more than point Sadie in the direction of the parlor. "Wait for him in there. He'll be in directly. Find you a seat where you please, but you will take them things off"— she'd looked down at the wet boots—"before you step onto my good parlor carpets. I got Orientals in there and they an import."

"Yes ma'am, Miss Zenobia," Sadie whispered, only too glad to be left alone for at least a moment. When she walked into the parlor she tried not to notice the others gathered in small groups around the long windows that stretched across the back of the room. The settee that faced the doorway was still empty, and she chose to sit there to wait.

When Weldon came in he was still dressed in his official uniform because he had only recently gotten back home himself. His formal look made Sadie's task feel even more overwhelming, but upon seeing him she stood and, with more assertiveness than she felt, extended her hand out to him. "Officer Thomas, I am Sadie Beulah Mathis."

Weldon was momentarily caught unawares because of course they had known each other since grade school. But he reached out his hand to shake hers and said, "Miss Sadie, how you doing? I want to take this occasion to say how sorry I am for the trouble that has come your way." Sadie grasped his offered hand and didn't let go. It was part of her plan to hold it firmly. Without letting go or letting the moment pass when she might lose any measure of her reserve, she looked straight into his eyes and delivered the speech she'd prepared and practiced.

"Officer Thomas, I thanks the Lord for having put you in this place." And then she invited him to sit down. On his own (well, on Miss Zenobia's) settee.

She didn't give Weldon a chance to speak. She faced him and said, "I don't know what you going to do about this thing that happened to my people, but you the po-lice now, and the only one we got. And you can't let it keep on like this. She didn't no more kill that lady than I did or your mama." The "mama" comment was LaVerne's advice. At first Sadie considered this to be disrespectful, but after some consideration she figured she had to say something to get the policeman's full attention. Weldon began to raise his hand to signal her to stop. But Sadie, whose home training meant that she ordinarily would not have touched a man apart from family, grabbed his hand and held it firmly down. "Like I say, you the only po-lice we got and I ain't seen no evidence that you done taken this terrible thing to heart. So I come here to tell you to remembers who you are, who your peoples is, and what your responsibility to the race be." Nobody else could have managed to use every form of the verb "to be" in the same sentence. But Sadie's seriousness was conveyed by her unchecked loquaciousness. "It is the likely reason the good Lord above done reached down and placed you in this position of importance to your people. And at this moment here His will is clear that whatever training they done gived you must be turned to the service of your people. Which is who this family be. These are fine folks—the kind of people that do us all good. They gave me a job and Dr. Scott, he done a bit of doctoring hisownself down here." Sadie was stretching the truth just a bit here. Reynolds Scott was known to put in a few hours giving medical advice and checking sore throats at the Community House at least a couple of times a year during the NWL's "professional volunteer days." But not much more than that. Nevertheless, Sadie and the HLC thought the point was worth making. "So what I am here to say is how will you be of service to us?" Before he could answer, much less think about it, she answered for him. "In fact of the matter, I will relieve you of that consideration in order to tell you what it is for you to do. What you has got to do is you have it on you to figure out for this fine and troubled family, and that would mean me too, who you known since we was kids together in Mrs. Stallings's classroom, you has got to figure out who it is in truth and the light of God done done this terrible thing that brung us all to this pitiful situation we have here before us today." It sounded as if someone in the back of the room may have whispered a muffled "amen," but it could have been a chair scraping back from the card table. "You know for a fact that what touches one touches us all so don't think this ain't about you and me an everbody else standing or sitting around in this here room. We be the people that uniform is representing. And we all wants to know is where our representation be." Sadie's voice, strong and commanding up to this point, began to lose the controlled edge she planned on maintaining. "You just got to do this because I knows from the bottom of my heart to the tip of my spirit that my missus could not do nothing like this what they have accused her of."

She didn't know that she had his attention in part because he didn't quite believe that Vera Scott was guilty either. In fact, if anything he thought the lady probably jumped just like he indicated in his unreceived official report, that it was a death by misadventure. And he also spent a considerable amount of thought on why Hughes Wellington hadn't even been questioned. Wellington was not without his own suspicions. But when the investigation turned up the matter of the handkerchief that did not belong to the deceased and how a few too many pointed out Miss Frelon's argument with the doctor's wife and, of course, the rumors of Dr. Scott's relations with the dead woman, he had to admit it looked pretty bad for Mrs. Scott.

Sadie didn't pause to consider what Weldon might be thinking. "And the pitiful thing that I knows for sure, even though she didn't say nothing to me of course and it is out of my role to report on my family like this, but we prayed on it and was told this is all right for me to say to the official investigator—that would be you—the thing is that something in me says that Dr. Scott thinks she mighta done done it and that's why he went and got one of those high lawyers from downtown."

Sadie stopped here to catch her breath and reach into her pocket for a hanky. But instead of using it to wipe her eyes, she used it to wave at him as she declared, "Weldon" (she'd reverted to the informality that ordinarily characterized their relationship), "Weldon, let me tell you this one thing. She don't need no defending from nobody. High class"—the hanky flew upwards at this statement—"or low class or no class," at which point the cloth fluttered back into her lap and she began to ball it up in frustration. "Them lawyers will take money from a dry stick in a riverbed. It don't matter that she innocent to them. But it matters to me. And to my family up in the Heights. And it ought to matter to you because my lady Mrs. Dr. Scott, my Mrs. Vera be as innocent as the newborn day. And with the doctor spending God knows how much money on this it sure will be the ruint of them. I feel it in my spirit. This fine family ruint and turned out from the place they earned up in the Heights. And not to mention this good job I had with them that you know goes to support my dear mother, who depends on me for this since the stroke you know she has suffered." She looked at Weldon with tear-filled eyes. "Weldon," she pleaded, "you has got to find out who done this thing because these my people which means these is your people as well."

She was weeping uncontrollably now, begging Weldon to use his "connects" to find the murderer. With her being so overcome that she couldn't speak, Weldon finally had time to make his own case.

"Miss Sadie. You listen to me now. I am so truly sorry about all this that has come down on your people, but you got to listen to me." He took the liberty of tipping her tear-streaked face up to look at him. "You just have to understand this one thing. I am not the detective on the case. In fact, I'm not a detective at all. Just a beat cop with no connections or nothing else that's going to get me in the mix of this thing. It's too big—with all the newspapers following everything that happens—and the captain, he has made it crystal clear he's going to be the one doing all the talking and assigning all the investigating. Folks downtown been looking into this thing. And you can be sure of one thing. My name is not nowhere on any list of his. And the fact is that the indictment by the grand jury means the police work is over and done except for the testifying." Sadie sobbed louder. But not so loud he couldn't hear the grumbling from across the sitting room.

"He a cop or not?"

"Bus drivers and elevator boys got them a uniform too, you don't catch them saying they cain't drive the bus or operate elevator doors and announce what floor it be."

He ignored the cluster of roomers seated at one of the game tables pretending like they were playing cards. Either it was the quietest bid whist game in history or they weren't playing worth a happy. But knowing he spoke to an audience, he turned his attention to Sadie, but with a bit less confidence than before. "Miss Sadie, they already done with the investigation, which is why your lady got herself arrested. Look, they had evidence. It was your lady's hanky they found all caught up with the body." He thought maybe not saying her name would make it better. Of course it didn't. Sadie began her sobs afresh with that recollection. She'd been the one to put the hanky into Vera's bag that night. The fact that it had been found somewhere in the place where Miss Olivia fell didn't make one bit of sense to her. Weldon spoke the rest of her worries aloud: "And you got to understand there were things that seemed mighty odd around what she did that night." At this, Sadie's retort was fierce and swift and despite the heaving sobs that seemed to hold her voiceless. But she spoke pretty clearly for someone so distraught: "Oh no sir. No siree. You is wrong as you can be about what it is that I got to do. I got to admit nothing of the sort. But maybe you can understand this, Mr. First Colored Po-lice. If my missus is convicted of this ungodly charge Dr. Scott will pick up and take those beautiful girls to live in his magic Brazil, wherever in tarnation that be; and that's the last any of us will see any of them. And so them and me will come to ruin all because you ain't the police they done made you out to be an ever one of us here in Harlem will know it don't mean diddly that you got you a badge or a uniform or that there stick you always twirling around like you in somebody's parade." He hated this allegation, as she suspected he would, because it reflected a failing on his part on his being a credit-to-the-race man. It's just that whenever he thought of alternatives to Vera Scott's involvement he could only think of Hughes Wellington. But if the man was off-limits to his captain how in the heck would he be on-limits to a colored cop?

117

Weldon started to offer Sadie another excuse when several thoughts crowded into his mind and threaded together like spooled silk. And at the same time he felt that old blossoming flutter in his chest. It could have been his heartburn. But maybe it was the other thing. He remembered the boy he caught that night lifting cigarette cases from the tables and how nobody had talked to him about what he might have seen. Second, the lines in his favorite book seemed to light up in his mind like a fluorescent sign: "The guiding of thought and the deft coordination of deed is the path of honor." And finally, he thought of his daddy, who told him that when somebody gives you a ticket, you got it to use, or you may well have tossed it in a trash can. And then his daddy would say that nobody in their right mind throws something away without determining its value. So maybe his uniform was like a ticket. And maybe it was about time he was the one to give it value.

He took Sadie's elbow, helped her up from the sofa, and escorted her to the door. "Sadie Beulah"—he called her by the name they'd used in elementary school because he thought it might remind her that he was still on her side—"you right. You more than right. And I'ma do what I can. But I can't be promising nothing right now because I don't know what there is, or is not. You've done your part by coming here and reminding me of the path of honor." Sadie looked at him with relief and puzzlement. She'd rehearsed her speech pretty well and didn't remember a thing in it about walking no paths or choosing honor. But she was smart enough to know she was closer to where she wanted to be than when she came in the door. When she left, she stood on the stoop, grabbed her coat at the collar, and pulled it tightly around her neck. She felt her whole circle of women breathe out with her. Either the brisk winds or her relief or the spirit held aloft by the HLC prompted her audible sigh. Inside, in the front parlor, a chorus of exhalations echoed Sadie's. Somebody said out loud what the rest of them were thinking. "Well done." And they weren't calling out his name.

PART III

Before the Fall

19

The Harlem Branch Library

I STARTED MY RESEARCH DOWN TO THE HARLEM BRANCH LIBRARY because that's how you tackle a problem like this one. I knew there had to be a book down there to be my "guiding thought" like it said in the quotation. The librarian, Miss Eulailah Silk, was a tiny little thing—just a wisp of a woman. But in her mannerisms, she was anything but diminutive. You could depend on her like clockwork. Like the way she always brushed her silver hair back into a neat braid that circled around into a bun. In summer, when the heat got to everybody else, she was "cool as a cucumber," like Mama would've said, except you could see the hair at the nape of her neck curl tight into its natural crimp just one good hot comb away from home. Whatever her age—me and my buddies used to guess old as dirt or somewhere near it—her nearly translucent skin bordered on a delicacy fully belied by her strict demeanor. It didn't matter how much lace was on her cuffs or collar, or how quietly she moved. Everybody was well aware that a fierce and proper spirit was steward of Harlem's branch library. It was Miss Silk who led me to the Conan Doyle mysteries and how I first got to read about Sherlock Holmes. Miss Silk was a guiding spirit for a lot of us kids.

Many of the grown-ups who brought their kids to the library would more likely than not stay to listen themselves and settle their backsides into the adult chairs that circled the little kids clustered around Miss Silk while she read. I remember Greek myths and travel stories, fairy tales and stories of India and emerald cities, and "Eureka!" moments accompanying inventions like the electric light bulb or the telephone. Miss Silk never just chose her books from the children's shelves; instead, she focused on books that would stretch our imaginations. Her only requirement was attentive listening; but she didn't mind at all the gasps when we learned about Magellan making it safe around the treacherous Cape of Good Hope and how he sailed into the calm of the Pacific—which is how we learned that "pacific" meant "peaceful." I liked learning things like that. She read about pyramids with buried tunnels and burial chambers filled with treasures. And how Peter Pan chose not to grow up. She read books that gave me pause and that made me laugh out loud and even some that made me mad. I got to be a reader because Miss Silk got me thinking how I could grow from a book as well as from a well-balanced meal. She gave all us kids rooms with a view.

That Harlem library was our quiet space. Miss Silk's infrequent "Shush!" and the dull thump of the date-due stamp were the only sounds that consistently betrayed the room's near silence. Us kids did our reading, and when Miss Silk wasn't reading aloud or walking down the aisles making sure we weren't holding our ink pens over the pages, she sat at her desk writing. We used to peek over at her papers, because if you could catch a glimpse before she slipped her work into a binder you could see how each letter and every word was perfectly formed. Some of the kids—girls mostly—knew she was a generous help in perfecting their own penmanship. The ones who had her assistance, especially with learning to master the cursive capital *W*, were more likely to win the annual school penmanship award.

The first time I laid eyes on her, Ellie Howard, she was standing at the checkout section of Miss Silk's desk explaining how she was trying to track down a book on African arts. "I know if I can just use your catalogue for a few moments more, I would find it for Mr. Wellington. We're rather on a deadline." I grinned in a sympathetic way at her effort. She was well spoken and all, but this girl obviously had no idea she was pleading with a person who lived by regulation rather than exception. Her request for just a few minutes to complete her task was out of order. The five-minutes-to-closing bell had already sounded. The only things left to do were to return books to shelving carts and check out. More time was not an option. I stood there waiting for her to be put in her place and ready to offer a sincere condolence and explanation when she did, but instead Miss Silk asked her a question. I nearly dropped my books. The checkout desk is for business, not for conversation. Miss Silk was breaking her own rules.

"Mr. Hughes Wellington?" she asked Ellie. "Is that your employer?"

"Yes ma'am. I'm his new research assistant. And I am trying really, really hard to do a good job and it would be so very helpful if I could just have a few more minutes to track this down." She showed Miss Silk something off a page from a book she held, and the two of them bent their heads over it like Miss Silk was as interested as Ellie was in whatever was on the page.

That seemed to go over pretty well because next thing Miss Silk said was about how she had noticed her in the library before. "You work mostly from the art history collection. Isn't that so?"

She and Ellie just kept on talking like it wasn't closing time and there hadn't been the five-minute bell, and like it wasn't a place for chitchat and like there wasn't no line of patrons, of which I was one, waiting to get our own books stamped. "Yes ma'am. That's the kind of research I am doing for Mr. Wellington. But I used to come here when I worked for Miss Olivia Frelon."

"Oh of course!" That was when Miss Silk tapped her desk with the tips of her fingers. Which means she had put down the due-date stamp. Which was way out of order. "I remember who you are. You are the young lady with the commendable habit of returning the books to the carts instead of attempting to reshelve them yourself."

Ellie would tell me later about how embarrassed she was when she was working for Miss Frelon and had to come to the library and check out books that looked good. "She didn't care one whit about the subject—fiction, nonfiction—all she wanted were books that matched her décor. Shades of blue for the front parlor. And yellow for the dayroom. It was decidedly superficial."

I told her it seemed like she was the fortunate one here and choosing the right color of book wasn't hurting her prospects in any way at all. She told me that her sensibilities were offended by having to choose books based on whether they matched the wallpaper. I told her she was too easily offended. That's the way a lot of our relationship happened, and I should've paid attention back then that we were not always on the same page with things. But back on that day when she and Miss Silk got into a conversation, once the librarian found out she had graduated from Fisk it was like heaven's gates had opened.

"Oh Fisk! How splendid. It's one of our finest!" I remember Ellie beaming, and when Miss Silk told her she had already made a "commendable step to a new position," which I suspected she said because working for a white man was always going to be better for some of our people. But by that time, as interested as I was in the way the two of them were chitchatting away like there wasn't a line (well, me and the kid behind me and the two ahead of me), I was also noticing how lovely this Ellie Howard was and then I got to figuring out a way to make my introductions.

Miss Silk was clearly won over, but I could hardly believe what she said next. "Well, my dear, your consistent good habits carry your reputation for you. And some of our patrons could learn by your example." She tilted her slight face just a bit to the side and scanned the line behind her. I knew she was signifying on me because one of her constant irritations with me was that I liked returning books to their places on the shelves, fitting them into the empty slot that seemed to be just waiting for the book to come back from wherever it had been. But Miss Silk, she wanted all books returned to a cart for her official reshelving and she never appreciated that I always got it right, she just repeated the rule. So it was me she tilted her head at. And yet here on this day Ellie Howard was soaking up more compliments than I ever knew Miss Silk had in her.

"Yes ma'am. Thank you so much for your kind notice of my efforts. I do appreciate it's important to follow your rules here." I gave a loud "ahem," but nobody was paying me any mind. "But it's just this one last item that I was hoping to track before I went back downtown."

I was still trying to think up some appropriate expression of condolence to offer to her when Miss Silk explained her rules were inviolable.

But in fact it would be weeks before I actually made Ellie's acquaintance and some time after that before we developed the kind of relationship church folk might call keeping company. But just at the point when I had decided out how to say, "Sorry—but Miss Silk got her ways. Maybe next time I could help you look? I'm really good with the Dewey Decimal," there was Miss Silk saying that she supposed she could look quickly, just this once, as long as she was able to complete her task before it was time for Miss Silk to turn off the table lights. I nearly choked and needed the handkerchief I'd taken out, ready to offer her when her disappointment led to tears. I used my handkerchief to cover my own cough, which of course ruined it for handing to anybody, especially Ellie Howard. By that time, she'd walked past me with the loveliest smile straight over to the card catalogues. Under my breath I muttered, "Well, I'll be damned."

I never knew Miss Silk to change her routine for anybody at all, but I was there the day Ellie Howard managed to stay in the library for "just a few more moments" while the librarian straightened her desk and checked the room for any stragglers. Which at that point was me. But I watched her while she slipped the long wooden sleeve out of the card catalogue files and placed it onto the shelf below with an ease that felt like allure. Miss Silk asked me if I needed a sip of water while she stamped my book with the date due. The only person I ended up speaking to was her. I thanked her kindly and said I was fine. There was nothing left to do but leave the library to Miss Silk and Ellie Howard's quiet conversating. I thought about Ellie Howard all the way back to Zenobia's rooming house.

Weeks later, I told Ellie this whole story to prove I had been there (she insisted she didn't remember). And then months past that, I had to bring her the devastating news about Miss Frelon. It was the whole of it—from knowing how she held things so deeply, having watched her before she knew me, having listened to her tell me about how embarrassing it had been to choose the right-colored books. I thought then that this Olivia Frelon death would be trouble nearly too difficult for us to manage. It was. And the fact that I had been there upon Miss Frelon's fall and seen what there was to be seen added to the trauma of the telling.

In fact, Ellie Howard's despair was a good part of the reason I told Sadie that I would look into the matter. There were folks I cared about mixed up some kind of way in this thing, not to mention my people that I represented as an officer of the law. We were all caught up in our feelings and sometimes that's exactly when you can get the most information about something.

IT TURNED OUT THAT WHAT FOLKS KNEW ABOUT OLIVIA WAS MORE than folks who actually knew her. For example, even though Earlene

Kinsdale came to blame Vera Scott for leaving her name off the list of invitees to Olivia's housewarming, it wasn't like she was entirely to blame, because it was Miss Frelon who made the instruction for Ellie to compile a list of Harlem's "best people," and Ellie had looked more at listing families. Mrs. Kinsdale in being a widow just didn't show up on the final register. It piqued Earlene to no end, but it was simply the happenstance of Ellie Howard's interpretation of her assignment.

The invitation list was one of the last tasks Ellie completed for Olivia before she left to go downtown to work for Hughes Wellington. Because she wanted to be as much help as she could before she took the new position, and because she did know what it was like being new in Harlem, Ellie was sympathetic to Olivia's attempts to navigate the very élite and exclusive social circles of Harlem's Sugar Hill Negroes. Given her criteria of "only the very best people and any details that might be helpful to me so I can get to know them," it was perfectly reasonable that Vera Scott's name would be first on the list. Mrs. Scott had been president of the Negro Welfare League, chaired its Women's Auxiliary, was the wife of a doctor with offices in Manhattan, was rumored to be Kyria, and, quite frankly, she looked as white as Olivia Frelon. Although she too was quite obviously an important member of the Harlem élite, as well as a dear friend of Vera Scott's, Earlene Kinsdale simply didn't make the first cut. And even though it came to be a consequential decision, it wasn't a malicious exclusion—just pragmatic.

As a consequence of what she felt to be an intentional snub, and one provoked by what Earlene would come to attach the unbecoming label of their relationship being about nothing more than "skinship," Earlene Kinsdale, former best friend of Vera Scott, spent most of her afternoon sulking by the punch bowl. Some of the younger, and therefore more foolish members, fluttered over to the table to show Earlene the perfectly lovely calling card that Olivia had selectively (but in accordance with Ellie's prepared list) distributed.

"Did you get one of these?" Diana Bingham held hers up as if it were something precious. Charlotte Woods immediately replied that she had, and together they admired the added flourish of the engraved blossom. "I do believe it's a magnolia," Diana declared. "Such an elegant touch!"

Mrs. Woods turned toward Mrs. Kinsdale and asked, "Earlene dearest, what do you think?"

"I think," Mrs. Kinsdale replied, "that a card from that thirsty strumpet is nothing to get quite so excited about and it causes me to wonder that you do." She punctuated her remark by dumping the contents of her silver cup back into the bowl.

Mrs. Bingham gasped at this unfortunate display of bad manners and said, "Well! I suspect this means that our dear Earlene didn't receive one."

"And she shouldn't, with unseemly habits like that!" Mrs. Woods signaled to the waiter to remove the bowl from the table.

The spring event that Vera and Olivia both attended sealed their friendship. The talk about them centered on how they became close so quickly—which was not unexpected because both were notably fashionable women, and both were endowed with a particular kind of attractiveness—a judgment absolutely attached to their especially fair skin. Olivia Frelon's hair was deep honey bronzed, an almost golden mass of thick and shining curls. Her wardrobe had been purchased overseas, so she was stylishly up-to-date. Mrs. Scott was more low-key but nonetheless fashionably attired. Miss Frelon was a bit more assertive in her colors and flourishes—like a few more ribbons and bows on her hats, or a lower décolletage. Vera Scott was more refined, or at least a bit more matronly. Her fashion expression was reasonably muted. After all, she had to help convey the seriousness of her husband's career. Their differences were actually helpful in distinguishing the two women. It was relatively easy to tell them apart when, after noting that they each could easily pass, one could say, "You know, the flashy one."

For the rest of the spring and well into the summer the two women's friendship grew over lingering lunches in Manhattan tearooms and visits to each other's homes. Sometimes Miss Frelon brought home one of the delicacies they had shared and giggled over how they had fooled the wait staff into thinking they belonged there. Ellie told Weldon that when she learned about their practiced deception it made her feel uncomfortable, like she was breaking some kind of law. It would have been one thing if they were doing it to engage in a social protest against the unfairness of rules that excluded colored women from the places they visited—like the dressing rooms in fine shops or the parlors of exclusive hotels. But it never occurred to either Vera or Olivia to make their forays into whites-only establishments a public issue. Their conduct was purely about their comfort and access. Their complexions and carriage assured them entrée to places forbidden to others of their race, and they quietly took advantage of the privilege.

Ellie tried to explain to Weldon how it was that she mostly felt sorry for her former employer. "It was odd," Ellie explained through tears, still stunned at the news of her death. "She didn't have anybody who came around who wasn't new to her. It was as if she had been set down in Harlem without anything or anybody to call her own. No wonder she went about making friends with such business-like precision. But I wish it had been less contrived—you know, more natural. And I wish it had been easier for her." She shook her head. "But no matter what we did to try to help her find her place, everything about her felt vulnerable and fleeting."

20

Passing

I KNOW I'VE GOT JUST ONE CHANCE WITH THESE FOLKS. USUALLY, AS A
tragedy works its way through, folks want to talk, until they don't. You got
to get there before the don't do. I'd done my reading and like Sherlock
always did, I planned on doing more listening than asking. Mrs. Doctor's
own lawyer advised her no talking to nobody. Once you get lawyered up,
police are usually so out-of-bounds we don't even count as a nobody. But
my being a colored cop worked just the opposite. I didn't count as being
anybody official in the ways that a white lawyer would worry about. The
situation included my being somebody with singular responsibilities to
my folks in Harlem. Whether they be up in the Heights or down around
125th, I was Harlem's colored cop. Of course Sadie helped in this regard,
being that these were her people and it was her that put me up to this.

And too, you couldn't discount that there was a measure of desperation mounting. Like Mr. Sherlock said, "If you eliminate the impos-
sible, whatever it is that's left, however improbable, must be what's true."
Everybody—me included—was looking for what was true. For that I
needed to hear from the principals, and that would clearly be the doctor's
wife. After the indictment, the Scotts' Manhattan lawyer wasn't doing
much but counting on his client's position in the community and what
he called her good looks (which meant her white looks). These, he said,
would help her plead nolo contendere—which is what the law calls no

contest—and get the sentence down to involuntary manslaughter, which was as good as saying she did it but she didn't mean to. Hearing that this was the plan, in my judgment—as a professional and a race man—it was right for this family to be concerned. Sadie too. That worked out for me because it got them concerned enough to where, after Sadie did her talking to me, Dr. Scott said I could have a bit of time with the Mrs. And she said yes too. It was the opening I needed, and that was how I found myself back up in the Heights.

I started out quiet like, just asking her to tell me what she remembered about the day. Every word made it apparent she was in pain. Her voice was small, but full. The kind of full the ladies say they feel in church where they can't speak because they're so close to overflowing. Mrs. Scott was deep into the wake.

BACK IN THAT SUMMER OF 1927, NEW YORK HAD RELINQUISHED ITSELF to unrelenting heat. Its searing blanket scorched neighborhoods, and residents poured out into the streets to escape the tinderbox tempers of their apartments and flats. Curtains draped listlessly from windowsills waiting without promise to be disturbed. Despite the heat, and with the characteristic resilience of the very young, children played hard from daylight to dusk on city streetscapes that, from a distance, shimmered a wet promise, then disappeared. Adults, more attuned to the weather's sultry dangers, refined wiping their sweaty brows or wringing their hands into aprons into an increasingly damp ritual.

Olivia Frelon and Vera Scott kept an appointment for tea in the rooftop gardens at the Astor. They found a gentle wind there that was cool and as different from the streets below as was their idyllic surround. Panels of intricately woven ivory lace framed the terraced gardens and moved easily in the breeze. Their drinks came first; a very proper waiter presented tall crystal glasses of iced tea with sprigs of mint floating in each to them on tiny silver coasters. Both ladies removed their gloves and eagerly grasped their glasses, anticipating a penetrating relief. Olivia laughed at their parallel moves, saying, "You know, we are so much alike we could indeed be sisters. I feel like I've known you forever." Vera agreed. "Dearest Livvy"—it had become her pet name for her friend—"you know how deeply I share your loving sentiment." And then she blithely added, with no intention of being provocative, "and it has nothing to do with our both being rather fair."

"You mean it doesn't have to do with the fact that we both look white," Olivia whispered the obvious with a characteristic straightforwardness. She reached over to Vera's hand, clasped it in her own, and suggested a more penetrating analysis of their relationship. Her tone took on an unanticipated seriousness. "Well I think it has everything to do with the color question," Olivia whispered, emphasizing the secrecies they engaged. "After all, the familiarity we share comes from our deep understanding of what it might mean if we were not born so biologically benighted." Then she sighed. Olivia's sighs always made strangers and friends empathetic, even when they had no idea as to what brought it on. She didn't notice Vera's tightening countenance and continued her unexpected (and unasked-for) philosophy. "I suspect we both have imagined what it would mean if we were as free as we are pretending to be at this moment. And yet, on these lovely occasions, we get to glimpse what it would be like to experience this freedom, this liberation into finer worlds." Olivia sighed again and looked away. This time Vera used the performance to abruptly draw her hand away from her friend's embrace.

"Wait. Wait. Exactly what kind of freedom is this that you long for? Isn't our work for the race important to you? Are not our access and our membership a privilege as well as a responsibility?" Vera's sharp questions clearly indicated she felt none of her friend's wistfulness. It was disconcerting to realize that Olivia would harbor a secret desire to pass in ways other than their clandestine teas and trying on the latest hats in the finest Manhattan department stores. Why couldn't the exclusive society of Harlem élite that she'd so generously brought Olivia into be sufficient? Vera heard enough wistful race talk from her husband. Olivia was supposed to offer her a sisterly respite from the racial miasmas she put up with at home, encouraged, she was certain, by the table talk at Reynolds's Omada lectures. But here, suddenly, was Olivia's admission of her own overindulgence of the value in her light skin, and this was as irritating to Vera as Reynolds's anger over the expectations attached to his place on the color line. She'd tolerated his complaints because she recognized and accepted that his darker color was undoubtedly a burden. But Olivia looked like her, and she'd mistakenly thought that mirrorlike reflection would erase the always-present issues of color from their relationship.

"No Vera, not at all. Gracious! I didn't mean to make you upset. Please don't be irritated. I couldn't bear your being angry with me! I just meant to suggest it would be . . . well, our lives could be somewhat easier."

Vera's response was sharp and unforgiving: "And exactly what would being white give you? A cucumber sandwich at the Biltmore? An icy drink up here without a whispered, 'So sorry, but we're unable to accommodate you'? Access to a dressing area at the new Saks store? I'm not quite as sure that any of this"—her gloved hands gestured to their surrounds—"how this compares at all to our responsibilities to the race."

"Oh of course it absolutely cannot!" Olivia quickly concurred, trying hard to rescue their conversation. "I just think it's a pity that our desires must be constricted by color, that's all." Vera thought she'd ask her exactly what desires she was thinking about, but just then a very deferential waiter served a tiered tray of savory and sweet delicacies. Olivia seemed more than happy to let the matter drop.

Unfortunately, the Astor revelation was but one of a series of remarks that made it increasingly difficult for Vera to ignore Olivia's lack of boundaries and an entitlement Vera suspected bordered on the reckless. Maybe she just wasn't well schooled in these things. After all, ever since Olivia arrived in Harlem, things had come easily for her, perhaps too easily. To be truthful, she never really took to the responsibilities of their social class with any obvious energy. Nevertheless, she adhered to the expected codes of conduct amongst their set. At the same time, Vera noticed Olivia's habit of dabbling in the luxuries of life among Harlem's élite that the rest of them had worked diligently to secure. Even her home indicated an unbecoming superficiality. Vera wasn't the only one to notice there were very few books on her shelves and an overabundance of knickknacks—clocks, miniature landscapes, and other decorative pieces. There were gossipy remarks—not always kind ones—regarding her décor. Those oversize art and travel books she kept on the tables—cover out, so people could admire her refined tastes—were clearly chosen for the colors of their covers rather than their content. The fact that they were library books was difficult to ignore. Even her participation in the duties taken up by the Women's Auxiliary of the Welfare League was offered on occasions only when she could be a part of some public display. In essence, it was rather apparent that there was something artificial about Olivia. Perhaps Earlene was right about her being a flirtatious fraud.

Vera sighed heavily and pushed these unpleasant thoughts away—after all, this was one of the last times she would see Olivia before she took the girls to Chicago for the summer. She had to admit that Olivia was a delightful partner for shopping and tea, and since in the past she had to do these tearooms by her self—or not at all when she was with Earlene, as her friend's coloring would not allow the deception—it was certainly better having some company. She smiled wanly at Olivia and apologized that the heat seemed to be taking a toll on her manners. Then as if in apology, she held out a sweet from among the delicate array of concoctions for her friend to taste. The slight flutter of excitement she got when Olivia's tongue caressed her fingers as she bit into the chocolate threatened other memories. Vera missed Earlene more than ever.

EARLENE GATES AND VERA WRIGHT WERE ROOMMATES DURING THEIR freshman year at Howard. It didn't take too many nights of Vera's quiet crying for Earlene to crawl into her bed to comfort the girl. Earlene knew loneliness; her mother's death had been devastating. This homesick girl from Chicago reminded Earlene how she had had no one to hold her in those months following her mother's passing.

It didn't take long for the two to find a comfort they had not intended. Earlene wiped tears away from Vera's eyes and moved her hand down to hold her around her waist. She hadn't expected to notice the gentle rise of her nipples as her hand slipped down the front of her gown, much less the excitement she felt when she touched them. It would not be long before Vera turned toward her when she came into her bed. They silently explored each other's bodies, fingers and lips brushed against damp folds and downy curls.

Each was the other's comfort but both knew that this unspoken dimension of their friendship would be unsustainable. So when Earlene introduced Vera to Edgar Kinsdale on graduation day, saying they were both going to New York and would be married, Vera's hug extended a sincere but bittersweet enthusiasm. "She's been my sister," she told Edgar,

"Now you may have her as your wife." Edgar Kinsdale never suspected that Vera's was a bequest that included an intimacy she'd long for but never again acknowledge.

OLIVIA LAUGHINGLY PULLED THE CANDY AWAY FROM HER LIPS AND Vera did remember. Their gay mood restored, the two women walked arm in arm back to the trolley. It was the last time Vera saw her before she and her daughters left for Chicago. When she returned, things were very, very different. By that time she'd reflected on the ease of Olivia's casual flirtatiousness and remembered the inquiries and compliments Olivia frequently directed toward Reynolds. Now there was a completely new context available for understanding her friend.

Eventually the summer's heat gave way to fall; and as the seasons changed things fell apart. It would take considerable thought to piece it all together again.

21

Rooms with a View

VERA SCOTT SAT WITH THE CURTAINS PULLED, A SHELTER FROM December's dreary excuse for daylight. An open desk drawer revealed the edge of a set of silver keys that had been pushed to the back of the drawer. She pulled them out, slowly drawing the blue silk ribbon that held them through her fingertips. It took her back to that day in September when she found the office keys. When her life was undone. Before Olivia died. And before the fall.

SHE AND THE GIRLS WERE JUST RETURNED FROM VISITING HER MOTHER in Chicago. Despite the two months they had been away, and despite what one might have imagined would be a joyful reunion between them, there was no such happy meeting. In fact, Reynolds was late picking them up, and she couldn't tell whether he was distracted or simply uninterested in their lively chatter about their holiday.

Vera found the keys about the same time that she'd finally reached her wit's end puzzling over Reynolds's increasingly cool behavior. But on that day, holding the keys in her hand, it occurred to her that perhaps something at his office was causing his distress. Her frequent calls to her mother in Chicago always ended with a reminder as to her wifely duties. And this she did, albeit with less and less interest. But perhaps their personal life was not the source of their problems. Maybe the office staff was not functioning as they should, or it could be his patient load was problematic. Whatever the case, if something could explain his distance and moodiness, Vera resolved to discover it.

There were two sets of keys to Reynolds's offices. He had one and she kept the other. She remembered looking for a place to keep them after she finalized the contracts for his offices on the upper edges of Manhattan, including the flat above, which gave him perhaps the greatest excitement of the entire plans. "They will be absolutely perfect for an office and library!" he exclaimed, walking over to the nook that neatly framed the shelves. "Darling, look at these built-ins—I could put a whole medical library here!" Vera was pleased that she'd been able to secure the rooms with little of the usual drama that accompanied Negro leases downtown. When she entered the banks and realty offices, no one thought she was a colored woman and once she mentioned her husband was a doctor, their attentions were unimpeachable. The unspoken racial identity that allowed her to secure the contracts seemed not to trouble Reynolds in the least—in fact, he congratulated her savvy. His excitement fully washed away the discomfiture of her engagements with the bankers and property agents. "With these rooms I'll have no excuse but to create dozens upon dozens of articles on the health and disease of the Negro. Nobody from our side is writing these articles for the journals!" He envisioned being invited into the Medical Association, and not just the Negro auxiliary group. Reynolds never thought to ask Vera if it was difficult keeping up a charade of whiteness, or what it felt like to have to mask her color. Nor did he thank her for that sacrifice. It was just one of the reasons he married her. Access.

On the day after Labor Day, when the girls returned to school, Vera decided she could do some shopping downtown and, being so close, make a brief stop at her husband's office. Reynolds was scheduled to be in the hospital for the day, so the office was closed to patients and empty of staff. Vera let herself into the office building, walked through the meticulously appointed waiting rooms, and, despite the concern that brought her there, could not help but smile with approval. Her decorative touches were still very much in evidence. In fact, it looked just as it had when she completed the task and left Reynolds to assume the role of a doctor "with offices in Manhattan."

She wandered into his private office, sank into the plush leather desk chair, and slowly took in its serene orderliness. Nothing cluttered the surface of his large mahogany desk. Vera chose it thinking that patients sitting on the other side could not help but notice the ornate lion's-claw feet and be respectfully appreciative of his authority. The clean desk was a habit Reynolds actually bragged about. Other than the polished brass spyglass, inkstand, and fountain pen, it was clear of the usual clutter that often managed to find its way onto a work surface.

The desk, like the cabinetry and bookshelves behind it, were all spotless and smelled faintly of leather polish. There were just three chairs in the office—his own slate-blue tufted leather desk chair and the two side chairs, also in leather but of considerably smaller dimensions where his patients would be seated to receive the doctor's orders and diagnoses.

At first Vera felt guilty opening the desk drawers and looking through Reynolds's papers. She didn't even know what she was looking for, except that it would be out of place, just as his recent conduct was out of character. Finding nothing there and peeking only briefly into the nurses' station, appointments area, and examination rooms—noting that they were in pristine condition and everything was in good order—she found herself in the back hallway of the suite facing the door that allowed Dr. Scott to enter his offices without passing through the waiting room. With her hand on what she thought was the doorknob to the outside stairway, Vera began to berate herself for harboring mistrust instead of remembering Reynolds's hard work for the social and financial stability that the family enjoyed.

Throughout their marriage, he had treated her and the girls with every indulgence and followed her guidance on what social groups to join, which church should become their church home, and how to strategically guide their family's ambitions. Reynolds trusted and depended on her social savvy.

Of course, his membership in the Omada assured their family's social success. Reynolds knew she was the reason he was selected for final induction; she was light enough to pass and in that way actually exceeded the membership's objective to marry the most beautiful and accomplished women of the race, which of course meant the lightest women graduates of the élite Negro colleges. Her Howard University degree and membership in the most selective sorority were also helpful. But her assessment of the substantial contributions she'd made to their marriage did not dissipate the shame she felt then, standing alone in the antechamber to her husband's offices. Whatever had she thought she would find?

She turned away from the back door, looking around to make certain everything was in place, and was startled when a basement door opened and the cleaning man pulled his supplies into the hallway. He was as surprised as she but regained his composure first. "Ma'am? Can I be of some help to you this morning? These offices be closed."

"Well, I—that is—no, thank you. I was just coming to check on something for the doctor." The janitor looked at her quizzically. There was nothing in her hand but her handbag and he didn't recognize her as one of the nurses or receptionists that worked for Dr. Scott. She seemed a whole lot more fancified than any of those ladies anyway.

Franklin Evans had been the janitor in the building even before the doctor's offices were leased. He was a wiry and wrinkled elderly man with bushy gray eyebrows and a mustache so thick that it didn't matter that there wasn't a single hair on his round brown head. He was proud of his relationship with the building staff; they recognized the importance of his services and treated him well. If this was some kind of intruder it was going to be his job to call a halt to the trespass. Vera noticed Franklin's puzzlement and thought she ought to introduce herself quickly, before he rushed to some unfortunate presumption.

"I am Mrs. Scott, the doctor's wife. Aren't you Franklin Evans?" She was relieved that she managed to recall his name.

"Oh yes'm—of course. I didn't know that was you, Mrs. Doctor. You the last person I expected to see up in these parts. You sure I can't do something for you?"

"No, no thank you, Franklin. Everything is in good order here. I was just leaving." Vera had her hand on the doorknob and paused for just a moment, watching Franklin work his way down the hallway, pushing the wheeled bucket with the handle of the mop.

"Well, nice to see you, Mrs. Doctor. Very nice to see you today." He pushed the rag mop in front of him mumbling just under his breath, "No telling what is going on this day with Mrs. Doctor here. I'm just going to keep to my ownself and get on with my business. No matter that I never seen the lady over here before. Heard tell of her, but never laid eyes on her. And good goodness, she just like they say, white as rice." He chuckled to himself and shook his head. "But ain't none of this any part of my business at all."

Vera thought she heard him saying something to her, but then she realized he may just have been talking to himself, as was the habit of people of that class and his age. She turned to grasp the knob of the outside door. But it would not budge. That's odd, she thought. She fully remembered during the building tour that the back entrances locked only from the outside, not the inside, as a protection for emergency egress. But when she tried the knob again, it still didn't open. Then she noticed that she hadn't grasped the outside door's knob but that of the door that led upstairs to the flat Reynolds used as his private office. She'd nearly forgotten it. So she reached into her pocket and took out the keys on the blue ribbon. The door opened to a small dark stairwell that led to the upstairs flat. She held on to the walls as she made her way up the staircase.

Had anyone been there with her they would have heard Vera's slight and involuntary gasp. She fell back against the door. She'd expected at least a room stacked with medical books and papers, or perhaps one that was still empty; but she had not anticipated this, well . . . this boudoir.

A large iron bed stood at the center of the room and everything else seemed designed around it. Exotic carpets covered the floor, one overlapping the other and each rivaling the next in luxurious elegance and design. There were paintings on the walls by artists she did not recognize—strange geometries of limbs and faces with unintelligible but boldly colored designs. She did recognize the naked brown-skinned women that were Paul Gauguin's objects of interest. The Women's Auxiliary had held long (and rather titillating) discussions of his art, and there was engaged and lively debate about whether or not his nudes were good for the race.

Vera was as embarrassed as she was drawn to the casualness of their exposure. They weren't the only nudes in the room. Small portraits of nut-brown women sat on the mahogany shelves where she anticipated that medical texts and various journals would have been shelved. But instead they were populated with masks, statues of women with African faces and braids, as well as the voluptuous bodies with exaggerated anatomies. Vera hesitantly touched the bed's satin draping as if she could not believe the riot of colors before her—the crimson and heavily tasseled pillows of gold, vermilion, and emerald. Scarlet-scarfed shades covered the lamps, and the bedding was layered with plush mattresses and duvets. It was so unlike Reynolds, who was usually so circumspect, controlled, cautious, and whose meticulous habits could have been described as boring. She looked around, hoping for but not finding any medical books at all. In front of a fireplace there were oversize atlases splayed out open to scenes of tropical climes and countries as if ready for a kind of casual browsing totally uncharacteristic of her husband. Her breathing grew more and more labored the longer she stayed in the room. Eventually she turned, trying to find the door. But it was almost buried in the dense expanse of draperies that covered the walls. She nearly tripped over a collection of pillows, plush velvet duvets, and glamorous animal skins. She struggled, feeling trapped in the wild blend of textures and colors and the lingering haze of incense. Finally she found the door's glass knob and managed to stumble back down the staircase, her chest heaving from the shocking encounter.

The whole event brought Vera to tears, and memories she'd dutifully placed in her past came rushing forward. More than anything she wanted her friend and confidante, the girl who had known her as a girl. She wanted Earlene's comforting understanding and solace. After all these months, Vera allowed herself to acknowledge how she missed her and deeply regretted the way she'd allowed—and even encouraged—Earlene to move away from the center of her social circle. Once she was home she asked Sadie to contact Mrs. Kinsdale, but Earlene never came. So Vera fell asleep sobbing, wishing for nothing more than the solace of her friend's calming caress and intimate understanding.

As the weeks passed, Vera never spoke to Reynolds about her discovery. Eventually, the moment when she could have shared her horror with Earlene slipped away and two silences—hers and Reynolds's—maintained themselves in the house.

It hadn't taken Vera long to determine who was being indulged in that room. The disarray of the bed linens confirmed that. The room was sultry and overly aggressive in color, texture, and opulence. Everything was a figurative rendering, a reproduction, of the indulgences practiced by Olivia Frelon.

After discovering this excess real estate, Vera refined her increasing facility in quieting the storm in her spirit. Instead of being assertive and socially engaged, she grew increasingly still. She allowed and even encouraged Sadie's taking over many of her duties with the children. In one of their Sunday telephone calls, after noticing the strain in her daughter's voice, Vera's mother asked if everything was all right.

"It's fine, Mother. It's fine. I'm just very tired."

"Well, tired I can understand, sweetheart. Being a doctor's wife comes with obligations. It's not an easy life you took on, but your father was so proud of you. If you've got troubles, wear them loosely. Just keep on keeping on. That's what your Grandmama used to say—remember? Keep on keeping on." How could she tell her mother that that was the problem? That she felt kept. Kept away. Kept trapped in a life she thought they had created together. Kept quiet by his providing and his prowling. And kept quiet by the irony that Olivia had been the only friend of hers Reynolds spoke about, wondering over her background, inquiring as to whether Vera knew anything about her apparently substantial finances, and pointing out her exquisite taste in clothing with suggestions that Vera "brighten up her wardrobe like Olivia's." Standing in that exotic paradise of a flat, Vera finally understood what desires had been satisfied there, what brightness indulged. Her Livvy had been the one doing the satisfying. Even after she'd given up everything for him—arranging each aspect of his life so he could be the race man that everyone seemed to aspire towards. Vera could have been a very different kind of woman and now, these many years past, it was too late.

Instead, Vera attached to the quiet in her rooms. She rarely came out and she never received company. She cut off all contact with Olivia and ignored all her pretty little pleadings.

Weldon

Mrs. Scott told me all this and more after she agreed to meet with me. It came pouring out so fast I wanted to slow her down, but it was also true that this was a time to just let her talk. You could hear the despair coming right through her voice. She said she was chilled that morning. And it wasn't because she had a visit from Mrs. Kinsdale that was "rather disconcerting." I wanted to know more about this, but I knew better than to interrupt. If Mrs. Doctor stopped to explain, she might never get back to the story I needed to hear. She said it came to her that the banquet would be the time to carry out her plan. She'd even circled it in the daybook she kept by her bedside table—December 17. I could've asked her for the daybook, it would have made a good entry for my evidence and also indicated prior intent, which these matters would ask for in court-room proceedings, but things were going too well with her deciding to talk so I just kept still and took notes. I could always go back and get the corroborating materials. Sadie sat right down with us, although I wished it was just me and Mrs. Doctor. But it was also plain that I wasn't the one in charge of how this could go. So I listened, and my note pages turned almost as fast as she was talking.

She said that she remembered how on that day Sadie had come into her room, pulled the draperies, and said that the skies almost certainly meant snow. I looked over to where Sadie was sitting, and she nodded an affirmation. Sadie told her that the doctor had telephoned and left a message that he would not be able to accompany her to the banquet. Sadie nodded that this was also correct, but, like me, she was keeping quiet.

"But I already anticipated that," she said, kind of sad like, "it's the way things happen in this household. No surprise there. The hospital. A patient. A professional obligation. Whatever. It no longer mattered." She sighed and looked away. "I already knew more than I could bear." She said she asked Sadie to take down her winter-white velvet and to make sure a car had been arranged. She remembered how Sadie was surprised she was still going. But Mrs. Doctor explained she had obligations and how she had "business of my own to attend to." Then Sadie told her Miss Frelon wanted to ride with her. I looked over at Sadie, who shuddered and started to rock back and forth in her chair, clasping and unclasping her hands.

Mrs. Vera explained that she was actually surprised it took her only a moment to decide to attend the banquet despite her husband's absence, to decide that tonight was as good a time as any to finally confront Olivia. And I couldn't help but interrupt there. "You two ladies had a confrontation?" I asked, keeping my voice low and kind of quiet so my question wouldn't seem overly important, even though it was.

"We did. I knew I'd have her all to myself in the motorcar so she wouldn't be able to escape the conversation. I expected it would be emotional and trying, but my mother's words—'keep on keeping on'—had to mean something. And this time, Officer Thomas, it was going to mean that this sorry creature could not invade my family without consequence."

"Yes ma'am," I said, trying to make it ordinary even though it was close to the exact opposite.

"No, Officer Thomas. I don't think you do understand. What I meant was that if there was a way to break the hold she had over my family, a way to make her realize the costs of her flirtations, I would find it. I am the wife of the doctor with offices in Manhattan. I deserve better. I intended to claim it back that night."

"Yes, ma'am. I see." Although I didn't. What she said bordered on confession.

She told Sadie she was tired. And that was all she had to say, except that of course she didn't kill her. She might have wished her gone, but not dead and gone. I thanked her kindly and Sadie showed me the way out. She tried to get me to say what I thought, but it was too soon. I needed to think it through, to be orderly. And after hearing from Mrs. Doctor Scott, this mess here was a long ways from orderly.

22

Cinnamon and Salt

THERE WAS MORE TO THAT DECEMBER DAY THAN VERA SCOTT SHARED with Officer Thomas. It might've helped—might have, if he had asked about the visit with Mrs. Kinsdale. Nevertheless, Harlem has its own ways of things being told, found, or simply leaked.

The full truth was that the Scott household had gone quiet. It started out solemn in September. By October and November a steady dreariness was long past settled in, and by December everybody either tiptoed around Vera's bedroom suite or avoided it altogether. Doctor Scott would come home, question the girls about their day, have dinner with them if it wasn't too late, and as quickly as he could, retire to his desk in the front parlor. He didn't even get to calm until he'd pulled the stained-glass pocket doors closed and turned his chair away from the doors to face the outside windows. The routine and silences were as predictable as clockwork.

But one day in early December, about a week before the banquet, a commotion broke through the quiet. Even Vera, as cosseted as she was in her rooms, could hear Sadie's pleas getting uncharacteristically loud and then louder. The other voice matched hers in volume, but it was irritatingly shrill. Vera realized immediately it was Earlene Kinsdale.

"I'm sorry but that won't be all right today," Earlene declared. "She absolutely will see me, and see me immediately. I insist that you move aside or I shall step over or on you. It doesn't matter to me which." Vera held her breath. The next thing she knew Earlene Kinsdale was standing in the doorway of her boudoir with her hands on her hips, looking absolutely lovely, a bit petulant, and frankly, a bit disheveled. "You've kept away from us for too long, Vera, and I won't let you disappear on us. Not one day longer! I have come here to tell you that I totally forgive you for ignoring me all last season to play with your pretty little Olivia. But I want our friendship back and I am here to claim it, and you. You are perfectly selfish not to have looked in on me. And here I am trying to be considerate of you!"

Vera was so taken by Earlene's sudden appearance, her sympathy, and even her generous but punishing forgiveness that she opened her arms wide and Earlene settled into an old and familiar embrace. Vera thought Earlene looked just a tad anxious and was concerned that her carelessness regarding their friendship might have something to do with it. She wanted to tell Earlene she'd tried to reach out but there was no way to interrupt, so she allowed herself to be chastised, and then, when it was clear Earlene had exhausted her pique, she insisted that she stay for tea. Vera rang Sadie for tea and a decanter of brandy. Earlene took off her gloves and a beautifully feathered hat and, in her careless way, tossed them across the chair by the fireplace. She announced that she wanted to catch up on everything, and she would not leave until they did. But as soon as they started talking, no matter whom Vera inquired after, it seemed all Earlene wanted to talk about was Olivia Frelon—especially after Vera explained how close she had become with Reynolds and the girls during the summer past.

Not for a moment did Vera consider that Earlene probably knew more of the story than she did. Vera did notice how the mention of Reynolds made Earlene flinch, and she hugged her for the empathy evident in her response. She must know, she said to herself silently, I expect that everybody does. So it wasn't long before Vera told her, in quiet, hesitating sentences, what had happened between Olivia and Reynolds. She was just a little surprised, and more than disappointed, that Earlene didn't try to argue her out of the notion.

"Really? You let them spend time alone together?" Earlene exclaimed. She looked at Vera over the rim of her teacup.. "Well, you and I both know quite well what kind of intimacies come from loneliness."

Vera tried to ignore the memory she prompted. "It's just she had so much energy and interest in the girls. I knew I'd been neglecting them. And it was also true that I felt sorry for her. You know how that can be." She looked at Earlene expectantly, hoping at least that she might find some empathy. But Earlene made no comment, so Vera filled in the quiet. "But, oh my dearest Lene"—she hadn't called her this since college, but it slipped out, along with the memories. "Of course I see what I have done. I see it all. I opened the door and welcomed her into our home, and she's taken it over completely. And she took Reynolds along with it." Vera whispered the last part, realizing that her fears about Olivia and the unspeakable display of Reynolds's upper rooms were not at all unreasonable. Earlene didn't say a thing to dispel the notion.

"Well, there's something to be said for character." Earlene turned away from the window but, because the sun was spilling into the room, Vera could barely see her through the glare. Nevertheless, she heard her clearly. "She had a taking way about her. And it looks as if you just handed it to her." Earlene sat back down on the divan and took one of the sandwiches Sadie brought to accompany their tea. She didn't wait for an answer. "What are these little delicacies?" she asked. "Sadie must stop keeping them a secret from me."

"It's, ummm . . . well I can't say for sure. It's cook's recipe," Vera replied, puzzled that this was the substance of her best friend's response after spilling the most intimate details of the room above her husband's office and how it was designed to accommodate Reynolds's affair. She didn't know what she wanted to hear, but she hadn't anticipated it would be about the tea sandwich.

"Come now, Vera. Shan't we be honest here? It's just the two of us. Frankly, it seems just a bit late for you to have noticed your friend Olivia's character. Me personally? I've never trusted that bitch. Light ain't always right." She looked quickly over at Vera, realizing it wouldn't be unreasonable for her to take a personal offense considering the two women's coloring was indistinguishable. "Oh Vera, darling, of course I didn't mean you, but a woman like that with no background and who is, we've agreed, ridiculously flirtatious—"

Vera tried to interrupt, "I never said ridiculously—"

"No, of course you didn't, dear one. That just wouldn't be you. That's why I am here to say it for you." She laughed at her own impertinence.

146

"I've so missed you these many months. Here it is December and I find you sitting all closed up in your rooms and unhappy and worried and looking poorly! Have you looked at all in a mirror?" Vera was trying to figure out how the focus had shifted. Hadn't she in fact invited Earlene to stay and offered tea because her friend seemed a bit overwrought? But Earlene was clearly invested in reminding Vera of her own failings. "And it's time for me to say bluntly, even though you treated me terribly when you got all tied up with your lovely little Livvy—and even though you left me out of all your fun at the infamous and poorly appointed little bungalow of hers—I would never want something that hurtful to happen to you!" She took a sip of her tea but kept her eyes on Vera, trying to gauge her response.

Why did it always seem that even when Earlene was sympathizing with Vera she was punishing her for inattention? She had to admit, though, that despite the slightly manic edge to Earlene's gaiety, she felt better with her in the room. The sudden change from her cultivated quiet was a stark relief from her self-pitying isolation. Even Sadie seemed relieved that she had a visitor. When she appeared at the door to ask if they would take more hot water for their tea, Earlene declined but pointed to the decanter and asked her to bring a real glass rather than these annoying little cups. Sadie was so relieved she didn't even raise her eyebrows to query the response.

In fact, Earlene's frankness was helpful. Back in September, Vera had wanted independent confirmation regarding her suspicions about Olivia, and she certainly couldn't ask the staff. She tried to explain to Earlene that she'd wanted to reach her then, but Earlene was fully in charge of how their conversation would, or would not, proceed. Vera remembered how she had reached her judgment about who was sharing that room with Reynolds rather quickly. More than once she wondered if she was wrong to have thought ill of the two. Almost as if she had spoken the last thought aloud (she hadn't), Earlene placed her teacup in its saucer and pronounced, "And as our mothers always said, the truth will out. No doubt, she's a slut."

Vera was startled by Earlene's choice of vocabulary, but she didn't interrupt. Instead she took a hanky from her sleeve and tapped across her brow, trying to avoid Earlene's piercing stare.

"You know, to be kind, maybe it can't be helped. Women that light—

147

not you of course, but women who haven't the social stability and advantages that you and I have had—still act as if everyone has to bow down and worship their pretty pink toes. Fact is, they don't give as good as what they get offered. Some of us have to wait for the kind of adulation they get with no effort whatsoever. And by that time, it isn't all that . . ." She looked slyly over at Vera to see if she was listening, but by that time Vera was lying back in the divan with her eyes closed, somewhat overwhelmed with her friend's chatter. "Well never mind. It doesn't matter now anyway." She shuffled through the perfume bottles on Vera's bureau. "Have you any of that new Eve Arden scent? It's quite the talk amongst our group."

As far as Vera was concerned, everything Earlene said confirmed and encouraged her suspicions. She thought better of her harshness given Earlene's overtures. To be kind, this visit had to be somewhat difficult for Earlene. After all, she and Reynolds had always gotten along well. Both women had always taken great care to be thoughtful and attentive to each other's spouses—especially because neither had forgotten or frankly quite forgiven themselves the indulgences they enjoyed when they were roommates. So their husbands deserved a kind of attention and focus that might otherwise be challenged by their own relationship. Earlene so easily became friends with both of them, and their daughters, and she had proved it countless times over. If this situation led her to become critical of Reynolds, he'd obviously earned it. This was as clear an indication as she could have that Vera's slighting of their friendship had done some damage—at least to their family circle. So she listened without complaint as Earlene chattered on. Vera closed her eyes, trying to keep the riot of thoughts in her mind in check.

In one way, Earlene Kinsdale felt rather sorry for Vera. For a woman who was usually so carefully put together, she looked carelessly pitiful. But then, she had to remember that Vera had brought a lot of this on herself by being disloyal to their friendship when she chose Olivia over her. It was probably just because the new girl was a mirror image of what Vera admired the most. Even though she publicly celebrated what she called the sweet chocolate and spice colors of the race, Earlene had always known Vera did it only because she looked more like salt than cinnamon. What was it they had learned about Lear's daughters? There's always a favorite. And she was there first. And it should have mattered to Vera that since Earlene lost her Edgar, her once secure place amongst their set was fragile. She didn't have the companion that gave every other woman their social legitimacy. Even when the Omada had their annual winter affair, where the festivities were called "Christmas Is for the Kyria," she was relegated to the widows' table. It was humiliating. Her friend should have sensed her need. After all, Vera understood that it was Edgar Kinsdale's wealth rather than his wife's coloring that secured her membership. He was Omada and as his Kyria, she was someone worth, well, worth her own salt. To lose Vera's attentions and affection after Edgar died threatened her own social position. Edgar had been her entrée into the élite. It was clear that Vera was selfish. And she should have been needed as well—certainly a lot more than Miss mystery-becomes-me-Olivia Frelon, whose coloring was her only calling card.

23

Color Struck

REYNOLDS SAT GLUMLY IN THE FRONT PARLOR WAITING FOR HIS WIFE'S guest to leave. At first he was delighted to hear that she was taking company, but when Sadie told him who it was, he moved as quickly as he could back into the parlor and pulled the pocket doors closed. He sat in the advancing dark and sighed wistfully, recalling the happiness of his glistening and full summer. But when those days faded into the drear of late fall and the trees lining the streets seemed like dark sentinels watching things fall apart, the summer's warm pleasures lost their appeal. It wasn't long after that he thought better of his folly.

The treescapes were the only reliable measure of the season given that most of the days were gray and cloudy. Late autumn rains pounded the roofs and windows, or splattered in quieter rhythms on Harlem streets. Eventually fat wet snowflakes drifted lazily against windowpanes and augured an early winter.

It was, he was now certain, that long spate of especially gloomy days that led him to realize the error in his conduct. He wished now he had ended it earlier. Or better yet, never gotten involved at all. He didn't love her, but of course they both knew it had never been about love. Their relationship risked more than it ever gained either of them. While he waited for her to come up the stairs he sensed his heart pounding and anticipated how its rhythms would soon be matched by his embrace and her fevered response. It was always about the sex—never the intimacy, certainly the desire, and the risk, and, especially for Reynolds, the difference. In public their casual chatter was about the weather, politics, the advancement of the race, or the business of race work that those in their positions were obliged to engage in. Eventually, they'd cut these conversations short, aware that a look, a comment, or a glance that seemed too familiar might be detected. But in the privacy of the room they secretly shared, it was always the same—before and after.

She arrived shortly after he opened the blinds, allowing whatever light there was to gently scatter diffuse and dusty shadows through the air. He loved the way that the light had the effect of making even the dark colors more intense. When she came in, every aspect of the room—its tone, the sculptures and prints, came to life as if she embodied the spirit that he'd wanted the room to capture. Eventually it was almost as if her presence was necessary—almost essential to the room's design.

He was more than ready to succumb. His lover's striking skin and her easy laughter were hard to ignore. Between patient visits, Reynolds often sat at the massive desk in his spare but sophisticated office imagining what it would be like to touch a woman whose skin was as warm as her laughter. What does brown feel like? So when her affectionate attentions fell across the line of propriety, a gloved hand left a bit too long on his arm, a glance that went beyond lingering, he fell willingly into her dusky arms.

It was as if she embodied all the exotic allure of Brazil and his fantasy was fully executed. When she walked into the light he'd ask her to stand motionless. Eventually, and without saying anything at all, she'd disrobe, but only down to her carefully selected undergarments. Then she'd stop. At first he found it surprising; not, of course, that she could stop at this moment, but that he would want this pause. He had never given a thought to the idea that women's flimsy undergarments mattered. With Vera he always considered them in the way. And more often than not, she acted as if she was fulfilling some wifely duty rather than committing to the intimacy of sex. But his lover encouraged his focus on each item—the intricacies of the lace or the seams of satin-scalloped edges. Each had a role in the slow unfolding of her allure.

Afterwards, when there was nothing left between them but the sheen of her coppery skin, glistening from the intensity of their lovemaking, he'd let himself notice how the late afternoon light bathed the bed linens and illumined the room's exotic appointments—including her.

Reynolds hadn't figured at how much his fascination came from the way her skin took to the summer's heat, or how the drops of sweat that sparkled on her forehead and, after their lovemaking, on her belly caught the sun's rays and glistened. He was hypnotized by how light was caught in each droplet and melted onto her bronzed skin just so. His tongue rushed to capture its trace before it trailed off, a gleaming golden rivulet of honey. His tongue followed the trail it left into each fragrant fold of her body. He was sure that he could fully sense her color; touch, smell, and even taste the narcotic duskiness of her skin as she lay naked and exhausted, her honeyed body fading languorously into the shadows of the late afternoon sun. He slipped between her legs, pushing them gently apart, and after pausing to brush back the matted curls between her legs, he disappeared into the indelicate torrents of her dark and downy hair. When he dared to open his eyes and actually look at her, he sank helplessly into her breasts, certain that their warmth was due fully to the beautiful brown they held so perfectly. He turned her over and clasped her warm bottom with both hands, moving them closer and closer together in circling rhythms until his thumbs disappeared into the dark, wet, and deep crevice.

But with the shortening days and the increasing fade of fall to the steely certainty of winter, she became less appealing. Not to mention the fact that his guilt over the matter was becoming more and more difficult to bear. Vera had noticed his moodiness, and the fact was that with each clandestine encounter his Omada brothers would be more likely to discover his break from their standards. For the Omada, reverence of family—especially the wives—"Kyria" in the affected vocabulary of the society—stood as the ultimate test of character. The affairs of the lower classes, their vices and uncontrolled emotional and physical neediness, opposed the Omada's stoic virtues.

Reynolds tried to remember when artistic renderings of brown and golden-skinned women no longer satisfied his imagination, when the idolatry of Vera's creamy complexion became annoying, and when he resolved to see if the way the books characterized the eroticism connected to skin tone. "The blacker the berry," he read in one of the Harlem novels, "the sweeter the juice." In summer, when their affair began, her skin leaned toward copper. She finally noticed his watching her and succumbed to his invitations to visit his secret room where the framed portraits of women looked, he promised, just like her. And when she finally visited and protested they didn't look like her at all, it was easier than it should have been to prove they did; she had only to disrobe to see the resemblance.

By late fall, he came to his senses and called it off. It wasn't just that her summer glow was fading and her color was no longer quite as seductive as it had been during the height of the season; their liaison threatened his home and family. The night he told her, he waited to say it until after their furious lovemaking, after their ragged breaths fell into a shared rhythm. She listened quietly to his pitiful explanation. Then she got up from the bed without turning to look at him. Her quiet was disconcerting. He was almost afraid while she languidly slipped into her gossamer undergarments and casually let the deep-violet frock fall over her head. In the late afternoon light its intricate beading had sparkled like a promise. But, like the woman who wore it, its embellishments faded into the evening's dusk. She walked over to his side of the bed and touched his face. Reynolds looked up. For just a moment, the streetlight caught her eyes. Their intensity and darkness unmanned him. He wondered if she was going to slap him and make a scene. But she just stood quietly in the fading light, long enough for any discomfort he might have to reach its apex. Just when he was about to break their silence with a pathetic plea for her to remember "their good times," she turned away and spoke so quietly that he had to strain to hear.

"Whatever made you think you were the one who could say when this would be over?" He tried to respond in some way that matched her unexpected tone. But she spoke first. "It appears you've made a most unfortunate misjudgment." She sat down on the edge of the bed and slipped on her shoes, crossing her legs in order to buckle the ankle straps. "Understand this, Reynolds." She stood and faced him, looking down since he was still lying in the bed. "I will not be toyed with. Neither will I be ignored. It seems you and that creamy bitch of yours both suffer from the same delusion." She lifted her coat from the rack at the door. "It's far past time that someone disabused you of it." Earlene walked out, leaving him to the dreariness of the overly decorated flat. Her words settled like grit into the room's thick shadows. Reynolds shivered and drew the sheets so tightly around him that they could have been a winding cloth. The worst part was, he already missed her.

Tonight, while his wife and Earlene Kinsdale met over tea at the other end of their apartments, Reynolds sat glumly in the darkened parlor, wondering how he managed to make such a complete mess of things and, worst of all, fighting his furious desire to see just one last glimpse of Earlene before she left.

PART IV

Just Spring

24

Witness

AFTER I TALKED WITH MRS. DOCTOR IT TOOK SOME TIME AND THOUGHT to figure out how to proceed. Folks had already got to talking—so it was important to let my thinking evolve on its own rather than be directed by the conversations at Zenobia's. I knew I needed to talk to someone who would not rope me in one way or the other—who had no particular stake in an outcome. So I met LT Mitchell down near Chasen's Grocery.

When I got word out that I wanted to see the boy it didn't take long for the neighborhood kids to get in touch with him. I could've easily tracked him down, and I told him this too when he dared to show up sporting an attitude. So to get him to a more proper demeanor I asked him if we wouldn't want to upset his moms by letting her know we was doing some conversating.

"No sir. But whatchu want with me? What I do?"

I didn't waste any time explaining how I knew he lied about the night at the hotel. I just told him I knew he did. I don't have much tolerance for working the truth out of kids. Given the chance, they lie. Not that they be weighing options. Sometimes, a lie was just more interesting. In fact, it's a shame the way grown folks invite kids to fabricate by asking, "Which one of y'all did this?" when we know good and well which one done done it. And it's not necessarily the one that peed in his pants when confronted. Grown-ups can be scary. I always give youngsters the respect of telling them straight out what I know, and, more often than not, they take the opportunity I'm offering. It eliminates them having to think about how they might could get away with it.

So I started out by telling the boy that he lied to me once, and he'd better not to waste any more of my time. LT walked along real quiet for a while, then he sat down on a bench and downed the rest of a red pop. He wiped the stain off his lips with his coat sleeve and leaned back on the bench, his arms stretched out across its rear panels. The boy was thin set and was going to be tall. He was close to the age when no good would come looking for him.

"Moms didn't know I was out that night. She moved us up here with just me and my twin baby sisters. She taking in some pressing, but it ain't enough to make ends meet. I hates seeing her bent over that board with that basket full of rolled-up shirts. She take one out an looks like another one just shows up in its place." LT folded his arms across his chest. "If she found out she wouldn't have none of it. All she wants is for me to just go to school, come home, go to church, come home, go back to school, and get ready to go back to church. She thinks all there is in the world is jails, schools, and churches. And only two of them on the list she got for me."

I left the boy's words to drift out across the park, not just because his mother had the right priorities but because it wasn't my place to comment. Instead I asked him to go ahead and use this time to talk about that night. And then I said that afterwards we could stop back by Mr. Chasen's and talk to him about a real job. LT looked up hopefully, but the way his eyes dimmed over real quick, you could tell something interrupted his excitement. I knew what it was. "I'll stop by to talk to your moms about the job."

His grin took up nearly his whole face. He was going to try to thank me, but I told him that all I needed to know was what it was that he had witnessed that night.

He let out a deep breath and finally said, "Well that's different, then. If I'm a witness, then that means something. Lemme get it out just like it all happened. Lessee . . ." He paused for a moment, clasped his hands both one way then the other, then he let it all out. "You see, Officer Thomas, sir, as a witness like what you say I is, I can tell you it all started when I was peeping out the kitchen watching the people come in for the dinner. My job was getting trays ready for the waiters. That and clean up. So between the servings, I had time to check them out." He looked over to see if I had anything to say, but I kept writing in my notebook so there wouldn't be any part of me coming between his story and its telling. When he saw I wasn't going to interrupt, he went right back to the place where he left off. "Man, I thought I had seed everything till them two ladies what I thought back then was white ladies come in. They was fussing in the way like you want to stay all proper, but you done got to a place way past hiding it, you know?" I put down in my notes how this detail did corroborate what Mrs. Scott said was her intention.

"Okay. So like I said, back then I was thinking they was white, and when I learned they wasn't it got me to thinking there's all kinds of coloreds up north. Moms even took me to the colored doctor what come to the community center. But, except for the scope around his neck, he looked kinda ordinary. Me, I'ma get me a job with a uniform. Maybe drive one of them trolleys. Or be a cop. These uniforms come with the job?"

He reached over to finger my lapel, and I had to put him back on track. I told him that he was doing fine but I needed him to go ahead with his witness report.

"Yeah well, okay. But I ain't stupid about what's been going down. I just read about the look-like-she-white lady that you arrested. She done done it, huh?"

I told him that's what I was trying to discern. He looked puzzled, so I wrote the word—"discern"—on a blank page, ripped it out, and gave it to him. I told him that the next time I see him I want to hear what the word means. That was my way of letting him know I wasn't going to just drop out of his life like I just dropped into it. But I didn't want to belabor that idea so I encouraged him to keep on with his witnessing. He looked at me to see if I meant it. Then he folded up and pocketed the paper and kept on talking.

"The ladies, well they went up to the banquet hall still fussing. One, I call her the dull lady—there wasn't nothing special about her. She walked away sniffling and went toward the ladies' toilets. The other one, the dead lady, there wasn't nothing dull about her at all. She was wearing this red dress. I mean she was *w-e-a-r-i-n-g* it." He looked over to see if I was in agreement, but I just kept writing in my notebook. "Well, like I was sayin, it was easy to follow where she went; she walked in like she owned the place and like there hadn't been no kinda fussing at all. Some folk got

159

that kinda chill." It would have been a good time to prompt him, but I just waited him out. A pigeon bobbed its way over to where we were sitting and LT reached down for some gravel. I caught the boy's hand and covered it with mine. The gravel spilled from his fingers. We sat quietly until LT went back to his story.

"Well, then I saw this real dandified white man. Now I know *he* was white. Mr. Shannon explained how this gent shows up at a lot of fancy colored affairs. At first, he looked kinda snobbish, but that's not how he was comin off to people who looked like they wanted to pee their pants when he went walkin over to folk clapping them on they backs and stuff. But when he saw the red-dress lady, he quit the glad-handing and got to watching her. What made me pay attention to him was how she started looking over at him. They just stood there for a minute kinda checking each other out. You got that down?" I could tell that he was getting more and more impressed that what he was saying was important enough to be recorded. He was right. It was.

"Well, next thing you know he gets over to her and then the two of them, they started their own set-to. I got to wondering what was it with this dame? Do she fuss at everybody?"

It seemed an appropriate time for follow-up, so I asked if he was certain it was arguing he saw.

"Well, seemed like it; but I couldn't exactly hear what they was saying. I did see when he took her hand real gracious like and kissed it. Like this." The kid actually kissed the back of his hand. "Then he left her there right in the middle of the room under one of them candle lyras. And she just stood there like she didn't know who to go talk to next."

I explained that the word was "chandeliers." He repeated it under his breath. It made me glad to see the boy was open to learning things. He already had at least three words on his paper. He unfolded it again and asked if I would write down "chandelier." After that I asked him to tell me whether he saw any of those folks later on that night.

"Well, most of the night I was on cleanup. But in between moving the dirty dishes and wiping down the trays I could peep out the sides of the screens we was working behind and see pretty much everything. When I got ahead of myself on the loading off and wiping down, that's what I did." I asked him what he saw.

"Well, that would be the banquet room and the door to the room where they was keeping the prizewinners. The colored doctor's wife went in there."

I asked him which room he meant and tried to keep my tone from sounding the interest I was feeling.

"She went in the prize waiting room after everybody but the dead lady got done with their speechifying. And then she rushed out and went back into the banquet hall. It was when the little girl was singing and I wasn't much interested in her—she waaaay too young. You know what I mean?" I didn't respond, so LT kept talking. "Yup. Well I saw her go in, and I saw her rush back out."

I asked him what he meant by "rush out," because Sherlock says notice when you get a descriptive word.

"Well, she come out real quick and she kept brushing down her dress and pulling at her gloves."

I needed him to explain, so he offered a bit more.

"It was like . . ." At first he couldn't get an image, but then the one he got was dead-on for my purposes. "Well, like if she had been a guy with lapels, she woulda tugged on them. Like a 'so there' kind of move. Like an attitude adjustment." I wrote that down and asked if there was anything else he noticed.

"Well, I didn't see anything else until that libary lady came out, and Will Angus—the other boy what was working with me that night—we was cracking up about something and she shook that umbrella she be carrying all the time right up in our face and told us to 'shush' like she do in the libary."

I asked him if he meant Miss Silk.

"Yeah, I know her because when our class goes to the li-bary we all have to say, 'Good morning, Miss Silk.' And then when we leave we gotta say, 'Thank you, Miss Silk.' So I knowed who that was. Even so, I coulda told it was her by the way she said 'shush.' Ain't nobody can shush you up like a li-barian or a church lady."

I nodded yes but didn't stop my note-taking. I did pause long enough to ask him to practice saying "li-brary" and explained how it's got an "r" sound in the middle. I didn't want him to feel picked on so I explained how lots of folks gets it wrong. I heard him try it out under his breath, "library"; but I didn't act like I noticed. I just asked him if there was anything else he had to tell me.

161

"Well nothin till everything went to hell in a handbasket. After most of the folk had run out I scooped me up some cake and got the cigarette case you done took from me and then ran down the stairs cause I wanted to see what happened too. That was when you found me." He paused before he asked, "You still got my case?" I ignored the question and instead asked him about the white man.

LT was clear on this. "He left before dinner. I didn't have much chance to think about him with everything going on. And too, he started to feel creepy to me. He kept kinda looking back at the dead lady. Of course, she wasn't dead when he did that but the lady that would end up dead; he kept on looking back at her whilst he was making his way out the room. I watched him ride away in one of those fancy cars."

I said, 'Hold up just one minute,' checked my notes, and reminded him that he'd said the white man left early. And that he didn't come downstairs until after the lady fell. "So how can you know what kind of car the man was in?"

LT looked irritated. "I *was* upstairs like I said. But after she went out the window and after I came down to see, an before you got holt to me, I seen him standing cross the street by the back door of this car. It was a real limousine with a driver and everything. The driver, he had on a uniform. Wasn't near as fancy as I like; but the man stood there watching all them people and then he got in the back door, and his man closed it, and the car took off. After that I didn't pay it any attention because I had a dead lady to look at an who knows when I get to do that again! She was way more interesting than that limousine. Wonder if he was out there all night?" Then the boy got excited and ahead of himself. "Oh, I get it, Officer T! That white man coulda been there all night just waiting, then snuck upstairs and done her in!" I cautioned the boy that that would be a precipitous judgment. Anticipating his puzzlement, I took his paper, scribbled the word down, and handed it back.

"I gotta look that one up too?"

I didn't answer, but that's when I told him we could walk down to Mr. Chasen's. On our way to the grocer's I taught him how to do a firm handshake and we practiced it before we got to the store.

LT's story left a lot of questions—especially concerning Hughes Wellington. And that's a problem. Anything leading toward white folks was bound to be trouble. And anything leading toward the white folk my Ellie worked for is trouble on top of itself.

I crossed off LT's name in my notebook. Sadie and Vera Scott were already marked through. Mamie Walker, the one Miss Frelon hired to do the work Ellie once did for her, was next on my list. I added Miss Silk and Hughes Wellington. Soon as I got back to Zenobia's Ellie rang up to let me know that Mamie Walker was willing to talk. But I knew I needed to talk to Sadie again and before anybody else. It was looking more and more like the investigation she asked me for—but it's also getting to be that this might not be the investigation she wanted.

25

Keys

WELDON ASKED SADIE TO MEET AT ZENOBIA'S. AS WAS HER HABIT, Zenobia used the occasion to shout way too loudly down the hall that Weldon had a caller. But everybody already knew he was representing Harlem in doing the "Lord's work," and that earned him some privacy. It didn't help that the word on the street—"Officer Thomas, he looking into this thing"—was, in fact, more pressure than taking the police exam or the Lord's oversight.

Sadie listened intently while he explained that, having gotten a good sense of the atmosphere up in the Heights, how it would help his investigation if she could answer some questions. He needed background and context. Sadie wasn't central, but she worked in the house where this thing kept winding its way back to.

As soon as Sadie heard him say "investigation" she mouthed, "Thank you, Jesus." Nevertheless, this task was difficult. Sadie wasn't comfortable talking about her people except with the Harlem Ladies Club women. In that place whatever they said was hushed under the rock of the church. They'd all agreed to that, knowing a loose word could lose a job for any one of them. Sadie was correctly closemouthed. But since she was the one that brought Officer Weldon into this thing, and since the good Lord Hisownself had turned the policeman's heart, it was her duty to help.

So she answered that her people was doing pretty good until the day

Mrs. Scott returned from Manhattan, when she went to Dr. Scott's office even though he wasn't there and the office was closed. She told how her lady had come home and gone straight to her sitting room and asked Sadie to pull the drapes. She remembers because it wasn't like her to go to her rooms in the middle of the day and especially to be cross. "She tossed them keys at me like I had done something, but I didn't mind much because I knew it wasn't me that did something upsetting." Sadie added quietly, "Truth is, she tole me to get rid of them. She never wanted to see them again. I knew something had gone way off track, but I wasn't about to be throwing out no household keys." Weldon nodded when she explained how she shoved them way back in the drawer of her writing desk in case she changed up her mind. "Her moods was so topsy-turvy: one day this, one day that, who knowed but she coulda blamed me if it turnt out she wanted them back. An too they looked to be kinda special; they the onliest ones in the house that she kep tied with a ribbon." Weldon asked her how she knew what they were for.

"Well, of course I goes to church." Inside Weldon groaned. Sadie, young as she was, was a church lady in training. Which to him meant she would end up being just like his mother, there all day Sunday, leading midweek prayers, organizing Sunday school and Vacation Bible School, and already the current recording secretary for the YAAPWSYSC (Young Adults A Prayer Will Save Your Soul Club—and yes, there was a pronunciation for it). Church ladies, even young ones, had a way of seeing everything through the eyes of the Lord's special intervention. So Weldon thought for sure she was going to tell him she prayed on it and the Lord showed her the answer. He was more than grateful when she explained that Dr. Scott's janitor, Franklin Evans, goes to St. John's and he told her that "Mrs. Doctor" visited the office and it seemed strange because she shoulda known the office wasn't open that day.

Weldon knew his next question was going to be a challenge, but it was a necessity. He asked her for the keys—"the ones on that ribbon."

Sadie flared back. "Have you done finished losing your mind? Who you think you is asking me for my people's house keys?" He knew this was a critical moment, so he couldn't be at all wishy-washy about it.

"Look here, Miss Sadie. If you want me to help you, then you got to help me. And it seems to me you should already have in your mind that I wouldn't be asking for anything that I don't absolutely need." Sadie brushed at a tear that was trickling down her cheek. Weldon didn't want to upset her, so he continued in a gentler tone: "Didn't neither one of us think this thing here was going to be easy. You helped a lot by getting me in there to talk to Mrs. Doctor. And I'm taking this thing on. So I need the keys and something else on top of that." He thought he'd better get all his asks out on the table now. She was the kind who might pray on it and wait for the Lord to tell him what he could and could not have. He was right, because Sadie looked over at him shaking her head, wondering what she'd gotten herself into. But her Lord answered prayers. She wasn't about to get in the way of His ways.

Sadie gulped while explaining how frightening it was when Mrs. Scott returned from the banquet in such a state. And how Mrs. Earlene, who had brought her into the house, was pretty much undone as well. And how the doctor come running down the hall to grab her up (the fur coat had already done finished falling to the floor, but she hadn't) . . . "Wait, just a sec here, Miss Sadie. You mean Dr. Scott didn't come in there with her?"

"No sir. He come home just before they did. He couldn't quite make it to the banquet like he planned."

"Why not?"

"Now look here, Weldon Haynie. I don't make it no kind of habit to ask my people where they going when they get gone. If they want me to know something they tell me. An that night he didn't have nothing to say to me. In fact, when he come home I asked him if he wanted his dinner now, and he didn't even answer that question. Just gived me his coat and hat and went into the front parlor like usual."

"Okay then . . ." Weldon wrote in his notes that the doctor had come home sometime after the dinner hour. "Let me ask you about Mrs. Scott. What did she have?"

"What you mean what did she have? She didn't have nothing. It wasn't like she caught a cold. She was what they call overcome and near fainted away."

"No, I mean what did she have with her. You said a fur coat. Anything else?"

"Well, just that and her evening bag. She had it in her hands in a death grip, if you will excuse me for saying so, because I had to near pry it outta her hands to get her gloves off."

"Where's the bag now?"

"Right where it should be up there in the chiffarobe put away with her evening things. Now I will be the first one to admit that I might of not done it right then, given the circumstances and all; but it's up there where it belongs now."

"Uh-huh." Weldon was focused on the bag. He was trying very hard to keep from hoping there still might be a handkerchief in it and then maybe that could go to make a question out of the one the police found and showed him at the indictment. But hope wasn't the kind of thinking that Sherlock used to solve cases.

"So what is it you guess happened, Officer Weldon?" Sadie's question brought Weldon out of his thoughts. The answer he gave was straight from Sherlock Holmes.

"I never guess. It would be a shock to my logical facilities." Or something like that. Luckily, it impressed Sadie enough not to pursue it further.

SADIE RETURNED TO ZENOBIA'S LATER THAT EVENING AND DROPPED the keys into Weldon's hand. Anticipating his question, she offered, "And there wasn't nothing in that bag neither ceptin this here lipstick, her compact mirror, some folding money, and a cigarette case."

"You got these things with you too?"

"I do. But what you want to know for?"

"Don't worry, Miss Sadie. It is official to my investigation. I've got an evidence box right here for whatever comes up in this case. You can watch me put it in here, and you have my word that everything will be safe and kept in place until it gets back to you." Sadie watched him gather the things she'd brought. He understood her nervousness. He was nervous himself. "Miss Sadie, with these things . . ."—he said it as if he had the experience he wished he had—"with these things, sometimes you don't know what makes sense until it makes sense." Weldon figured that if that wasn't in the Sherlock book it ought to be. Sadie thought his "evidence box" looked more like a shoebox but kept it to herself. And even though he gave her a list of the items to make her feel better, when he put the money in she spoke up.

"Now Officer Weldon, I want you to know that I know exactly how much folding money that is that I'm turning over for your evidence."

"Miss Sadie, if you got to be warning me about the count of her folding money you don't want me working on this here case. Either you trust me or you don't. We have to have that clear or this here thing stops right here and right now."

She regretted it immediately. "I'm so sorry, Weldon. It's just I'm trusting you with all the things I care about the most in the world right now. That's God's truth I'm not myself—none of us is while this thing has got us all twisted up. You do have my trust and my most sincere thanks as well."

He patted her hand and gave it a small squeeze. The two of them had entered an arrangement of sorts, and, as he was to learn, it came with its own set of happenstances.

26

Office Visit

IT WASN'T LONG AFTER I MET WITH SADIE THAT I STOOD IN THE BACK hallway outside Dr. Scott's office wondering what in the hell I was doing breaking into a Manhattan doctor's office. It wasn't technically a break-in since I had the keys, but it wasn't technically legal either. I was on the far side of the law and it didn't feel right at all. I decided not to wear my uniform, thinking folks would be more likely to ignore me if I wore everyday clothes. And too, if I got caught, I wouldn't be claiming police business. I didn't know what I would claim, so I thought it best to plan not to be caught. That would simplify a whole lot of things. So when I got downtown to his building I just went right on up to where the glass door had gold and black lettering that said, "Reynolds Scott, M.D. Medicine and General Surgery," looked around once, used the key Sadie gave me, and let myself in like I was supposed to be doing nothing other than what I was engaged in. I did let out a breath once I got inside and saw it was a fact the offices were closed and quiet. Seemed I was the only somebody with business there today.

I couldn't help but to admire the way the place was set up. In my mind I had the image of the community clinic where moms used to take me. But there wasn't any comparison between that and to Dr. Scott's place. The one-room clinic we went to didn't have plush chairs, just those folding chairs the church loaned out. When the doctor was there, the kitchen was the exam room. It sure could make a difference if my folks had rooms like this to bring their coughs and rheumatisms to, and to get their pressure taken. Even moms might agree to go see a doctor once in a while if she didn't have to go through somebody's kitchen door and sit next to a stove, which she told me wasn't much different from what she could do at her own house.

Dr. Scott's offices were so pristine that it was hard to say what I needed to find. But the Sherlock books agreed on looking for something out of place. And you don't know how to see that until you take a good surveillance of what there is. The nurses' station was positioned behind the reception desk. Right out in the open were neat rows of patient files stacked in cabinets. Large letters in alphabetical order jutted out from different places in the files. I was thinking that this man takes orderliness to a whole new level, but in fact, for this place Holmes would probably call it status quo. I let my hands flick across the tops of the files, but I didn't pull any out. For just a minute, I did wonder whether there was anybody with the letter X that started their name; and just like I thought, the letter was there but there were no files between it and the Y. It was just like one of those spaces on the library shelf where a book was missing—a space was ready for some X's, but looks like nobody came with that name yet. There wasn't too many in the Y group, but I knew a Yellin, Yarborough, and a Young from church, so it made sense. X was rare—and the emptiness messed with my wanting something to put in that space. But that was a leftover library sensibility. This was a doctor's office. Two different places.

The examination rooms looked pretty much like I expected given the fancy waiting room. The black and white tiling put me in the mind of what I'd seen downtown at the coroner's. I knew then I needed to get the familiar out of my head if I was going to bring an unfettered—that was Holmes's word—perspective to these offices. I walked back through the waiting area. It looked comfy and I could see myself spending some time there going over a magazine or putting my feet up on a footstool. It was just that fancy. I bet folks start holding on to their wallets when they walk in here. This place is set up so people think they are someplace special. My experience is that special costs. I left the reception area, the exam rooms, and walked down a long hall that ended with a large mahogany door. Dr. Scott's name was on it too, like somebody wouldn't already know this was his place. It added to the whole effect.

My unfettered perspective—that this Dr. Scott was an orderly man— was verified when I saw that the large desk in there didn't have a single thing on it except an inkstand, a fountain pen, and a notepad. That was when I began thinking that he is tidy to a fault. Neat is okay. Orderly is fine. Fastidiousness is a whole nother level that suggests there's mess somewhere else. And in my assessment of the environs I inspected at the office, Dr. Reynolds Scott was fastidious. And of course that took me right to the rumors about the doctor and the dead lady, and, since my thinking was leading me there and the stuff around me didn't lead me away, I stayed with the thought for just a moment until I decided that I could not make a judgment on something I didn't independently know.

That was when I sat myself down in the doctor's chair—to get a sense of his perspective. I pulled out his desk's center drawer. Things in there were just as neat as everything else. In place. Some notepads, prescription pad, a matching gold fountain pen, gold cigarette case, and a gold-rimmed magnifying glass, a silver cigarette case, and a thermometer in a glass case with a little band of gold where it opened. I picked each item up but lingered over the thermometer, tilting it from side to side so the mercury could slip from one end to the other. I wondered if there was something else I should notice, but nothing came to mind, so I just wrote down everything I saw. Some folks doing this would go reaching up under and inside things looking for secret drawers and envelopes taped to the bottom of something. But the Sherlock books explained that most things that you need to know hide in plain sight, and that saved me a whole lot of time rather than my having to turn things all upside down and backwards looking for what I didn't even know about.

I took my time in his chair. I leaned back and tried to consider the kind of man I was dealing with. If the doctor done this thing and then set back and let his wife get blamed it wouldn't be the first time. But my instincts were leading me away from him as a suspect. I could say for sure the man was meticulous. And that took me back to wondering about which side of meticulous he was on—neat and particular or where he needed this kind of control because he was troubled elsewhere. Trouble brought me back to thinking about Miss Frelon. She was different from these surrounds. But then, some people find themselves needing something different. And maybe people as neat as this doctor would need it a bit more. Still and all, as crazy as tipping out on a pretty lady like Mrs. Vera was, it wasn't the kind of crazy that made people suddenly go and push somebody out a window. I needed something that would tell me if this man was crazy and, if so, which kind of crazy it was. It wasn't going to be here. So after I checked to make sure I left everything like I found it, I walked out his back door trying to leave the premises from the way the doctor would. That was when I put my hand on a doorknob that didn't turn and didn't unlock with the building key. But there were two keys on the ribbon Sadie gave me. The smaller one fit into the keyhole quite easily.

Only a few moments later, just as long as it took me to close the door behind me, head up the staircase, and open the door at the top, I was standing in the middle of a room that left me speechless. Well, not really. I heard myownself say, "Holy shit." Out loud. And like the word "holy" had three syllables. And "shit" had two. It took me a while to take in the scene, but it didn't take me long at all to realize that the fastidious Doctor Scott was not particularly fastidious up in here. In fact, this was just the counterweight his fastidious needed if I was going to take him off my crazy list. It didn't mean he didn't stay on my suspicions list. But it was exactly what I was worried about earlier, and if this wasn't confirmation of an independent judgment I didn't know what could be. I loved it when the books I read corresponded with what I needed to know. If you wait, information will come get you. If you go looking for it, it's more likely than not you find what you want, not what is. This was most certainly information. But I needed somebody to hear it with me—to consult. Which was why Holmes had Watson. I should be so lucky.

So after I left, again making sure nothing was disturbed (although up in these rooms, it would be hard to tell), I went to a corner booth and rang up Ellie and asked if she would meet me at the library. She said yes, as soon as she and Mr. Wellington finished their meeting. That was okay by me because she was a working girl; but it didn't feel like how I wanted to feel right then. I was excited and worried both. And to my mind, her Mr. Wellington still had some kinda role in this as long as I didn't get information that he didn't.

27

Evidence

LATER THAT DAY, WELDON SHARED HIS NOTES WITH ELLIE. SHE WAS grateful he was looking into Miss Olivia's death and promised to do anything to help him, and that included getting Mamie, the young woman she'd hired to help Miss Frelon, to talk to him. He wanted to talk about his visit downtown, but she was busy with her own research. While she finished at the card catalogue, he started gathering detective books. When she finally got back to the table, he explained his dilemma. "I'm going to need your help, Baby Girl. I need somebody to listen to the things I find out. It's what Sherlock calls objective listening. Like what Watson did for him."

"Who?" Ellie asked.

"Watson. His sidekick."

"You think I'm a sidekick?"

"It ain—It's not like that, Baby Girl. Just listen so's I don't depend on thinking something through only by what I saw. You can be objective. It means that . . ."

"I know what it means." Ellie looked over to the desk. "Well, if we need to talk, we need to leave here. Miss Silk won't let a conversation get past a simple hello." She was right, of course, and as if to confirm it, Miss Silk looked up from the desk with a finger across her lips. So they left and walked together back toward Zenobia's while he told her what he found.

"So Miss Frelon and Dr. Scott were . . ."

173

"No, not at all. She wasn't the one he entertained there."

"Entertained? That's what you're calling it?"

"What does that matter? And can't you just listen to what I say before you take it apart and turn it upside down and whichaways?"

"Sorry. I just really wondered how you know that Miss Frelon wasn't his . . ."

"His paramour?" He handed Ellie his notebook. "See here's what I wrote about what was framed all across the walls. Pictures hanging on top of the drapery. It looked like a gallery. That should be of interest to you given all your art." She saw his notes detailing the tropical scenes and unclothed brown girls. She read one note out loud: "Oversized picture, forests and jungles, brown women lying in front of large leaves . . ." She couldn't help herself. "Are you sure that shouldn't be 'laying'?"

"I'm certain. Looks like you the one that might need a redo on grammar. Just keep on reading through. For substance. These just my notes."

She read aloud: "Dark lady in white dress with yellow girl behind her, in a blue cloth. One bre—oh, never mind. Exposed." She blushed slightly, knowing the painting well. "Must you write that word?"

"Which one annoys you the most?" he asked, with just the edge of sarcasm. He didn't wait for her reply. "Ellie, these are notes. They have to be accurate. They're not meant for Sunday school," he said with some annoyance, snatching the book back. Weldon was trying really hard to keep the conversation focused, and she wasn't helping. He took a deep breath and tried to let go of his pique. "Baby Girl, the walls were covered with pictures like these. And then there were his books. See what I wrote here?" He pointed to the next pages where he listed a series of books about Africa and South America. "This is how I know those rooms weren't about Miss Frelon. This was the doctor's precious space—his sanctuary, and she wasn't what he valued. She was waaay too bright."

Ellie was trying to digest what he said. "But Weldon, everybody, including the district attorney, is saying Mrs. Scott killed her because Miss Olivia was having an affair with Dr. Scott."

"Well, yeah, it looks to me that everybody got the wrong somebody in their mind, at least as far as this duo is concerned."

"But wait a minute." She asked her next question slowly, as if the revelation was just occurring to her. "Wait. What if . . . what if Mrs. Scott believed it? I mean what if she thought it was Miss Olivia? Even if it wasn't true, it could be that . . . I mean, could it possibly be that she would have done something like this acting from a mistaken belief?" The chilling potential showed in her voice.

"Hold on now. Don't get ahead of us yet. An investigation means a step at a time. There could be a lot of things that room could reveal. Mostly it suggests that things are different from what they first seem to be. And that's what I have to ponder next."

"Think about something you don't know?"

"Nope. Reflect on things we probably do know, but that might be different from what we think now."

"Like what?"

"Well, first thing is eliminate the doctor as a suspect. If he wasn't having an affair with Miss Olivia, he wouldn't have reason to kill her. No motive."

"And, he wasn't there that night."

"Well, the only thing we know for sure is that he wasn't seen in the banquet hall. But still, he or somebody else might have been there back near the winners' room. And that tells me who to talk to next."

"I guess you're not going to share that with me," Ellie said, somewhat petulantly. But Weldon didn't bother to answer. They were close to Zenobia's, but Ellie, in what was getting to be a habit, said she wouldn't be able to come in and paused at the trolley stop.

"That's okay, Baby Girl. There's some leads I need to track down. And I also want to go back to the branch to check out some more books."

"So what happens next?" she asked.

"Well, its time to find somebody who was there that night who was curious enough to be where he wasn't supposed to be and who might have seen something he doesn't know is important. And I've a suspicion about who that's going to be."

The trolley's bell signaled its approach, and Weldon watched until Ellie found a seat. He could tell she was worried. He was as well.

THAT NIGHT HE REMOVED THE SHOEBOX FROM HIS SHELF AND TOOK out the few items that were in it. Once he lined them up he immediately knew what the matter was. There's one too many of these! he thought. He shook his head in puzzlement as he methodically replaced everything on the desk inside the box and lifted it back to the place he'd made for it on his shelf.

28

Eyes on
the Prize

"I REMEMBERS THAT DAY LIKE IT WAS BURNED INTO MY HEART." MAMIE
Walker sat in the hearth room of the Wellington mansion's servant quarters. After Olivia's death, Ellie spoke to Hughes about a place for her
in his household staff. Mamie was offered a position as an assistant to
Ellie. Given the circumstance that brought them back together again,
each took comfort in the other's company.

Mamie loved her new place, especially how Ellie was giving her
tasks that would refine her skills. It was Mamie who handled the
correspondence—sorting through the mail and determining which
should be in Mr. Hughes's pile and which Ellie would want to attend
to. She was also responsible for Ellie's rooms, her private office, and her
personal requirements. Having a lady's assistant took Ellie some getting
used to, especially since that was what she had so recently been herself,
but Hughes said that with the responsibilities she had for the collection,
if the girl was to join the staff, this was the most reasonable way to do so.

Mamie was especially attentive to Ellie's office. It was a delicate and
lovely sun-splashed room at the break of the grand front staircase. When
you entered the vestibule, marble stairs swept upwards in graceful curves
on each side of the room. They met at a landing that opened into a

176

barrel-vaulted hallway leading to the rest of the mansion. Ellie's office door and the smaller office that was Mamie's were left of the center.

Ellie finally had her walls covered in a canary-yellow and cream-flocked paper to complement the dark woods of the antique desk that Mr. Wellington said would be hers if she wanted it. A Persian carpet with gold and blue patterns spiraling out into exotic designs covered nearly all the black and white tiled marble floor, and her desk faced the window. Just outside an umbrella-leafed chestnut marked the seasons. Blossoming pyramids were giving way to broad leafy summer fans when she moved in. In August, spiky pods swollen with fruit dropped beneath the dense canopy. Mamie made certain that the table by her favorite chair, the one Ellie had re-covered in a French blue brocade (to match the shades of the rug), always had a small bouquet of fresh flowers.

That morning, cook left a tray in the hearth room for Mamie and the policeman. Ellie explained that Officer Thomas wanted to talk to Mamie about the death of their former employer. Cook left shaking her head, worried that some Harlem trouble was creeping downtown.

They sat in rockers that faced the hearth and Mamie, grateful that Officer Thomas was looking into the affair, explained how clearly she remembered the day. When she asked him what he needed to know, Weldon responded honestly. .

"Miss Mamie, the truth is I don't rightly know. So if you would just start out by telling me your story, that would be of most help."

Mamie's telling was spoken with a clarity and passion that indicated that she needed the telling as much as Weldon needed to hear her perspective. She'd held it in, partially in respect for Ellie, partially because of the hurt.

On the morning of the banquet Miss Frelon was still lying in her bed when she came in to raise the shades and then pull the drapes before she asked if she would take tea and toast in her rooms or downstairs in the dayroom. She started a fire in the grate at daybreak to make certain there would be no chill in the room. Miss Olivia chose to take her tea in the bedroom: "She was just as likely to choose the other room. She liked to use all the rooms in the house, she said. It was so big and all that she may as well get the most from it." Weldon said that made total sense. "Of course it do," Mamie replied with just a bit of huffiness. But then she remembered his intent and her more reflective and thoughtful tone

177

returned. "I went to the downstairs kitchen to order her tray," she said, explaining that when Miss Ellie gave her notice so she could take the position in Manhattan, the Frelon household was Mamie's responsibility. She was used to the upstairs work as well as supervising the kitchen. "When I come back to the room she was sitting on the edge of the bed. So I went on over to open up the drapes, because she always did like the light and how her rooms they gave her a good view of the park."

"Miss Olivia spent a lot of time in the park. Did you know that?" Weldon shook his head and kept writing. "She used to say how it reminded her of home. But that doesn't mean I know where she came from," Mamie added, as if anticipating Weldon's next question. "She was real closemouthed about that." She reached over to the tray and poured a cup of tea, asking if he wanted more. Weldon declined but did reach for another biscuit while Mamie stirred sugar cubes into her cup. She was careful to use the tongs, the way Miss Ellie had taught her, and to replace the spoon carefully back onto her saucer. She smoothed the napkin in her lap.

"So what is it I was saying? Oh yes. My story about that day." She sighed deeply, speaking from a memory that clearly still hurt. "Well, that morning was of those gray days that looked like nothing good at all was going to happen. An dear Lord, that was just what did occur." Weldon gave her a moment to collect herself before asking if there was anything else she recalled.

"Well, yes. She asked me, 'Mamie, would you please'—she was always so polite like that, didn't matter who she was talking to. High or low. She talked the same to everybody. Miss Frelon asked me if I would please take out her evening attire. 'Pull out the red silk and the black. I'll decide which later,' she said. And then I said that on an occasion such as this I would sure wear that red dress. It looks so beautiful against your skin. She got kinda quiet and I thought maybe I had overstepped you know, talking about her skin color and all. But then I saw the most beautifulest smile on her face, and that made me really happy because back then she had a lot that was making her sad."

"What do you mean by that, Miss Mamie?" Weldon asked.

"Well, it was like she so popular when she got there an opened the house an had tea parties and all. And especially her an Mrs. Doctor Scott. They was like sisters—always going out together and everything.

And she dropped by their place like it was her own. But then something happened betwixt them and it got to when I would telephone for Mrs. Doctor , Sadie would say she weren't available. I don't know what it was come between those two, but my Miss Olivia tried mighty hard to find a way to get to see her, and Mrs. Scott wasn't having none of it. So when I knowed she was going to the banquet, and that the two of them would be together again, it made me happy to see her so excited. I pulled her long black mink . . ." She took a breath and paused, as if for effect.

"Now let me tell you something. That was a coat like you and me never seen the likes of. Blacker than a midnight swamp. You could put your hand right into all that fur an then go lookin for it. It was a fine, fine fur. And I told her that when she showed up at that affair she would be a drop-dead knockout." Weldon looked up from his notes, and Mamie, realizing what she'd just said, broke down.

"I didn't mean that. Lord knows I didn't, but you know that's just what I said to her, and all these weeks it just keeps coming back to me that I told her that on the very day that the good Lord took her." Weldon tried to intervene.

"Now, now, Miss Mamie, you didn't mean nothing but good from that. And let me tell you this." He watched as her glistening eyes looked directly at him and he could tell that she hoped he had something important to say. "I caught a glimpse of her when she come in the hotel. And you are absolutely right. She was very beautiful. And what you can know for sure is that your careful attention made her look as good as she did that night."

"Well, yes. That is true. I even told her that . . . you know how they talk about 'making an entrance'?" Weldon nodded his head yes. "Well I tole her she would make the very front page of the *Amsterdam News* itself." By this time, Mamie was sobbing, remembering how pitifully true her prediction had been.

"But Miss Mamie, from what you say, it seems to me that you ensured that last day of hers would be very happy." Weldon tried his best to alleviate the guilt that in his mind was completely misplaced. "Is there anything else you remember?" Mamie reached over for a biscuit, broke it open, and spread both sides with marmalade. She took a bite and sipped her tea before answering.

"Yes. I suspect that is so." She nodded in agreement. "But still she didn't know I heard her, but when I was pulling out the jewelry from the wardrobe I heard her say, 'How can she be so selfish, and on this night of all nights?' and I knew she was talking about Mrs. Doctor and there was an unhappiness about that thing there I could do not one thing about. She got to where she was keepin it to herownself. Like when I aksed her what she said, she told me that she was just practicing her thank-you talk for the night. But that was how I knowed that Mrs. Scott was still on her mind." She took another bite and explained to Weldon that Olivia had told her about the award. "I didn't tell a living soul. But I tole her that soon as everbody knowed about it that I was going to get me a bunch of papers to show off to people about her prize. An that's when I aksed her if she was still going with Mrs. Scott, she said yes and I sorta kinda rolled my eyes, you know, remembering how she had done treated my lady. But she explained how maybe Mrs. Scott was a little bit jealous of her prize. She said she wasn't married or anything and couldn't be one of them Omada wives, so she had to make her own way and that this prize would help her get all the best invitations again and it wouldn't matter anymore that Mrs. Scott wasn't interested in helping her to get up with the society folks."

"What did you know about the prize?" Weldon turned to a new page in his notebook and titled it, "Notes on the Prize."

"Well, her and I talked a lot about things. Like when Miss Ellie left she had to take matters into her own hands about how she would get and keep her a society place." Mamie's voice dropped to a whisper.

"You know, I was the one what mailed the story for her to the judges. It was a quick decision. One minute she was sittin downstairs in the morning room and the next minute she gave me the story and aksed me to post it. I said, 'Oh Miss Olivia, you a writer!' And I aksed her to please tell me the story. She said it was called 'Sanctified.' It was about a lady who passed, you know, who crossed over into the other side—not dead, but joined the white folks." Weldon shook his head while making sure his note-taking kept up with Mamie's memories. "An the thing is, it was something Miss Olivia coulda gone and done herownself light an bright as she was. But she didn't. She stayed loyal with her people no matter how mean some of us could get when youse a bit high yellow on the creamy side. Bright skinded. You know." He nodded, not wanting to interrupt her telling. "Well, she wrote a story about it. And that shoulda tole anybody

180

that she was a good race woman who made her choice to stand with us." She paused, looking over at Weldon until it occurred to him this was an appropriate time for him to express his hearty agreement, and so he did.

"It was some few weeks later when I brought her the tray with the letter on it saying she won the prize. My goodness was we happy around here on that day! I jus knew this was going to be a fine new start for her independence. That's what she called it. Her freedom story. Bless her eternal soul."

Weldon gave the moment its appropriate respect. He just had one more question—whether Miss Olivia knew any of the people at the banquet.

"Well of course, she knowed all of them. Or most of them. They was all in the Welfare for the Negroes Club—the ladies section. Oh, and she did say something about Mr. Hughes." She looked nervous. Weldon wanted to keep the conversation going and mentioned that given that Miss Frelon was given to saying only the kindest things about people, he was sure whatever she had to say about her new employer fell into that category. It eased Mamie just enough to continue the story.

"Well now, that is true. And her kindness did pass on to Mr. Hughes just like it did to everybody else." She munched on the biscuit and said a bit more quietly, "Or woulda did if folks had not let their jealousy get to the best of them. But yes. She did have some plans to meet him and she can't be faulted for having them. They was perfectly innocent and even necessary by her accounting, and I can't say I disagree. She even practiced her speech for me. It was the prettiest little speech! So polite and grateful. She was going to tell people how she just got there to Harlem back in the spring and say thank you for the 'kind attentions she had received.' I remember that part because it was such nice words. Then she planned to say 'a special thank-you' to everbody who had been especially nice and welcoming to her, and she was even going to include Mrs. Scott, and I aksed her, 'Are you sure, with the way she been acting to you and all?' and she told me that was what being gracious meant."

"And Mr. Wellington?" Weldon asked.

"Oh yes. She was teaching me, because you know I don't have anybody like you and Ellie." Weldon was thinking it was feeling lately a bit more like the relationship he and Ellie "had" rather than "have," but it wasn't relevant. Mamie didn't notice his sigh. "Miss Frelon, she was teaching me how to do a bit of flirtatiousing. She said she would pretend to make him feel bad because he stoled Miss Ellie from us and then how she would flutter her eyelashes and how he would be shamed into doing something like offering her a cocktail to make up for it. And then they would get to be friendly and she could be in his circle. There wasn't nothing wrong with her wanting her own circle, you know. Mrs. Scott made everything harder for her to be included in all those social events when she took her attitude."

"Why do you think they fell apart?"

"Since you aks me I'll tell you. I've done some thinking on the matter myownself. It wasn't about nobody's color. They both was the same kind of bright. Myself, I believe it was just she was what folks call new blood and Mrs. Scott was old blood, and plus Miss Olivia had all the new things from Europe and, if I do say so myself, Mrs. Scott didn't dress quite as bright and fresh as she did."

"Now Miss Mamie, are you telling me that you didn't hear anything else about why they might have fallen out with each other?"

Mamie's demeanor changed quickly. "Now you wait one minute here, Mr. Officer Thomas. You do not speak ill of the dead. Let me tell you one thing. All of them rumors about my Miss Olivia and Mrs. Doctor's husband did not have one single bit of truth telling to any of it. Not a single word. My Miss Olivia was a lady born and bred." She paused for the briefest of moments and added, "Well, nobody knowed about the bred part. But you can tell good breeding and she had it coming and going. And she did not betray her friends and she did not have any goings-on with anybody at all. Especially not no married mens. I lived in that house, I would've known if she had visitors. Plus and all, I took care of her personal effects, so to speak. It was me who changed the linens if you get my meaning with that. And I would've known if anything was not, well, not in order. So we are done with this here interview if you thinks there is any truth at all to that which people been saying about my poor sweet dead angel. Folks got some ugly ways. And if this is what you been choosing to write down in that notebook, it is just not becoming of who you be, Officer Thomas. Not becoming at all."

Weldon tried to explain he just wanted to know what she thought. Mamie settled some, and he was careful not to upset her again. He couldn't help but notice how close her large brown eyes came to overflowing with tears and how they now glistened when she spoke. He wished he had a handkerchief to offer her but then remembered it was a hanky that was at the base of this whole mess anyway. He told her how lucky Miss Frelon was to have somebody like her to look after her. By that time Weldon had taken her hand, which seemed a natural gesture of comfort, and he couldn't help but notice how smooth and warm it was. She let him hold it for just a moment but then took it back to reach for her cup.

"Yes, that is true," Mamie sniffed. "That is how I helped and Lord knows she came to have a special place in my heart. Always will."

"And mine as well," Ellie said as she came into the room to see if there was a way she might be helpful to Weldon and Mamie. Weldon flinched for just a moment, grateful for no particular reason that he was no longer holding her hand and explained that they were just finishing up and maybe Ellie would sit a while with Mamie after he left. Ellie said she would, and the two women sat in the chairs holding hands and rocking their grief back and forth until it settled back into that still and solemn space each had made for their memories.

29

The Palmer Method

ELLIE HAD BEEN AT THE LIBRARY FOR A WHILE. SHE WAS PAGING through a large art catalogue when he tapped her on the shoulder and apologized for making her wait. Ellie noticed his spiral notebook was out, and that her name was circled.

"What? So now I'm a suspect?" she whispered.

"No, Baby Girl, but there's something you and me have to talk about." Before he could explain any further, Miss Silk was shushing the two of them, so they gathered their books and took them up to the checkout desk, where Miss Silk was engrossed in her writing. Ellie couldn't help but remark on her beautiful penmanship.

"Well, that's the Palmer method, my dear," she explained. "Anyone of consequence masters this script." She slid the papers into a folder, pulled out a file drawer, and briefly fingered through the alphabetized folders before slipping her pages into a file. "Now, what have you found to take out?" Weldon and Ellie each presented three books, a single borrower's limit. She looked up at them and smiled. "I expect these detective tomes really are just for one of you," she said knowingly—"Officer Thomas?" Weldon appeared to be distracted.

"Ummm, yes ma'am. We'd like to check out these books, please."

"That's not what I asked, Officer Thomas. I expressed a concern that you two appear to be bypassing the regulations."

"No ma'am. I mean yes ma'am. I understand. I mean we understand."
Ellie was busy opening the books to the back stamp page. She gave him
an exasperated look.

"Thank you, Miss Silk," Ellie said, "we appreciate this accommodation."

"So, are all these detective books necessary because of police work, or
are you looking for clues as to how to track down a piece of art for your
patron?" Ellie blushed. Weldon spoke up.

"Ummm, well really, Miss Silk, I'm reading these so I can learn about
the kinds of thinking a detective has to master for an investigation." And
then he told her he was actually looking into Miss Frelon's death. Miss
Silk paused for a moment and then reached over her desk and sympa-
thetically took Ellie's hand in hers.

"Oh, my dear child. This must be very difficult for you," she said kindly.
"I remember when you first came in here back last spring looking for
books for your Miss Frelon's study. And how embarrassed you were to say
you just wanted books that matched her upholstery."

"Yes ma'am. Miss Frelon was very considerate to me."

The librarian's comment was unrelated to Ellie's acknowledgment.
"She wasn't a reader herself, though. I never saw her here and"—the firm
thud of the date stamp punctuated her whisper—"she just didn't seem to
have the temperament." She paused, perhaps aware that her comments
might not seem generous. "But I do know she was somewhat active in our
uplift groups."

"Yes ma'am, she was," replied Ellie. She handed the books to Weldon
and shouldered her pocketbook. "And I will miss her."

"Of course you will, my dear. We will all miss her very unique contributions to our community." Miss Silk pushed the stamped books toward
the couple and opened a folder on her desk. By the time they left she
already had her fountain pen in her hand and was filling a page with
beautifully executed script.

Weldon was almost out the door when he stopped, asked Ellie to "wait
a sec" while he returned to the desk. Miss Silk looked up inquisitively.
"Miss Silk?" Weldon inquired. "Could I ask you just one thing?"

"Certainly Weldon. How can I be of help?"

"It's since you was at the party that night."

"You should say 'were at the party.'"

"Yes ma'am. We both was."

"We both were."

"Yes ma'am. I know. I did see you for just a minute going upstairs. You looked very well done up that evening."

"Thank you, Weldon. It was a formal occasion that called for a certain attire."

"Yes ma'am. Well, I have in my notes here that you was talking . . . I mean were talking to some young kitchen boys that night."

"I just wondered, could you tell me anything about the prizes? See, I've got a section in my notes for prizes, but not much there." He flipped his book open to the page that said, "Notes on the Prize."

"Weldon, I notice you are struggling with your grammar. I'm surprised. Your reading should help you with that."

"Yes ma'am. It do. I mean, it does."

"You should catch these errors before you speak. But as to that night, it is the fact that Miss Frelon was to win an award. In fact, short fiction was the top writing award."

"A short fiction story?"

"Yes. For her piece titled 'Sanctuary.'"

"Yes ma'am." He was busy writing in his notebook. "'S-a-n-c-t-u-a-r-y.' That's what it was called?" The librarian nodded her head in affirmation. "Umm, I guess you don't know what it was about? It could help me fill out this page some. It's still pretty much empty."

"I do. It was about a young woman who suffered the consequences of losing her family and her people when she decided to pass. Her deceit is discovered, so she returns to her home seeking forgiveness and sanctuary."

"It sounds like it could've been real interesting," Weldon offered.

"Well, the judges believed it to be award-worthy."

"Thanks, Miss Silk. Thanks for your help."

"My pleasure, Officer Thomas."

Ellie nudged Weldon with her elbow when he left the library. "This is the second time in the past hour you've kept me waiting," she said, visibly irritated.

"It's just that I had a thought I was trying to get back, but then I lost it."

"My mother used to say if it is important it will come back."

"Mine says if it's true it comes back."

"Mother wit," Ellie volunteered. They walked back toward Zenobia's. She deliberately slowed the pace of their walk because what she had to say next was going to be hard. And she didn't want to pass the trolley stop. She needed to tell Weldon that, once again, their plans for the afternoon weren't going to work out. She thought she'd ease it into their conversation, but when they reached the corner she simply blurted out, "I can't come to Zenobia's. I have to get back downtown because Hughes has something he wants to discuss."

Weldon heard the slip, and resented it. They'd had the argument before and he should have known this wasn't a time to reengage it. But the realization followed, rather than preceded, his response. "Baby Girl, you already up there working up under this man. You're available night and day. And now here you go calling him 'Hughes.' Well how about this? How about you tell me how I am supposed to think about all the ways your rather extraordinary availability to your Hughes Mr. Wellington is interrupting your attentions to me?" He immediately regretted what he said but couldn't help thinking about the soft difference in the conversation he'd had with Mamie—it seemed so easy compared with the challenge and caution he had to bring to his recent encounters with Ellie.

"Excuse me? Did you say I was 'available' to him?"

"Oh, shoot, Baby Girl. I didn't mean it like that."

"How about you think about how I am sick and tired of your calling me Baby Girl." She paused as much for effect as for the courage to continue. "I'm grown. And, well . . . I am certainly not anybody's baby. Especially not yours. At least Mr. Wellington treats me like an adult . . ." Weldon knew he was in trouble, and by the tone in her voice knew that the situation was unsalvageable. But what he said next didn't help.

"You mean 'Hughes,' don't you?"

"How about it's none of your business what I mean?" Ellie dropped his books on the bench at the trolley stop. Weldon could see his plans for the afternoon evaporating in front of him. He tried to rescue things.

"Baby—I mean Ellie, I need you for this. And it comes to me that I might even deserve it given that these folks I'm dealing with come more from your side than mine. Unless I can talk to your Hu . . . Mr. Wellington, I'm at a dead end. You can be as mad as you want about you and me, even if it might be that there's not a you and me to worry about." (Later, he wished he hadn't put it that plainly.) "But it doesn't change the fact that what I am doing is about the one who was your lady. So in large measure, this is for you. And with regards to however I characterize things with the man you're working for . . . well, I have feelings about that. But it doesn't belie the fact that I need your help."

Ellie's retort was biting. She told him that her employer wasn't "her Hughes." And then she went on a bit about whether their relationship should matter with regard to an investigation he'd assumed of his own free will. There was no way to interrupt to explain anything about the expectations of his position or his people. But it didn't matter, because she at least ended up where he needed her—she would help him for the sake of Miss Olivia. Just when he was about to express his relief, she followed it up by saying that when this was over the two of them would have to talk about two things: his attitude and their relationship. Weldon was on the other side of angry when she said that bit about his attitude. It was her tone, as much as her substance.

"My attitude? Baby Girl, let me explain this so maybe we can get this straight between us. This thing is not about my attitude. What it is about is whatever you have got going on in Manhattan that is so supersensitive to you that you try to make it about us. It's not." Weldon probably should have stopped there, but there was a lot he'd held back, and he figured this might be the last time he'd get to be blunt. "Let me tell you what this is about. And unlike your two things, I've just got one thing on my list. Or one person. One dude down there in Manhattan that has made a habit of hanging around whenever colored society folks get together and that you say you work for that seems to have you significantly figured into his concerns. And it doesn't matter to me one iota whether they are business concerns or personal concerns or personal business concerns. What matters is that you seem determined to misunderstand if not to misrepresent them. And frankly, that is your prerogative. But I want you to be fully aware that I am fully aware." He knew the last statement was a bit convoluted, but he was angry. So was she.

"I say I work for? A 'dude' I say I work for? Excuse me?"

This was certainly not the conversation he'd planned out for them. But things were so complicated that he could barely separate the mess in Harlem from the mess their relationship had become. Things were tangled: her employment, her employer, his duties to the race, his suspicions, what he needed to know, what he was afraid to know, and his growing angst about where this was leading. And now Ellie here saying she thought it was a good time to explain things that had been on her mind. She couldn't have chosen a worse time.

"Weldon, you have to know how special I think our friendship is."

Weldon thought, Did she just say "friendship"?

"It's just that I haven't seen all the things I want to. Miss Frelon was always telling me how she traveled everywhere on the Continent. And how free she felt. How she didn't have one single solitary reminder of our race problems. I want that too. I want to feel what it feels like to think through my soul—to feel what's in my spirit, not my color."

Ellie's thinking was getting as close to foolishness as he could stand. "You know, I've tried like the dickens to keep this color stuff away from us. Like Professor Dr. Du Bois says. I don't want us worrying about how it feels to be somebody's problem. But that doesn't mitigate against its relevance. There's nothing invisible about us. Just like all those e-lights (he deliberately used his mother's pronunciation) like your Miss Frelon. Seems like she mighta got a bit too close in trying to figure out how to be like them!"

"You don't get it at all. I just don't want to feel like this country makes us feel—like the only thing that is our responsibility to do is stay colored and stay put. I don't want my race dictating my place."

Weldon knew he had lost and there was no use arguing. The real problem for the two of them was not about travel or art or her romanticized view of "the Continent." His problem with her was that she was living in a mansion where she could describe every room and every piece of expensive this and cherished that and he could only be on the outside and listening to her goings-on about the man who lived there and how it sounded to him like she was one of the prized possessions. And she likely had gotten to the point where she'd take that as a compliment.

They heard the ring of the approaching trolley and both turned to watch it make its way toward them. Weldon sighed as Ellie gathered up her things. He felt edgy and uncomfortable. He needed some quiet to figure out why his common sense had left him. And whatever happened between the two of them, Hughes Wellington was still somebody he needed and Ellie was his only access to the man. Well, Ellie and Mamie. But Mamie hadn't known him as long and also . . .

The trolley rescued both of them.

"I need you to talk to him." She reached for the trolley's side bar.

"I know that you do. I will."

Ellie sank worriedly into the car's clutch of passengers. She had no idea how she would raise the matter with her employer.

189

When she finally reached the mansion, Meade met her in the vestibule and let her know that Mr. Hughes had a guest, "a Mr. Jefferson Duplessis." He explained he wished for her to meet his company but the gentlemen had not yet returned from a walk. Ellie waited in the solarium. She chose a seat near the fountain and hoped that the quiet trickle of water might still and focus her thoughts.

It wasn't long before she heard their arrival. She rose from her chair with no evidence of the burden she felt from her argument with Weldon, or the necessary conversation that loomed before her. She walked quickly down the length of the solarium to meet them in the vestibule.

Weldon

I knew I never should've said she was working "up under" her boss. It just slipped out. Most likely because that was what I'd been thinking, but saying it with that particular wording started a roll I couldn't pull back.

What she didn't know was how I already had it in my mind how I would invite her back to my room and show her the shelf where I was planning to collect more evidence boxes like the one already up there with "Scott" typed out on a label facing forward. And too, I wanted her to see my books. What I had up there was impressive. Even to myownself. I'd built shelves to frame the window that looked out to the street. They were nearly full of my nonfiction collection. I stored my plates and two coffee cups inside the oven because I used the kitchenette's cabinets for fiction books. All my oversize books were lined up underneath the china cabinet Moms left to me. I put all my books that still had outside covers inside the cabinet's leaded-glass doors. But I laid the oversize ones down on their sides rather than up on the edges. That way I could stack them higher. And all of them—every single one—was catalogued with index cards in the wood file box I kept on the coffee table.

This evening could've been the first time for Ellie to see my book collection, and although asking her to step out of the parlor to go back to my rooms had the potential of going left, it was still an honest request. Seeing my books might could help her appreciate that I had something more going for me than a career job and a reputation that other folks still seemed to have some respect for. Given how she was always talking about traveling here or there and visiting that place or another, I figured we could spend some time with the atlas I'd got from the used bookshop an old professor who had been living in Harlem since the early days had set up. These days, I spent nearly as much time in the library as I did when I was a kid.

But when I told Ellie what I wanted she told me what she had planned, reminding me that "Hughes" had asked to meet with her. So of what all I said after that, my starting with a "look here, Baby Girl" was a problem because that just gave her the chance to explain how she was grown and nobody's baby and to run through her bona fides that began with Fisk and ended up with how she graduated with Latins, from which I told her maybe she should've held her own folks in the same regard as she gave to them continentals, because from what I knew Fisk was a colored college, and just because it had some Italians mixed up in there was no reason to abandon her race.

Here I got this investigation in front of me that in large measure involved her folks, and she was making herself more available to that man in Manhattan than to this man in Harlem. I shouldn't have said that either. Ellie lit into me because I said she was available—a word I shouldn't have used at all with regard to him or me. But it was what it was.

The thing was, I was just getting to the point of finding the gaps. Not that this investigation that had found its way to me made the kinda sense it needed to, but like Sherlock said, there was going to be traces, and they might not be the ones you expect. I was seeing traces. Almost like the river sketched into that old lady's table where I could see the water tracing its way—tributaries and all—from one edge of the table to off the other side. I had to work hard to displace my own suspicions so I could see the traces. But it was getting to feel like Ellie was working just as hard to displace me. She went on and on about how she wanted the freedom to travel the Continent, like her Miss Frelon.

Given where we was in the argument, it probably was inappropriate (but it didn't seem so at the time) to remind her that North America on which the U.S. of A. is placed is a continent with things to see worth anticipating. I told her how I wanted to see Niagara Falls and the Grand Canyon. I even threw in Smith's Museum in Washington in order to let her see I could do culture as well, but all she could do was correct me and say it was the Smithsonian. Like that made a difference.

I was shook by her attitude and told her so. I could've said something

191

about e-light thinking was all about leaving the U.S. instead of staying here and fixing the state of race relations. She came back at me with some nonsense about how free her lady felt on the Continent not having to have any reminders of race problems and how she deserved her chance to feel the same way. Seems like to me it was not only necessary but absolutely appropriate to remind her that Miss Frelon didn't have race problems in Europe because (and it might could be that I raised my voice just a bit when I reminded her that her lady looked like anybody's white lady looked) I said with a bit of emphasis that "ain't nobody could tell she was colored!" And too, maybe it wasn't so necessary to grab her hand and put it up to her face when I asked her what she thought those continental folks would see when she was on a train in France; but I meant it more like an illustration than the disrespect she accused me of when she snatched her hand back out of mine and pulled on her gloves like that would hide the fact she was brown skinned. Whatever. Here I was with a case that had its own necessities, a girl that couldn't see past her own situation, and feelings on my part that seemed more tilted than I would've liked. And what's more, it's not like I shouldn't have expected this given she was living in a mansion. My shelves of books, whether they were borrowed from the library or bought with my own savings from the professor's used book shop, didn't have a chance against a whole room called a "library" upstairs in the Wellingtons' Fifth Avenue digs.

But none of this made the investigation go away. And I still needed some access to the man. And I also needed to spend some time thinking of that push I been getting when I go to the library. It was getting to feel like an irritation, or an itch more than anything else. But with whatever is going on between me and Ellie, I can't tell the difference between irritation and instigation. At the library there's too many folks watching me and expecting me to shout out, "Eureka!" or some such nonsense. So between folks' expectations, my own irritation, and Ellie's touchiness, it's got to where I can't do my thinking like I need to. And what makes it all complicated is that she's still my means to get to Wellington.

But on the other hand, so is Mamie. And Mamie don't leave me feeling at all like I need to explain anything at all. In fact, the more I think on her, the more the tilt seems to shift back to being more like something balanced just right.

30

Vermilion Parish

JEFFERSON DUPLESSIS, ESQ., ARRIVED IN NEW YORK CITY MIDMORNING on one of those getting-mighty-close-to-spring days. Despite the fact that his home and practice were in Louisiana, he enjoyed trips like this one, especially during seasons when a cold and brittle air swept away the bayou's sultry climes.

This visit, however, was mixed with a personal sadness. Having learned of the death of Olivia Frelon, he'd felt the loss deeply. The *Times* carried the story of the awards banquet and the death of the young woman who was to have won the night's most coveted award. That news, as distressing and puzzling as it was, could have been the sorry end of the whole unfortunate business. After getting an official confirmation from the state coroner, his office closed the accounts they had been responsible for. But shortly thereafter, a visit to his office from a private detective hired by Hughes Wellington occasioned Duplessis's own trip to the city.

Sanders Campbell thought the lack of information about the background of the deceased to be curious. It usually wasn't hard to trace these coloreds. Just the talk amongst them of mother's son from Selma or Uncle Brother from Dayton was useful. These people kept up with family. But with the Frelon gal, there were more unknowns than knowns. He got it down to two major questions: Who were her people? And what was the source of her considerable finances? The last question was almost too easily resolved. It hadn't been difficult to latch on to the banknotes that were deposited monthly into Olivia's accounts and, since she was deceased, to secure information about their origin. That put him on the right track.

Although it didn't take a lot of time to get this information, he figured its value to the investigation was worth him doubling (and then some) the hours he'd worked for his report to his client. Just because he was skilled didn't mean he shouldn't make some dollars on the deal. A gent like Wellington wouldn't miss the cash. He chuckled when he went over his first expense report while his sister Ida Belle made arrangements for him to get down to Louisiana and check out the Abbeville Bank in Vermilion Parish that was printed on the checks.

The first easy thing once he got situated down in Abbeville was getting the personal attention of the bank teller, Lucy Mosley. Her days were boring repetitions of the same people, the same gossip, the same "How's your people doing?" "Fair to middlin." "Yours?" This New York gentleman's difference was his politeness—asking for her confidence and showing her a business card and everything. The manager excused her from her window to show him personally where he needed to deliver the confidential information that he'd brought with him from New York. It was always easier when he said he had something to give to somebody than something to ask. Lucy led Campbell outside, where centuries-old magnolias arched across both sides of the narrow street. Through their softening filter of Spanish moss she pointed out the town hall, the high school, the place where he could get a room and assured him the town was safe—day and night. "Don't worry none," she assured her visitor, "our coloreds can come in on Tuesdays and Thursdays. If they in town, they usually taking care of our business for us." As if to prove her point, they passed by a brown-skinned woman pushing the back of a toddler's tricycle. The little girl's blue eyes were bright with irritation.

"Faster, Hattie! You too slow!" The colored woman's admonishment was louder than the toddler's high-pitched whine.

"You hush now, Miss Katherine. What kind of white lady you going to grow up to be hollerin like that?" She looked up when Lucy Mosley cleared her throat and cut her eyes at her. The woman looked back to the little girl and, with a decidedly gentler tone, said, "Just hush your voice down some and I'ma push you fast; just like you aksed. You is such a smart one. And impo'tant as they come!" Lucy shook her head.

"You got to let them know their place," she said. But Sanders focused on the elegant brick building at the end of the block—the law offices of Fontenôt and Duplessis. Hopefully the attorneys would be as impressed with his New York credentials as Miss Mosley.

He failed. It took Campbell a full week of repeated visits and unsuccessful requests for an interview before he was told not to return to the law office. It was Friday, and closing hour at the bank. His last idea was actually his best. He thought he may as well revisit Lucy Mosley. "Just wanted to thank you for your help with things, Miss Mosley." He caught her as she was buttoning her gloves at the wrist, her pocketbook appropriately tucked under her arm. "I think I've got things all wrapped up. But, well . . . you see . . ."

"What is it I can do for you, Mr. Campbell? You sure have made yourself scarce this week." She was hoping he'd ask her to dinner or a walk through Park Square. It was obvious that he was not there coincidentally; she'd seen him from the window and took the time to freshen her makeup before she left. Just in case.

"I was just about to say that I wouldn't be surprised at all if a bright gal like you didn't already know all about the business I have just brought to conclusion given you're the one who was selected to handle the monthly 'correspondence' from the law office, if, between us, we can call it that." He gave her a conspiratorial wink. She wondered if it was a New York come-on, so her response was measured.

"Well . . . yes. My manager is respectful of the way I handle my window." She hoped he would understand her reply as genteel. "That's why he give it to me to handle correspondence. I have a good sense of the proprietaries." Since she was talking, Sanders knew better than to interrupt. His instinct paid off. "Daryl Lynn, the secretary, she used to give me the checks. I can't keep her from talking about what a shame it is to have all that good money going to waste up to that gal in New York. She don't have my professional training so she just talks on and on about the firm's business." Sanders correctly sensed that he was about to hit pay dirt.

"Miss Mosley, I don't even have to tell you that, me being a detective, just like an officer of the court, you already know how to deal with confidential business matters. Professionals like us understand business."

She liked his notice of her capabilities.

"Of course you right, Mr. Campbell. I knows my p's and q's. I suspect you fully understand that what I have to say is that ours is what we call one of the off-the-record conversations. Seein it involves Attorney Fontenôt." Campbell cleared his throat. "That be the old man."

"Miss Lucy"—she liked that he'd gotten familiar with her name—"your potential just shines right through. Even knowing about the required 'off the record.' It's not every day I have the honor of talking with another professional about matters like the one you are telling me about . . . ?" He phrased it as a question just to nudge her a bit.

"Why of course you quite welcome. Now like I was sayin, Daryl Lynn she told me how Mr. Jefferson done stepped in to take care of some of the old man's outside the family 'missteps,' we might can say. He's one that's got chirren inside and outside. He been cattin around the coloreds ever since I was little. 'Round here it's not like these chirren is a total surprise. Usually, they keep to they place. But not this gal. She might be his blood daughter, but that don't make it right. And it absolutely don't mean she can take to prancing around all out in the open like she don't have nothing to hide. It only took a couple of times for her to come down to the law office and walk on in like she was up there in line with his own family before things got to change. Like as not, that's when the missus made it clear it would be a good thing for her to go on an get herself up outta here. And that's when things changed. Real quick. One day the girl here, walkin through town and in the front doors of the law firm like she don't have nothin to hide, next day she gone. And then right behind that happening, the old man retires. One plus one. It add up."

"And you know this for a fact?" Campbell asked.

"Oh yes siree. It didn't take us much figurin out. These outside families a bane to Christian living. So a lady like Mrs. Fontenôt, well, you can only stands for so much disrespect. When the girl be so brash as to think she can show herself in town . . ."

"Of course. His wife should not have to abide that." Campbell could barely hide his glee at getting at the town's secrets. "You've been quite helpful, Lucy."

"You most welcome," she said, slightly blushing. "It seems Mr. Jeff at least got enough sense to cut off the checks going up there to New York. It wasn't right takin away from his real family like that. Ain't been no New York transfers for a couple of months now."

"Seems you've got it all figured out, Miss Lucy." They'd reached the train station and for the first time she noticed the edge of a ticket in his front pocket. "It was a pleasure to have made your acquaintance."

"And the same to you, I'm sure, Mr. Campbell," said a slightly piqued Lucy Mosley when she realized their relationship, as it was, had come to its conclusion.

CAMPBELL PREPARED THE REPORT ON THE TRAIN BACK. THESE THINGS always come back to family. This one, though, had a twist. It was clear to him Wellington had had his eye on the girl from what he'd heard about the banquet. What he couldn't figure out, though, was why he was still interested enough to hire him to track her down when the newspapers let everybody know she was colored. No matter how white she looked it wasn't a secret down here. That's why the daddy sent her away and paid for her to stay that way. So why and how did she still figure in Wellington's interest?

In Wellington's office Campbell explained that "the girl come from Louisiana, and some bigwig lawyer down there is doing his best to protect the family name."

"Through the auspices of his firm?" Wellington inquired, making certain his voice reflected an appropriate level of incredulity. He placed the newspaper down on his desk, folded back to the section where he'd been reading the article about the vice mayor's son's misadventures. It seemed that Wyckomb deBaun's new wife had been killed in a car accident on their British honeymoon. The circumstances were suspicious enough to require a coroner's inquest.

But Campbell had his attention now, and as he suspected, he'd have to manage the situation carefully. He folded the paper on his desk. Only then did he look directly at the increasingly uncomfortable detective, who had not been invited to sit. He gestured to the chair and Campbell sank into it, unsure where his relief was coming from. After all he was the one who got the goods, so to speak. These rich bastards could make you nervous by paying attention to you, or ignoring you. It sure made a difference who you were in the world.

Wellington buzzed for Meade.

"Is this the report?" Wellington asked, reaching for the papers Campbell had placed onto the desk.

"Yes sir, it's all there."

Wellington spoke with what he hoped was an assertive and righteous anger. "So it seems you have uncovered a frank case of fraud, perpetrated

197

by a firm that is bound by the ethics of the legal profession to act other-wise. Between the two of us—the detective sat forward in his seat, app-reciative of the implied intimacy—I have made it a practice to track these matters down. I can't tolerate any form of fraud. My companies and asso-ciations cannot afford it. Do you understand?" Sanders said he thought he did.

"The gal—I mean the young woman who died—she was being fraud-ulent with you, sir, wasn't she?" Wellington did not react. The conversa-tion was advancing as he'd intended. "Between us, and with appropriate notice of the confines of our confidential relationship, I had invited her to the vice mayor's home that night. She, shall I say, represented herself differently than I came to discover. I could not let that be the end of the matter. I had to get to its roots. Your very satisfactory work has uncovered that misrepresentation and her coconspirators."

"Exactly," the detective replied. He hoped it didn't sound like a question.

Wellington reflected for a moment. "Well. Now you understand that I have no recourse."

"No sir. I mean yes sir. None whatsoever. No recourse but to . . . to . . ." Wellington filled in the blank for him.

"To make certain this firm's business interests in this city will come to an immediate and permanent closure."

"Shut it down. Right. I was about to say as much. Absolutely."

"I've no need for your affirmation of my decision, Campbell." The detective was momentarily chagrined. Wellington's admonition was stra-tegic. "Although I do not think this was a particularly arduous assignment, it was an indication to me that your offices might be of additional use."

"Is that so?" Campbell tried not to let the excitement show in his voice.

"I've some business in Brazil you might handle for me—nothing like this, some contract and land-use and property matters and the like that need the kind of attention you have shown yourself capable of. Are you free to travel?"

"Me sir? Oh yes sir!"

"It could be for a considerable period of time, some of my holdings are rather remote. But I don't anticipate you'll have any trouble." He reached into his drawer and placed a check in front of the detective. "I expect that this will cover your expenses and your report on this matter. You can stop by my downtown offices when you've made the arrangements for travel—purchase a one-way fare, it's always easier in these international cases to make travel arrangements from points of departure. My secretary will have the files ready for you by the end of the week?" It was framed as a question; but both men understood it was a conclusion to their conversation.

Campbell looked down at the extra zero on the payment and swallowed quickly. There's a whole lot of difference that a zero can make.

"Yes sir, Mr. Wellington. It sure will. That will take everything into consideration." Campbell had become comfortable again. "Me old mother, the good Lord rest her soul, would all the time say, 'Blood will out.'"

Wellington didn't reply. He simply said, "Bon voyage, Mr. Campbell" and left it to Meade to see the man out. He took up his desk phone. The operator didn't take long to make a connection for him to Abbeville Parish and the law offices of Mr. Jefferson Duplessis, Esq. Although the attorney was not in, he left word that he should anticipate a letter of invitation to New York City. That correspondence arrived on the same day that Sanders Campbell waved to his sister, having booked a second-class cabin, because he was moving up in the professional world, on what would become a very long trip to Brazil. And who knows, he might just find out that he liked the place. As soon as he figured out where it was.

JEFFERSON DUPLESSIS ALSO MADE TRAVEL ARRANGEMENTS. THE intriguing letter regarding Miss Frelon combined with his office's recent encounter with a New York detective and with what he had been able to learn of Mr. Wellington left him rather eager to meet the man.

31

Blood Will Out

DUPLESSIS FORWARDED A GRACIOUSLY SCRIPTED ACCEPTANCE OF Wellington's kind invitation and instructed his office to secure the necessary tickets and to prepare some notes on Hughes Wellington to brief him for their meeting. He was not surprised at all to be ushered into such an elegant mansion. Meade showed him into the solarium and Wellington didn't keep him waiting. His welcome and thanks for undertaking the mysterious journey were sincere and effusive.

"But I could not help but be intrigued by your offer of conversation regarding Miss Frelon. She was a beautiful and sad young woman. Our professional relationship did not cover many years, but no one who met her would fail to be moved by her . . . her story. Might I ask, sir, your interest in the matter?"

Wellington had turned toward the window. He still did not know how and to what extent he was going to apprise the lawyer of his interests, and his history. Duplessis did not urge him to break the silence. Instead, he looked down the long shadow of his host as it stretched across the floor and then upwards at his profile. Wellington could hear his sharp intake of air before he said, "Ah monsieur, mai j'offre mes sincères condoléances à la mort de votre sœur." Sanders Campbell had the circumstances right, but not the lineage.

"Vous êtes bien aimable, je vous remercie," Hughes replied, realizing immediately what he had done, and wondered if it was not the irrepressible expression of his own desires. He turned back to his guest, his arms crossed against his chest. "You know," he sighed, with resignation.

"I must admit I did not until just now. But I have been your father's counsel for many years. You and he have the same physique and bearing. It is strikingly apparent that you must be Carteret Fontenôt, the son of my senior partner, Cameron Fontenôt, and, if Olivia Frelon was your sister, you are the son of his . . . well, the son of Belle Chartier. Please forgive the liberty I have assumed. But now we will be able to have a frank conversation about these matters . . . and your sister Désirée."

"C'est vrai. And if I might request from you the same professional privilege of confidence that my . . . that Monsieur Fontenôt has enjoyed, we can discuss the matter that has brought us together."

The two southern gentlemen crossed the vestibule's marbled foyer and walked through the solarium to the study. Meade closed the double doors behind them. The men took seats at the small conference table rather than by the desk and opened their napkins to take in the small repast prepared for the gentlemen. Duplessis broke their silence.

"I was deeply distressed to learn of the death of Mademoiselle Frelon." Duplessis was keenly aware that his host had just revealed a secret he'd dedicated many years to preserving. He anticipated that he would need some time to regain his composure, so he continued speaking. "I met your sister on the occasion of your mother's death, but of course I have been aware for many years of the situation of your family. I knew your dear mother well. In fact it was she who insisted upon your tutor."

"Monsieur Cadêt!" Hughes interrupted with surprised remembrance of the tiny and animated brown-skinned man who spoke impeccable French and who came to their home to educate him and Désirée about a world arguably unavailable to either of them.

"Oui. Yes. Your mother and I met frequently about this. Your tutor had to be willing to maintain the appropriate discretions regarding your unique circumstances as well as to offer you and your sister the finest private education." Wellington seemed lost in the memory. "Frankly, your father had to be persuaded on this matter. Your mother prevailed. Given your situation, it was a rather unusual accommodation."

Wellington winced with the painful recognition. One day, the elderly Negro man assigned to take Désirée and Carteret whenever their father visited took them on a longer ride than usual. Their horse-drawn wagon moved at a quick clip down Abbeville's Main Street, but when they came to a particular corner, it slowed. They passed a large white mansion with stately pillars framed by a grove of magnolias. Laughter from a cluster of white children echoed out onto the street. The man driving the wagon mumbled loudly enough for the children behind him to hear: "That's a natchl bo'n pity an a shame. All y'all looks jus like the other ones. But none a y'all in dis wagon ever gwine be up in there. Things stay the way they is. There be house chirren and outside chirren. You two on the outside. Umph umph umph. It's a pity an a shame." The man shook his head and the wagon moved on down the street, picking up its pace after it passed the house. Désirée would have been too young to understand his message, but Carteret was well aware of the secret that had been revealed to him.

That was how Hughes Wellington (né Carteret Fontenôt) learned there was a white Fontenôt family in town. When he and his sister were returned to their cabin after the conclusion of their father's visit with their mother, he looked around at their meager surrounds and felt quite keenly the imbalance of the comparison. The anger that began that day simmered throughout his youth and eventually drove him away. There was no future for him in their tiny cabin nestled behind the grove of cedars.

Jefferson could only imagine what it would have been to have to live with that kind of isolation and understanding. Perhaps that was why he fought so hard for every privilege Belle's children might receive. His own father's indiscretions lay heavily on him, but there was no intercession he could make in his family. He suggested the arrangement for Désirée and Carteret Fontenôt. With Belle's death, his father was easily convinced that their daughter might well threaten the inheritance of his legal kin. Any such inquiry, even if unsuccessful, would be an unacceptable burden to his family.

Wellington asked how it was that his sister came to live here in Harlem. "She was a world away from the world I have chosen to inhabit." He closed his eyes, feeling again the painful depths of his loss. "And yet, she was close."

"Je comprends," the attorney replied. "I thought you had passed on. No one knew that it was your death as a colored man that you arranged."

"She spoke to you about me?" Wellington asked.

"Only that they had received the devastating news of your passing."

202

The lawyer cleared his throat, perhaps strategically. Wellington shuddered with the memory of his having arranged that deceit.

"And Mother?"

Duplessis told him how she'd passed after a long and painful illness. He suggested that his sister's mourning had to have been mixed with some measure of relief for the end of their mother's suffering.

"When I met with her in my offices," Jefferson explained, "I could see the grief had taken its toll. She came in to sign some papers that turned over the land and the cottage your mother occupied to her name." Hughes started to say something but Duplessis continued.

"When I first heard of your mother's declining health, I thought Désirée was at Spelman Seminary in Atlanta. Your father offered to pay for her schooling there, but it seems that instead she chose to remain home."

Hughes buried his face in his hands, remembering the day he left home fully aware that if he did not leave first, the lot of caretaking that his sister inherited would fall to him. It was both an act of absolute selfishness and, as far as he was concerned, absolute necessity. Even at this moment, so many years past the pathetic moment, he could remember his sister's plea echoing out into the swampy darkness. On the evening of his sixteenth birthday he opened the door to his mother's bedchamber with an unshakable intent. He held the porcelain knob with one hand and in his other he clasped a worn valise. Désirée immediately realized his intent. The book in her lap slipped to the floor as she stood up. She didn't bother to retrieve it. She just stood, stilled by the reality of her brother's deceit and its consequence to her.

"Monsieur, shall I continue?"

"S'il vous plait," Wellington mumbled.

"Your sister was quite beautiful. But her visits to my office visibly displayed the painful effects of her mourning. She looked, shall I say, triste et fatiguée." He took the liberty of pouring more coffee into his host's and then into his own cup. "On her subsequent visit I was able to present to her the contract that allowed for her substantial support as long as she moved away from the parish, with the caveat that she must also change her name so that your father's legal—I mean his heirs—would not anticipate any potential claim that might arise regarding his estates. It was not that the potential was legally viable, but it was the best I could do for her."

Wellington leaned forward. "His money supported her?"

"Yes. Your father was persuaded that the arrangement would be a security for his family—the legal one." The two gentlemen were both quiet for a time before Jefferson asked Hughes if he might now learn something of their situation in New York given their différence.

"The truth is," Hughes explained, "I have never been able to fully separate myself from my people. Something in me knows and needs my race." Wellington explained how his society here believed his interests in the affairs of the coloreds to be an expression of a currently allowed eccentricity. "It is an odd moment here for Harlem," he explained. "It is as if the coloreds are à la mode . . . Harlem est en vogue. For a wealthy man, certain eccentricities are overlooked."

"Odd indeed," Jefferson replied thoughtfully.

"My sister and I discovered each other on the night of her death. Désirée—that is, Olivia—was furious and everyone was watching her. Who could not? Her entrance into the banquet hall caused something of a stir. I could not help but notice, and then appreciate that her attentions had focused on me. Apparently she recognized me almost immediately. I wish I could say the same. But when I saw her, frankly, I thought she was white. There were but a few of us there."

Duplessis noticed that Wellington's "us" meant whites.

"But even with the decided oddities of these times, there are codes of conduct. Some have taken up the Negro as a pastime. So, when I noticed this ethereal creature, I walked over to introduce myself and frankly to warn her of the social vulnerability of attending a Harlem event. My presence would be seen as an eccentricity. Hers could be . . ." Duplessis nodded his understanding, so Wellington continued. "So, you might appreciate my shock when she responded by calling my name—my given name—and quickly followed it with every derogation imaginable. There was a brittle, unforgiving hardness to her." Hughes paused, recalling the emotional upheaval of that moment. "But of course, I absolutely deserved those and more. All I wanted to do was to pull her into my arms and beg her apology. But we were already making a scene. So I reached down to her hand, brought it to my lips, and begged her to hush, people were watching. I told her I would send for her and then I left the affair."

"And you heard of her death?"

"I went to a holiday soiree in the village. But I barely remember it. I spent my time trying to determine how and when I could arrange for us to meet. Soon there was some indelicate conversation—no more than party gossip really—regarding the apparent death of a young white woman at a Harlem affair. I was desperate to think that Désirée could be involved. I left immediately and returned to Harlem. Sadly, it was so. It was my Désirée. Ma sœur bénie."

"Je suis tellement désolé."

"Merci bien. But your kind expression of sympathy does nothing to alleviate my great guilt . . ." He looked away from the table. "However, I, in fact, have every reason to thank you. The professional courtesies you directed toward my sister did much to allow her some of life's pleasure. For those brief moments I am most humbly grateful."

Wellington paused, and eventually Jefferson took up the silence. He reached into his attaché and pulled out a photograph of a grave site. "The cemetery personnel told me she visited the site before she left. It is the largest and loveliest memorial in the churchyard. You'll notice a partially opened magnolia blossom carved next to her name? It was your sister's own design." Wellington recalled her fondness for drawing. "The only task I had was to transfer bimonthly funds to her here in New York. When the bank informed me that her account had been frozen, my office looked into the matter. Discovering her demise, we of course closed the account. But then came your investigator. And then your invitation. Et nous voici."

"Yes. Here we are indeed," Hughes replied. The two men talked well into the afternoon. They even left for a walk through Central Park, Duplessis sharing stories of the parish and Wellington telling of his travels, his time in Brazil, Europe, and the Mediterranean, and his eventual arrival in New York. He even told him about his having hired Ellie Howard, explaining that she worked for Olivia before he hired her. Jefferson was duly impressed with the coincidence of associations but sensed in Hughes's engaged telling that there was something else about his assistant. He asked Hughes to forgive his question if it felt inappropriate, but did he discern correctly that Hughes had feelings for the young woman?

"You are unfailingly perceptive, my friend. I have not shared my feelings. The racial barrier I have so carefully maintained now becomes a barrier to my own desires."

"Are you certain? These things sometimes work differently than social conventions dictate. And you are here in New York where the conventions have some flexibilities . . ."

"That is of course true. But how could I begin a relationship of deception? Especially after . . ." He also thought that he might share his secret with Ellie. Given the confidentiality of the collection, "perhaps, this could be just another secret she held."

"Forgive my being so blunt so early in our acquaintance," Duplessis replied. "But I doubt that would be the case. In my experience, a professional confidence is quite different from a personal one. Isn't it possible that you could earn her affections as the man you are today? After all, with your sister's death, your ties are now completely undone."

Hughes looked troubled and Jefferson immediately apologized for reminding him, in that way, of his losses.

"It's not that. Not that at all. It's just that, how could I ask her to take on the burden of a cross-racial relationship? It seems a great deal to ask."

"May I make a suggestion?"

"Mais bien sûr. Indeed, I am grateful for your candor. Our conversation already leaves me feeling more liberated than I can recall. I could only appreciate your consideration."

"Hughes, you have just suffered two losses. This knowledge of your mother's death may well affect you as if it just happened. And your sister's death is a particularly grievous tragedy. In fact, you have arguably suffered the loss of your racial identity as well. This does not seem to me to be the time to reveal such a carefully maintained secret. Your response to these matters needs time. And time without the complication of the young lady's response to you."

"But I have already asked that she meet with me this afternoon. I was going to introduce you to her and, my intent had been, to use this meeting to tell her of my own past."

After some contemplation Duplessis suggested, "If there is nothing that compels that particular conversation at this time, my advice would be to wait."

They'd reached the mansion again. Meade opened the doors as they walked under the iron portico. He let Wellington know that "Miss Ellie" had recently arrived and was waiting for them in the solarium. It was just at that moment that Ellie Howard walked out into the vestibule. She followed the path lit by the final rays of the late-afternoon sun that framed her as she stood in the arched doorway. She was wearing a dress of coppery gabardine with a softly pleated skirt beginning just below her waistline and falling midcalf. Her collar and cuffs were edged with a border of creamy lace, and the satin cuffs were turned up over the long sleeves of her dress and fastened with pearl-like buttons. Because she'd recently removed her hat, her hair, tied back with a brown satin ribbon, was somewhat tousled, but instead of looking unkempt the stray ringlets fell over her cheeks in appealing disarray. She reached up and combed her fingers back through her hair in an effort to return them to their place, but it didn't work at all. Her unconscious gesture was fully endearing. Duplessis looked over at Wellington and nodded, an acknowledgment that he understood the attraction. Wellington walked over, took Ellie's arm, and asked if he might introduce her to his guest, Mr. Jefferson Duplessis, Esquire, of Vermilion Parish, Louisiana. Duplessis took her extended hand and brought it to his lips. He bowed slightly. "Je suis très heureux de faire votre connaissance." Duplessis was touched when Ellie returned the courtesy, in perfect French. He then turned to Hughes.

"Shall I anticipate, sir, that this brings our visit to its conclusion? I am certain we will be able to correspond about any of the matters we have discussed." It was an opportunity, and he hoped a slight encouragement, to follow the advice he'd recently imparted. He was surprised that he felt some anxiety waiting for Wellington's response.

After a hesitation that was nearly uncomfortable, Hughes sighed, and replied, "It is." He took Jefferson's extended hand in a grateful clasp. "I deeply appreciate the conversation we have had. And, mon cher ami, may I say that I sincerely hope our relationship extends past this all-too-brief visit."

"The same is true for me." He turned to Ellie and said, "Il a été un plaisir de faire votre connaissance, Mademoiselle Howard."

"Pour moi aussi. Merci," she said quietly. But she was looking over at Hughes and noticed his troubled brow. After Mr. Duplessis left she turned to ask him if everything was all right.

"Yes, thank you. It is."

"You wanted to talk with me?"

"I thought that Mr. Duplessis would have some . . . well, some business matters that you might handle for us. But it seems that will not be necessary at the moment."

"I see," she replied, and then, before her courage dissipated, she said, "then perhaps I might have a moment of your time?"

"Of course, Ellie. Let's talk in the gallery."

"That would be fine. It's just that, well . . . I want to ask you something about the night you met my former employer, Miss Frelon. The night she died. My, umm, Officer Weldon Thomas is looking into the matter. He asked me to see if you might have any information since you had attended the gala."

The fateful collision of moments regarding Désirée and the coincidence of his request left him feeling uneasy. Out of habit they walked to the gallery's center, where a delicate chandelier of Murano glass hovered over a small, round table. He pulled out one of the two chairs for her and began the story he'd decided to share.

"I remember that night well. And of course you should hear about it from me."

32

One Too Many

WHEN I CALLED ON MRS. EARLENE KINSDALE FOR MY INTERVIEW WITH her, I made sure to wear my uniform. This lady needed to see me as official. She could get casual too quick. Her apartment was at the top of the Heights. Seems like the dead husband left her in good shape. Her building had limestone cornices built up around the windows and doors, and a goodly part of the sidewalk was fenced with ironwork railing. High cotton my moms would say. I was a bit surprised, though, when LaVerne Caver opened the door. I been knowing the Caver family since I was a kid. Me and LaVerne went to P.S. 89 together. She warned me not to be bringing any of the Scott mess over here. I tried to explain I couldn't know how things would end up, but I was doing this for all of us. Yeah, I know. It didn't make much sense to me either.

Unlike LaVerne, Mrs. Kinsdale was more than happy to see me. Over-the-top happy. Worrisome happy. She offered me a drink from a chest that was decorated like a Chinese painting. Its brilliant red interior was lined with glass shelves and a lot of liquor. Not a book in sight.

Polite as I could be, I told her, "No ma'am, Mrs. Kinsdale. But thank you kindly for offering. I'm here to . . ." She sat down right next to me without a breathing space between us and gave me something to drink anyway. I set the glass on her side table, took out my notebook, and got right to the matter at hand. First thing I said was that I already knew it was her that brought Mrs. Scott home that night after the banquet. "Can tell me about bringing her back up to the Heights?" I asked.

I don't think she was happy I was trying to keep it professional. She tried to get me off track talking about how we "knew each other" from the grand jury before the funeral, although I told her my recollection was that it wasn't exactly a formal meeting, I just saw her in the hallway. And to my memory she didn't seem to have much time for me. But to her it was apparently enough for us to be on a first-name basis. I agreed because it might be the onliest way to make some progress. Good thing I did. Because "Earlene" volunteered she had talked to a private detective about Miss Frelon. I tried to find out more about that.

"Nothing I could say or do would get him to tell me who hired him. But it was surely Reynolds."

"That would be Dr. Scott?" I asked, making sure I was writing something in my notebook to try to get closer to an unvarnished reaction. Sherlock said unvarnished truth was better than the proffered truth. It didn't seem right that there could be a truth on the one hand and another truth on the other. But I was still new to detecting work. Earlene was tripping on my mention of Dr. Scott.

"No, that would be 'Reynolds.' I believe I've earned that familiarity."

I didn't say much more than "Yes ma'am." At that point I was still waiting for her to tell me more. The more a question could just lay there the more likely the person being interviewed would fill in the silence. That's in the Sherlock books too.

"I believe I can say that you will come to understand that Olivia Frelon was nothing if not strategic. She maneuvered herself into our social set like she had a map. And in spite of it all, Vera latched on to her."

I was careful how I asked my next question, seeing as she was willing to tell me more than what I was directly asking. So I just said, as matter-of-fact as I could, that it seemed like she didn't much like Miss Frelon. She said I was "intuitive." I couldn't quite tell if she was making fun of me, like I didn't know the word, so I let my quiet be her prompt again. It worked.

"The fact is," she set her drink down on the table. Not directly on the table. There was a coaster up under it. That's the way it was with these e-lights. They just like the rest of us, except they have their ways. And use coasters. "The fact is that I hated the bitch."

I tried mightily not to respond to that. Instead I took a bit of a pause and reached over to stir the cubes in my drink that I had put to the side. Then I asked her about the night of the banquet and whether she saw Miss Frelon there. It's what we investigators call distraction and displacement. Her answer was worth my self-control.

"Well of course I did. We all saw her go into that 'secret' room. What a farce that is."

"So the short fiction wasn't secret?" I asked. "You knew about her prize?"

"Frankly, it's not as much a secret as they pretend. Remember, that's what we're good at. Actually, both those things. Secrets and pretense. Everybody can see who's missing from the tables. We're not stupid. Pretentious? Yes. But not stupid." She ran her tongue across the rim of her glass. I tried not to notice. "To answer your other question. I did not know she would be awarded the prize for fiction. That was confidential. I only knew there was to be a prize."

She leaned back into the sofa. "Nobody knows who the winners are in each category until the card gets opened up onstage. It's part of the performance we paid for. Staged, but, well what about us isn't?"

So from what she was saying, only the judges and Miss Silk had the winners' names. The librarian did the writing and the Opportunity head honcho did the pronouncing. I put it down in my book mostly so I could keep writing and Mrs. Kinsdale wouldn't take untoward advantage of a pause in my process. By that time, she was well into her telling and that's when you just let folks talk it out. Even though a good deal of what they say is going to be useless, sometimes something is important. Right then I had no way to determine good info from bad. And Mrs. K. had already moved on from Miss Frelon and got to ripping the library lady.

"That old biddy always makes a big to-do of excusing herself from whatever table they've seated her at saying, 'Well, honor calls' or 'my task is upon me' or some such nonsense. I've been at the table with her for the past few years, and this year I demanded that they put me anywhere other than with that insufferably dusty little librarian." She took a sip from her glass and noticed me again. It made me sweat. "Gracious, Weldon! For someone who was there, you really do know very little about that night."

I tried to explain that it was a professional obligation for me, that I was on duty, and also how much I appreciated her breaking it all down. I tried to avoid making it sound like chitchat.

"Oh, of course. I can respect that. You must understand that, for them, it's all about money. Their little magazine is almost totally funded by that one event. The banquet fees include a subscription. And next month's issue will have all our photographs as well as publish the awardees' pieces. But it's all about our pictures. That prompts our buy of multiple copies. Then we leave the magazine on our coffee tables for the rest of the season just accidentally open to the page that has our photograph on it. Come next December, we'll do it all again. It's quite a little moneymaking enterprise. You know, when we don't ruin it, every once in a while our people can be quite entrepreneurial."

I thought she was getting near to being unhelpful, so I tried to move the conversation back to the principals. "And Miss Frelon?"

"Well now. How to say it? Frankly, she was quite the little no-talent freeloader." Then she backtracked with a decidedly ugly insinuation. "But, that's not quite fair. I'm sure she had some talents." She emphasized the "some." I took that opportunity to slip in a question about the rumors floating around about Miss Frelon and Dr. Scott. I kind of matched her tone, even though it made me kind of uncomfortable. I asked if these were the kind of talents a gentleman like Dr. Scott might appreciate.

"Oh please." She nearly choked on her drink when she told me that the only thing Reynolds Scott was good at is "furnishing the elaborate and otherwise vacant rooms of his own imagination." I thought it was creative phrasing, so I wrote it down exactly like she said it. Then she said, not particularly to me it seemed like, "He's a selfish bastard." She downed what was left in her glass, stood up, and walked dramatically over to the bar to mix another.

"I see," I said. I didn't want to do too much shaping of the conversation myself, so I tried to keep it neutral. Fact of the matter is, I was beginning to see something that had eluded me. But I still hadn't gotten around to asking her about her own whereabouts that night. When I did, it didn't seem to bother her. And that was important.

"Ask anyone at our table and they will tell you that I was either at the bar or seated with them."

"So they would all account for your whereabouts?" I asked that wrong. This time, she got testy—but not so much on the insinuation as on how it seemed like I didn't seem to appreciate her independence.

"Well, Officer Thomas. I don't have anyone I have to account to for my time anymore." I needed to be specific. This lady could take her emotions from here to there with no warning and I couldn't afford to lose total control of the interview.

"So let me ask it this way," I said to her directly, looking her in the eye to show I was serious. "Were you in the room with Olivia Frelon at any point?"

That's when she got a bit haughty. Or it could have been shifty. I'll have to think on which. "Well, I don't think I have to tell you that. And it doesn't much seem to matter since the arrest means Vera certainly was with her. Those 'real' policemen and attorneys and all those folk that probably do a good job of ignoring you downtown have decided there is reason good enough for them to have indicted her. So what I do, or did that night, seems to be something I get to keep to myself."

I'd heard enough, plus I needed to figure out her tone and where her attitude came from in order to assess the value (if any) in what she was telling me. So I closed my book and told her that indeed she did get to keep whatever she wished to herself. But just before I got to the door I clarified it. "For the time being." That was strategic, my walking like I'm leaving and then turning back around toward her with what Mr. Sherlock called dramatic effect. I had just one more thing to ask. Miss Earlene took it personal. I was not at all surprised.

I asked her if when she brought Mrs. Scott home, whether or not she and Dr. Scott had the opportunity to talk. That was when she got all attitudinal again and didn't directly answer me. So I decided to soften it up some and call her by her first name and tell her I didn't care one way or the other if she answered it, I was just there to give her the opportunity to be on the record like some of the other ladies in her circle whom I'd spoken with. That was stretching it some, but it worked. Her being in the thick of her own society folks was clearly important to her.

"Well, of course. I was waiting in the parlor until he got her properly sedated. When he came in we had drinks to calm our nerves. He offered me a cigarette and we took the moment to recover from the drama."

"You two both smoked?"

"I don't recall that being against the criminal code."

"It isn't," I said. Maybe a bit too eagerly, because something seemed like it was just on the verge of fitting together. I wanted to stay with that moment, so I asked her if it was Dr. Scott who offered her a cigarette or the reverse.

"Well, technically, they were mine. They gave them out at the banquet. I distinctly recall I gave the case to Reynolds and he opened it so I could select one. He lit it. We smoked. It was calming."

I pretended like I was stuttering, but the truth was I was fully in control when I asked her if she still had it.

"The case? That gaudy thing? It was plated—not sterling. Why would I keep a cheap souvenir? I left it with Reynolds. I recall how he just went and placed it in his pocket as if I hadn't been the one to offer the case to him. Characteristically cheeky. But given that he missed the evening's drama, perhaps he wanted a souvenir."

That's when the thing that was out of place in the doctor's office first made itself plain. If these cases were souvenirs, then why would Scott, who hadn't been there, have one in his office drawer? And especially why would such a fastidious man—whose preferences ran to bright brass desk accessories—choose a silver case? It was a mismatch from those in his desk, but it did match exactly the one I took from LT. In my thinking, there was no reason for Dr. Scott to have one of his own unless he had been at the banquet too. And that would have kept him a part of the puzzle. Until Earlene explained this, as well as confirmed his absence, it kept him on the suspect list. But now it looked like his silver case came from Earlene Kinsdale, not from a surreptitious trip to the banquet. It was a relief to figure something out. Things were roiling around in my head and I needed to get gone and get busy thinking on all this. In my notes I marked one of the cases as LT Mitchell's, one as Mrs. Scott's, and the one from the doctor's office as coming from Mrs. Kinsdale. I had my suspicions as to why he didn't leave it at his home and instead brought it to his office desk, but that wasn't at the head of my thinking.

By the time I got to the end of the block, I got to whistling. The thing was—and this surprised me nearly as much as what I just learned—of all my interviews, even after this lady's drama, Mamie's stayed with me. I was wishing I could go back and talk to her instead of Ellie. And that preference called for some thinking all on its own.

33

Reshelving

WELDON AND ELLIE MET IN ZENOBIA'S FRONT PARLOR. HE TOLD HER about his interview with Earlene Kinsdale.

"Gracious!" Ellie declared. "So she did it!"

Weldon replied carefully. "Tell me why you think so." It was important not to lead one way or the other.

"Well, she was there, but she wouldn't tell you where she was. That's opportunity. You said that was one of the criteria for guilt. Motive, opportunity, pattern, and . . . umm . . ."

"Intent. But go ahead."

"Right. So she told you straight out that she hated her. That sounds like motive to me. And she wouldn't give an accounting to you, an officer of the law. So she's obviously hiding something."

"I have to tell you that she didn't seem to hold a whole lot of respect for my being an 'officer of the law.'" Weldon briefly paused, not eager to broach the next subject. But when he did, he went into it head-on. "Did you talk to your boss yet? When it comes to motive it seems he and your Miss Frelon had an argument. So he could be as involved as anyone. And he's the one we know least about. At least most of us know least about." Ellie ignored his innuendo.

"He didn't."

"Do you know that, or hope that?"

"I know it," she replied sharply. "I did talk to him. And frankly, he was surprisingly honest considering . . ."

"Considering what?" Weldon asked, pulling out his pen and notebook.

"Well, considering they did have an argument, and considering why."

"He admitted to an argument?"

"Most assuredly."

"And you believed him?"

"It's not about that. His explanation was perfectly reasonable. I mean, I do keep my common sense with me when I'm downtown."

"That's good to know."

"I'll pretend I didn't hear that, Weldon Haynie Thomas. I believe him because he wouldn't lie to me about a race matter."

"Excuse me? What do you mean 'a race matter'?"

"Well, it seems they were arguing because when he went up to meet her, he assumed she was a white woman. And he made some comment about the two of them choosing to spend a perfectly good evening uptown in Harlem when they could have spent time amongst their own people."

"He said that to you?"

"Worse, he said it to her. And apparently it made Miss Olivia really angry. She told him she was as colored as everybody else there that night—with the exception of him and a few ladies—and that he should be careful because he was the only white man there."

"Dang. That's something to think on right there." Weldon was writing almost as fast as Ellie was talking.

"Indeed. And knowing Miss Olivia, she would have been incensed. I mean it goes without saying that she could have decided to pass if she wanted to. But she had race loyalty. Hughes made a terrible presumption." She tried to soften the judgment.

Weldon was pensive. "But he came back up to Harlem that night. Did you ask about that?"

"He told me without my asking. After the mayor's party he came back uptown to offer her a ride home and apologize. But it was such a chaotic scene that he didn't stay. And then, when he heard who it was he started worrying about me."

"What does that mean?"

"It means that, just like you, he remembered that I worked for her.

216

And like you, he was concerned about how I would hear about it. He didn't know you would tell me first."

"Oh. I guess that would make sense."

"You guess it would make sense? Weldon, this is a problem. Whenever we talk these days you question my judgment."

"Baby Girl—I mean Ellie—I don't mean to upset you! Thinking on those days has to be terrible. I don't mean to make it worse."

"Well, you are doing a good job of exactly that."

Weldon needed to change the subject. He gathered up the group of books on the coffee table and asked if she would accompany him down to the library. "It'll do us good to get some fresh air."

"It might do you some good," Ellie retorted, "but I am perfectly fine."

"Now that is something we can agree on." Weldon smiled and Ellie let her anger fade. He was grateful to lift the mood. But it didn't mean he wasn't distracted. Maybe the library's calm would help settle his thoughts. He was quiet the whole way there.

Miss Silk was sitting behind her desk, engrossed in her writing. Ellie and Weldon walked up to the returns desk, and, as they passed her, Weldon reached up to take off his cap. When he did so, the books fell from his hands and tumbled onto her desk, upsetting her ink and spilling it across her papers as well as onto the books he'd dropped.

"Oh my goodness! Oh Miss Silk, ma'am, I'm so sorry!" Weldon rushed behind the desk to help her. He pulled out file drawers to place her papers onto while he tried to mop up the ink on the desk. "I apologize! This is such a shame. I'm so sorry, Miss Silk. Did I get any on you?"

She pushed away from the desk trying to decide whether to shush him—his apologies were much too loud—or to check her blouse and sleeves for ink stains. She managed to do both. "I'm sure you didn't mean to, Officer Thomas. Oh my gracious! This *is* a mess!" she cried.

"Now, now, Miss Silk"—Ellie reached over the desk to reassure her—"please let us help. Your blouse is fine. See? There's no ink on it whatsoever." Ellie pulled a hanky from her purse. "Don't you keep a fresh blotter nearby?"

Miss Silk pointed to the table behind her, but she was still undone by the mess in front of her. Weldon folded the stained blotter and put it in the trash. He positioned a fresh one onto her desk, carefully moving her writing papers away from the blot. He tried not to turn around while

Ellie helped Miss Silk to check her clothing, so he took his time placing her pens back into their slotted wooden tray and sliding the file drawer closed. He righted the ink bottle. "It looks like I am going to have to get you some more ink. And at least one book seems stained."

"Let me inspect the damage," Miss Silk said, a bit more composed. "Ellie, dear, take the rest of these books to the cart. As for this one"—she gingerly held the stained volume of Doyle's *The Adventure of the Empty House* between her two fingers, careful not to touch the wet ink—"I'll have to wait until this dries to review the damage. There may be a cost to this accident, Weldon Haynie." He noticed that she called him by his two names like she did when he was a boy.

"Yes ma'am. I'm so sorry."

"Accidents do happen, Weldon."

"Yes ma'am. Some things is just an accident."

"'Are,' Weldon. Some things 'are' just an accident."

"Yes ma'am," Weldon said, "they certainly are." After he and Ellie finished clearing away items on the desk and cleaning up from the spill, they left the library quickly, embarrassed some by the scene they had just created.

ELLIE TOOK THE TROLLEY BACK DOWN TO MANHATTAN, AND OFFICER Thomas sat on a bench just at the edge of St. Nicholas Park and looked across the street at the apartment that Olivia Frelon bought that began this whole thing. It occurred to him that Ellie was living there even before he knew her. In a way, she was involved at the very beginning— even before Sadie Mathis asked him to investigate.

He slowly read through his notebook trying to layer the information he learned, but without forcing associations. This time he was trying to convince himself that he was wrong. He'd used deductive reasoning to organize his thoughts and notes. He was surprised at how helpful the method was, given that the Sherlock books were fiction. But in the dry brightness of late February, things were beginning to line up. The longer he sat the more it seemed like his notes were finding their places without his help, fitting together like stones on a garden wall or books returned to a library's shelves. Finally he understood the relationship that made sense—whether he wanted it to or not.

Weldon got up, walked through the park's gate and all the way back to Zenobia's. He could have taken the trolley, but the story needed to compose itself and Weldon needed time to accept it. The long rays of the late-afternoon sun stretched behind him. More hours had passed than he'd thought, so he wasn't fully surprised that there was a boy waiting for him on the stoop. He recognized the kid as one of the ones who hung around the library's reading room. And of course he immediately recognized the handwriting on the envelope the boy handed to him.

AT THE EDGES, MY PARKS ARE THE BEST PLACES TO NOTICE ONE SEASON'S struggle to hold on and the other's battle to emerge. An almost-early tree might threaten to blossom or bud and be chastised back into bark by just the right slap of cold.

In St. Nicholas Park large expanses of icy clear snow crusted over until it was mostly a vast expanse of glisten untouched by galoshes and rippling runs of children. The centuries-old grounds held the seasons' tension—winter's end and just spring—and for one last moment, neither had more claim or potential than the other.

Some layers beneath the snowy remains, under last season's grass and decades-deep dirt or slowly softening soils on sloping hillsides there had been villages. Those who were here before with habits long since disremembered. But habits mattered. And, quiet as it's kept, a close listen would let some sense slip through the clusters of centuries and into spaces saved for memories and play and, sometimes, a quietly whispered nudge.

34

Without Sanctuary

EULAILAH SILK CLOSED THE LIBRARY EARLY. THERE WAS MORE DAMAGE than she thought. It didn't take her long at all to realize what had happened. She'd seen Officer Thomas flipping through her files. Her "Gracious!" was the loudest word spoken in the library. Even some of her own patrons shushed her. Rather than the accident itself, it was an empty folder that provoked her. It prompted her recollection that she'd told Weldon about the story that would win the award the night of Olivia Frelon's death. The one that should have been in her folder. Of course he had seen its empty file. She knew him, he was neither careless nor clumsy. And grammatical errors in their conversations were uncharacteristic. It seemed more likely that he'd manufactured the distraction.

She sat at her desk recollecting each conversation she'd had with Officer Thomas over the past weeks. She remembered Ellie Howard's kind comments about her penmanship, and Weldon's interest. Miss Silk sighed, realizing it was only a matter of time before an inevitable encounter. She stood and cleared her throat loudly enough for the patrons to look towards her desk. Then she did something she hadn't done in the forty years of her librarianship. Eulailah Silk announced an early closing of the Harlem Branch.

Everyone gathered their belongings, returned books to carts, and checked out their selections. Miss Silk cleared and arranged her desk, counted the change in the fines drawer, leaving a slip of paper with the total atop the small collection of coins. She looked longingly at the files that held her own work and decided to leave them. She cleared the new desk blotter that Officer Thomas had so kindly placed onto her desk and made certain the pencils were freshly sharpened and the list of overdue books appropriately labeled. Then she slipped on her coat and gloves, buttoned them at the wrist, took her umbrella, and walked through the glass doors for the last time. She wasn't in any particular hurry, and if it hadn't been early afternoon no one would have thought anything unusual at all about her walk from the library to her apartment building. Just as she did every day, the tap of her black silk umbrella's metal ferule marked her way home. She didn't bother to recall the irony of the moment—that the umbrella whose tapping echoed down the Harlem blocks was the very same one that she'd used like a pointer to emphasize the matter that Olivia Frelon seemed unable, or unwilling, to understand.

She recalled the young woman's surprise when she appeared in the prizewinners' lounge, and especially her impolite demand to know why she was there. It took mere seconds for her ire to work its way out. "I'm here, young lady, because I found myself in the unconscionable position of writing the title of my very own story on the prizewinner's card, and then writing your name under it as if you were its author." Olivia was clearly startled. "As we both know, it's my story you are about to claim. That simply cannot happen." She didn't wait for Olivia's response. "How can it be that you would dare to submit a plagiarized story for this esteemed award?"

Olivia was defensive, which made her tone seem rude rather than afraid. "Well, it was in a book. Just lying there. How was I to know whose it was?" Then she added, petulantly, "And the book was in my house and on my coffee table."

"Indeed it was. But it clearly wasn't yours. Accident does not convey ownership. That book belonged to the Harlem Branch of the New York Public Library." She pronounced the name of the institution as if she were going to finish the phrase with "incorporated." "It was only on your coffee table because its colors matched what—your drapery? Or perhaps your sofa pillows? By no stretch of the imagination could you have honestly determined the papers inside belonged to you!" Miss Silk became uncharacteristically strident. "'Sanctuary' is mine! I'm the author! It was my creation, my composition, and . . . clearly my penmanship!" Then her tone softened some, as if she finally understood the likely series of events herself. "I knew I had misplaced it, but when the society that you have so blithely invaded requested me to prepare the card that carried the name of the award winner and the winning entry, I easily realized what must have occurred." Her tone was increasingly bitter. "You were either careless or so unprincipled that you didn't even bother to change my title."

Olivia's retort was a frightened bluster: "Well, if . . . if . . . that was true, why didn't you enter the contest?"

"I? Enter a contest?" Here she may have chuckled, or perhaps it was just a deep-throated sigh. "My dear, I write for the pleasure it brings. The urge of language, the excellence of script, the sweet release of fancy." She sighed deeply and shook her head with what seemed closer to disgust than pity. "How could I expect someone like you—who matches book covers to wall hangings—to understand that I've no need for public acknowledgment? *Ars gratia artis!* But—with standards. There are codes of conduct. I don't tolerate overdue books any more than I condone theft and fraud!" Miss Silk had worked herself into a fury. She emphasized the purloined provenance of the manuscript using her umbrella (which she carried everywhere, even to this elegant affair) as if it were a pointer, jabbing its ferule several times onto Olivia's breastbone to make her point. Olivia was already unsteady with the emotional toll of the evening's events—first with Vera's hurtful accusation about an imagined affair with her Reynolds, and then from the shock of seeing her brother back from the dead and walking around as a white man. It was all too much. She tried to back away from the accusation and the scene unfolding before her. Unfortunately, behind her was the gaping expanse of the window she'd opened to revive her spirits from the earlier encounter. On her third step back, she reached the window's short ledge and, because there was no impediment, Olivia Frelon, née Désirée Rose Fontenôt of Vermilion Parish, New Orleans, stumbled backwards and, with only the slightest whimper of surprise, fell into the willing embrace of the night.

Eulailah Silk was so startled by this unplanned outcome that she stood still for only the briefest of seconds before she turned around and walked out of the small waiting room, while deciding that in fact nothing of any consequence could have happened. Certainly not what she thought she saw. A momentary delusion produced by the evening's high emotion. It was just that Miss Frelon had become suddenly unavailable. Permanently so.

It was, in fact, quite helpful when she passed the kitchen and saw young LT Mitchell and some other boy giggling much too loudly. She walked up to the two and shook her umbrella at them, hushing them, reminding them there was a program going on.

She recalled both of Officer Thomas's recent visits to the library, first when he managed to discover that she knew not only the title but also the content of the winning story and second, when he surreptitiously managed to check her files to see if there was anything in the file she'd labeled "Sanctuary." He would have seen that it was empty. The likely consequences flashed into her mind like a series of clear-cut stereopticon slides.

Later, those who were fortunate enough to have been in the library on the occasion of Miss Silk's precipitous closing of the branch became quite popular. Again and again they shared how she stood over her desk, and what she said. They debated whether she looked composed or frantic. But all agreed it was uncharacteristic. When she cleared her throat and asked for everyone's attention, the patrons—adults and children alike—looked up and across the long oak reading tables to where she stood at her desk. Her long thin arms fully stretched out across the desk. The tips of her delicate fingers rested on either side of her desk and the lace edges of her billowy cuffs just brushed the desktop. They could see the shadow of her thin arms through her light silk sleeves. Some debated whether her fingers trembled when she politely asked patrons if they would kindly gather their things, explaining, "The Harlem Branch Library will close early this afternoon." Despite the unusual nature of the announcement, her tone was no different from the quietly assertive timbre they always heard from her. In fact, except for the timing, the closing routine had no irregularities. She still stood at the checkout desk stamping books with their due date. Some recalled that she whispered to more than one—especially the children whom she knew well—"Good-bye, now. Be well-read."

When Miss Silk arrived back to her small apartment she placed her umbrella into its stand and removed her coat, gloves, and cloche. She placed the latter two items onto an intricately tatted doily. She went over to the window, where her writing desk faced the street. She didn't bother to part the lace panels. She sat quietly, her hands folded in her lap. After a few moments she reached for her fountain pen and slipped sheets of linen stationery from the drawer. Then she wrote a lengthy letter to her beloved grandniece and only living relative, Miss Alondra Newsome of Selma, Alabama. Nothing but the content of her exquisitely penned epistle exposed the extraordinary story she narrated. There were no smudges from tears, no crossed-out words or letters that broke the uniform curvature of Palmer's formal script. No evidence of disarray. She folded the pages into an envelope and let sealing wax fall heavily onto the flap before she embossed it with her signature stamp—an open book with a quill lying across it. She then wrote a nearly identical letter (except for the intimate expressions of affection). This she addressed to "Officer Weldon Thomas, Esq." She used the handle of the broom she kept behind the icebox to tap on the ceiling. The youngster who ran errands for her came down and received instructions to deliver the letter. After the boy repeated to the librarian's satisfaction her instructions to wait at Miss Zenobia's until he could place the letter directly into Officer Thomas's hands, she looked around the tiny apartment for the last time. Finding nothing amiss she went into her bedroom. Before she lay down on top of her bed's lace counterpane, she poured a half glass of water from the pitcher on the nightstand, then carefully placed it back on the bedside tray and took all that was left of her medication. She lay down but almost immediately lifted herself back up, pulled her already heavy legs across the counterpane to the floor, and walked (unsteadily now) to the window for her final courtesy. She raised the window so that whoever entered the room next might appreciate the chilled air. Eulailah Silk lay down a final time. Her arms flailed slightly. She hugged her elbows close to her body, and then rested one arm gently across the other. It was quiet and still, but not unusually so. These rooms were already accustomed to her silences.

Near the end, the librarian attempted one last pitiful reach for the glass. Her frail hand, veins bulging with want, grasped almost mind-lessly for one last sip of life. She flailed, fluttered, then she finished. The crystal fell to the floor and broke into sharp and sparkling fragments. Old folks would have warned, "Careful! It will trap your spirit!" But it had already fled the room through the window. Glass prisms scattered across the wooden planks, splashing diffused rainbow rays of afternoon sun across the room. The final spill of water, that would inevitably find its way through Harlem's tributaries of loss, slipped through cracks in the planked floors with a sound too quiet, even for death.

35

Minding the Gap

I MET ELLIE ON THE PLATFORM AT PENN STATION. SHE WAS TRAVELING for one of her research projects. We didn't talk about much other than the resolution of my case and the repercussions up in the Heights. I was grateful we were still friends after all that had happened. It was an easier relationship for both of us—but you couldn't have told me back then that we was going to be better at friends than, well, what I was now heading toward with Mamie Walker.

Vera Scott and her daughters had "temporarily" relocated to Chicago and Dr. Scott was in Brazil. Sadie Mathis got the head housekeeper role at their Heights apartment, and other than making sure she'd keep her employment it also give her a chance to entertain members of the Household Ladies' Circle right up in the Scotts' front parlor. Mrs. Scott told her she absolutely "must have them over" and had even written what Sadie told me was a lovely and dignified a note of thanks on her best stationery in her own hand with a flawless Palmer script.

Ellie asked me when I figured I knew for sure who done it. I had to admit that I didn't know I had the clue when I was in Dr. Scott's office and was looking at his files betting that there wouldn't be a patient behind the letter X. Even if I didn't have all the information I needed at that point, it was a good lesson as to why it was important to keep notes. Ellie had a hard time believing I wrote down something about the letter X.

Me too. But it stuck in my mind how there were no names that I could think of that began with *X*. And then when we left the library that first time, something was bothering me, but I didn't know it was about gaps. I told her about using deduction. But it probably wasn't as important as my book was to my figuring it out.

Ellie thought I meant a Holmes detective book. But I meant Professor Du Bois. He wrote about two-ness, seeing things through a veil. Ellie tilted her head, in that way I used to love but now just see as one of her regular characteristics. Funny how things change in how we see folks. It's about twoness. And too, how I had to develop my perspective based on whether I could discern relationships. I had to see through the veil.

Ellie wasn't seeing any of this, and told me so.

She got it, though when I explained how my noticing the empty file at the doctor's office put me in the mind of things that are there, and things that are not. That's what made me look for what might be missing at the library files. Most folk notice what's there. It takes a certain kind of perception to even think on what's not present. Miss Silk had actual words separating her files. Not just letters like at the doctor's office. If I had kept to thinking that about words versus letters I wouldn't have noticed what was more important. But in fact I'd written the word "Sanctuary" on my "Notes on the Prize" page. Then in Mamie's interview pages I wrote down her recollection of the title that she misremembered as "Sanctified." It was close enough for me to discern their association. Ellie's eyes lifted some when I mentioned Mamie. She knew we were developing a relationship and I'd got past the fact that she didn't mind. I explained my sequence of discovery so as not to fixate on our past.

I didn't tell her how that last walk to the library my nudge had been pushing me something fierce. That was in the mix too, but I didn't have the words to say it. At the library I saw how Miss Silk's "Sanctuary" file was empty. When Ellie asked how I knew that I reminded her how I straightened her papers after I cleaned up the spilled ink.

She got kinda quiet, then startled. "Wait. You can't possibly mean that that whole scene at the library wasn't an accident!"

"Maybe." I said it kind of teasing, but really because it was that I wasn't sure myownself whether it was accidentally intentional or just accidental. Neither could I have predicted its outcome. But at least it gave me the time and the chance to notice that her files had a title that I remembered was in my notes.

"And . . . ?"

And that didn't follow Miss Silk's habit. Her files were titled based on what was in them. The doctor titled his files based on the alphabet, not on real people. You'd expect *X* could be empty. Ellie said she didn't know if she would have noticed that.

Things fell into place after that. Mamie and then Miss Silk both knew the name and content of the story that was supposed to win the award. It made sense for Mamie to know what it was about. Miss Frelon told her. But it didn't make sense for Miss Silk to know, because Mrs. Kinsdale said Miss Silk got the title and author information only just before the announcement. I told Ellie that keeping my notes was key. I didn't say how being nudged to distraction wasn't irrelevant.

"Okay," she said. "I get that."

We got quiet together then. Me, having known Miss Silk so well, trying to find a place in my spirit for the memories of years respecting and even loving the library lady. I had memories of being at her desk lots of times and seeing her slip what she was writing inside some book. In all probability, that's what she did with "Sanctuary," and then what happened was somebody took out the book.

It would've made sense for me to take Ellie's hand for the next thing I had to say; but our relationship had changed and too, she had her hands full with books and papers for her research. I took a deep breath and then I told her the rest of the story. How it was that she was probably the somebody that took out the book with Miss Silk's story slipped inside it. I watched her let out a long slow sigh as she figured out I was right.

"I did," Ellie said quietly. "She never went to the library on her own."

I didn't want her to leave with that rememory as her only focus. So I emphasized how Mamie told me about the day she mailed the story. How it all happened real quick. At first I thought she was just leaving some steps out. One minute she had an idea. The next minute the idea was in the mail. If she had been spending time writing, Mamie would have known it. But it just didn't seem to be amongst her habits.

Ellie shook her head sadly. "You're right. It wasn't. Not at all. She did write notes, but never anything at all that required me to get full-sized proper stationery for her desk. I hadn't thought of that."

"Listen, Ellie. There's not a single thing you could've done. She was a lady in a hurry. We don't know those whys and wherefores." I was surprised to hear myself say that. It was one of my mother's sayings. A reminder that book sense ain't necessarily common sense. Miss Frelon just took a wrong turn. And she was careless in a misraised kind of way. Sometimes when you go wrong like that, you leave yourself open to things that otherwise would've kept their distance.

Ellie was quiet for a long while before she said, "But Miss Silk a murderer? It doesn't make sense."

I asked her not to make a final decision on that just yet. Seemed to me that for all we know, the story could still end with what I wrote in my notes that very first night.

"Which was . . . ?"

I pulled my notebook out of my inside jacket pocket. Yeah. I still keep it about my person. No telling when something will need to go on the record. The ink was smudged but still readable. I showed her where I wrote, "Death by misadventure?"

"Yes. And I see you wrote it like a question."

"Yeah." I said it more like a whisper but it was okay for her to hear. "I know." We got quiet after that. Until the train whistle broke through our remembering.

36

The Omada Collection

ELLIE HOWARD WAS NEGOTIATING A PURCHASE OF A STUNNING COLLEC-
tion of passport masks when the charges against Vera Scott were dropped.
How they got to the basement of a house in Sag Harbor was a mystery.
But since she would not be back until after the weekend, it left the evening open and Hughes asked Meade to prepare supper for him and a
guest.

Protos Kenan Montgomery arrived promptly at six. After dinner the
two men retired to the private gallery. They walked alongside each other
with an ease built from a long-standing familiarity and trust. Wellington
was eager to show the collection's newest pieces.

Despite the stunning outcome of the Scott affair, they didn't spend
much time discussing it. Montgomery did thank him for the lawyer's fees
and for covering the Frelon funeral. Wellington just clasped him silently
around the shoulder. But this evening the two gentlemen—one still pre-
sumptively white—focused on the collection.

Kenan wandered through the exhibit. The quiet of the room never
failed to take him back to the evening when he was installed as the
Omada's protos. He'd left the ceremonies fully impressed with his newly
acquired position. The ritual was filled with appropriately complex ceremonial procedures. He watched as the elder brothers fit a small silver key into an intricately carved ivory chest and removed a scroll and

enthusiastically joined in the ceremony's ritual call and response. When it ended, he left the meeting rooms still under the influence of its solemnity. He didn't notice the limousine until he crossed Seventh Avenue. A white man stood at the back door of the automobile and introduced himself as "Meade." "Sir, I've been asked to escort you to the next services." Kenan was surprised and puzzled at this interruption—not to mention that it came from an impeccably dressed white man hanging out in the middle of Harlem well into the early hours of the morning. Not until Meade gave him a piece of parchment with the Omada seal attached did he trust this was another facet of the inauguration process.

The limousine moved downtown so rapidly that the new protos barely had time to consider what various scenarios might present themselves regarding the "next services" before he arrived at the Fifth Avenue mansion and was greeted at the door by Hughes Wellington. Kenan immediately recognized him. He knew Wellington's reputation for being involved and interested in the Negro; but he could not fathom what connection he might have to his fraternity.

When they entered the study, he recognized that the ornate box on Wellington's impressive desk was identical to the one that had held the scroll from the earlier ceremony. Hughes invited Montgomery to sit as he read a history of the Omada that Dr. Montgomery had not known. It explained that the group was formed from a partnership between Hughes Wellington, Esq., and the Omada's first protos, Walter J. Givens, as a response to the plunder, exploitation, and cultural loss of the arts of African peoples. The group's daily organizational matters and activities were turned over to the creativity and interests of Dr. Givens, who was instructed to enlist a cadre of men whose social standing could sustain the group "in perpetuity." But the organization would also have a private charter that would be known only to Mr. Wellington (and his heirs or designees) and the Alpha-chapter protos. They would coordinate the creation of what would "heretofore be known as the Omada Collection," with the express purpose of assuring that the arts of the Negro were collected and preserved in a manner that would form "the most convincing and extravagant collection of the arts, culture, and influences of Africa and its diasporas."

Montgomery was speechless. Wellington concluded his reading, took the edges of the parchment, and turned it to face Dr. Montgomery. He brought out a quill, blotter, and inkstand and indicated where he was to sign his own name, just below the signature of Walter Givens, whose recent passing created the vacancy in the office of the protos.

While he executed his signature, Wellington explained that one hundred years past its founding, whoever served as the protos for Omada's Alpha chapter would be assigned to take the collection public. But until that time, it was to be a confidential and jointly shared enterprise between the protos of the Omada's Alpha chapter and Hughes Wellington. His heirs, descendants, or the appointed executor of his estate would be responsible for its funding, upkeep, and collection. Ellie Howard had no idea that her destiny would be tied to one of those affiliations.

Dr. Montgomery was stunned to discover this significant purpose to the Omada. He'd understood and appreciated it as an élite social club that held discussions on the Negro affairs of the day, that facilitated business and social connections between the best men of his race, and that sponsored events that would maintain the integrity of their privileged bloodlines. In the short number of years since its founding, these affairs had become its focus. But the existence of the "Omada Collection" gave the organization an importance that only the Alpha protos would ever appreciate. The mission was a sacred trust.

During the early years of their association, Kenan spent a good deal of time wondering at Wellington's motivation. But after a while it finally just didn't matter. The meetings they held to discuss the newest acquisitions were cordial and always stimulating. Although he occasionally saw Wellington at some Negro social functions, neither betrayed their clandestine association.

Their meeting in the days following the librarian's indictment quickly took on the characteristic of the others they'd had. Wellington showed him the newest pieces, and the public events of the day were quickly dismissed as they discussed venues where important pieces might be discovered. The Scott matter soon receded into Harlem's histories. Certainly none of the residents of the Heights wanted it as their touchstone. Their social ambition could not afford it. And nobody in Harlem proper had time or energy to stay with it. There were too many other stories flowing into place.

Back at the gallery, Wellington returned the engraved box to its place on a glass shelf alongside other carved boxes from Nigeria. He turned back to look across the long expanse of the room to assure himself that everything was in its place. It always was. A mirrored cabinet briefly caught his image, and he paused, noticing with some surprise how he had aged. Slight strands of silver, evident in the lamplight, glistened from his dark wavy hair. He'd let it grow longer than most in his social set, preferring the gathered and tied with a slim satin ribbon style that he recalled from gentlemen of the Bayou, or perhaps it was from his travels. His skin was still smooth and unlined; but he could swear that his complexion was a bit duskier. When he was a child complaining that he didn't look enough like his mother, Belle, she would tell him that the older he grew, the darker he'd become. "By the time you reach my age, no one will know I am not your maman," she assured him. "They will say, 'Regardez ce jeune homme. Il est certainement le fils de Belle Chartier!'" Unsettled by the unexpected reminder of his years, and the uneasy memory of his mother, he turned away from the mirror and let the reflection pass back into the shadows. Back in his office, seated comfortably behind his desk, he quietly anticipated his young apprentice's return.

37

Common Ground

I'D WEATHERED CENTURIES OF SHAPE-SHIFTING. THIS SPRING STORY slipped through a summer, dropped into fall, and having weathered winter became another seasonal ritual. My grounds were used to the change. There were groves as pristine as the first morning broken over lush and virgin lands. Meticulously groomed farmlands had their time as well, but eventually they got pressed flat for the presumptive economy of roadways. Cobbled stones displaced them—they had the necessary heft and resilience—but the coming of asphalt, poured hot and spread steaming across and into their cracks and ridges, promised a ride without bruises. Horses—generations past field-free days—were left to decorate waysides for tourists or to respond to tugs from mounted uniforms.

As if giving ground were not enough, things took to the air. Iron grids, sketched like tracery, spiraled above and curved below to support trains that mapped up and then down into Manhattan.

But earth was a common ground. Walkway dust swept over slabs of concrete sidewalks. All manner of refuse found its way to the streets. Things lost and a few found then forgotten inevitably worked their way down, mixed together like pottage, and whorled into eddies that spread silent circles beneath the city. They migrated through the waterworks and finally spilled into the river.

In summers, opened hydrants gushed cool waters over sparkling brown bodies. In winter, detritus lay like sediment in iced suspension until the inevitable meltdown when everything that was waiting for warmth and sunlight joined a sloggy unwanted wash. There were early downtown days when autumn meant brilliant mounds of colored horizons. Uptown too, until somebody looked around at the people who matched the striations of colors in the damp bark and late fall leaves and decided these particular streets didn't need that many trees anyway and concrete was easier to contain than a spreading chestnut.

Sometimes really bad things happened. The earth held them no differently from an unspent penny or a strawberry ice dropped in wailing despair and a last longing for the sweet sticky thing melting and then slipping across the curb. Like the night the ladies' blood (and truth to tell, a bit of bodily tissue too) trickled into the street and became just another bit of waste in the mix of things fallen through grated gutters.

A seasoned wash of spring rains yielded to a forgiving green fully ready for bound-north folks whose mix of fantasy and desire, fixity and finish, would find whatever could not be imagined. With each shimmering promise of new, Harlem held fast to memories of dusk and dawn and every season in between—right there, where the stories settled and marked their place.